GUITAR MUSIC BY WOMEN COMPOSERS

**Recent Titles in
the Music Reference Collection**

GUITAR MUSIC BY WOMEN COMPOSERS

An Annotated Catalog

Compiled by

Janna MacAuslan
and Kristan Aspen

Music Reference Collection, Number 61
Donald L. Hixon, Series Adviser

GREENWOOD PRESS
Westport, Connecticut • London

Library of Congress Cataloging-in-Publication Data

MacAuslan, Janna.
   Guitar music by women composers : an annotated catalog / compiled
by Janna MacAuslan and Kristan Aspen.
      p.   cm.—(Music reference collection, ISSN 0736–7740 ; no.
61)
   Includes bibliographical references and indexes.
   ISBN 0–313–29385–6 (alk. paper)
   1. Guitar music—Bibliography—Catalogs.   2. Women composers'
music—Bibliography—Catalogs.   3. Women composers—Biography.
I. Aspen, Kristan, 1948–   .   II. Title.   III. Series.
ML128.G8M33   1997
016.78787'082—DC21   97–10404

British Library Cataloguing in Publication Data is available.

Library of Congress Catalog Card Number: 97–10404
ISBN: 0–313–29385–6
ISSN: 0736–7740

First published in 1997

Greenwood Press, 88 Post Road West, Westport, CT 06881
An imprint of Greenwood Publishing Group, Inc.

Printed in the United States of America

The paper used in this book complies with the
Permanent Paper Standard issued by the National
Information Standards Organization (Z39.48–1984).

10 9 8 7 6 5 4 3 2 1

This catalog is dedicated to
all the composers whose works
are listed herein
with confidence that there will be
many wonderful performances for years to come.

Contents

Preface

In 1982 during graduate school at Lewis and Clark College, I was hard at work in a music practice room when a light bulb switched on in my head. Suddenly I became aware that in thirty years of guitar study I had never played a composition by a woman composer. I couldn't even think of one. This realization gave impetus to a search which has produced the present volume.

For the last twelve years, Kristan Aspen and I have toured the United States as the Musica Femina Flute Guitar Duo, playing the music and speaking about the lives of women composers. Everywhere we have traveled, we have been privileged to visit libraries and archives. This book is a listing of all the works I have found to date which include guitar. Some of these compositions I have played myself. Others I have only found referenced in books, catalogs, concert programs, or conference packets. In some cases, I have carried on a correspondence with the composer, obtaining scores from her and receiving accurate information about her life. But for some references I have been unable to locate any additional verification.

It is very apparent that women have written extensively for the guitar. It is also painfully clear that these works are rarely performed. The classical guitar is an extremely popular instrument which cries out for new repertoire. The fact that the works contained in this volume are not widely programmed suggests two obstacles: (1) ignorance among guitarists about what is available by women composers; and (2) sexism in the guitar world. With the publication of this research, I offer a tool to eliminate the first obstacle. The second one will eventually disappear, as more and more women enter the field.

It is the nature of such a catalog to be out of date as soon as it is available. The appendices of addresses are certain to contain some inaccuracies. When complete information was not available, incomplete clues were included to provide some direction for further searching. My apologies for any other errors, omissions, or inaccuracies. I have tried to include only original material, but some publishers do not differentiate between arrangements of traditional works and original compositions, making it impossible to be sure. As the scope of the book is international, there are many languages in the titles of works and composer names. Diacrytical marks have been used when available and proper markings were known. Errors and inconsistencies may reflect either unfamiliarity with the language or limitations of the fonts on our computer.

The volume is divided into two sections. First is the listing of compositions by instrumentation, with as much information about each work, including length, difficulty, and publisher, as was available. The music is listed by instrumentation to assist guitarists unfamiliar with women composers in more easily finding a potential recital piece. By looking under a heading for a specific ensemble, the reader will quickly discover several options of compositions by women from which to choose.

The second section contains composer biographies, brief paragraphs about as many of the composers as could be found in print or contacted in person. The biographies are not exhaustive. Following each paragraph are references which will lead the reader to additional sources. For some composers there is little or no biographical data. If the reader can supply any missing information, it will be gratefully accepted and included in the project database, to be made available in a subsequent edition. Works which I have overlooked and more recent compositions will also gladly be received.

There are a number of people who have worked with me in the making of this book. I thank each of them for the special contributions they have made. In the early stages of compilation, Bev Lipsitz, my computer tutor, guided me onto the internet and into library catalogs around the world; Elliot Rubin, my dear composer friend since undergraduate days, helped me describe some of the twentieth-century pieces; Melanie Plesch, a musicologist from Argentina, with whom I corresponded on the internet, sent me invaluable information about compositions by Argentine women; Cindy Richardson, author, music librarian, and colleague dedicated to greater public awareness of women in music, helped me verify some obscure references; Badi Assad, Brazilian guitarist and performer extraordinaire, kindly sent me original scores of several Brazilian women composers; Tee A. Corinne, artist, writer, and friend, provided years of enthusiastic support for all of Musica Femina's endeavors including this book; Thomas Heck, archivist and librarian for the Guitar Foundation of America, convinced me that the project would have value for the whole guitar world; Don Hixon, series editor, recognized the need for such a volume and recommended me to Greenwood Press; and the editorial staff at Greenwood Press, including Alicia Merritt, acquisitions editor, Liz Leiba, production editor, and Irene Lebov, production assistant, kept the project on track with empathy and clarity.

Finally, I offer my deep gratitude to my partner, Kristan Aspen, whose patience and commitment to detail have made it possible to complete the manuscript in this century. As my editor and consultant, she has tackled the computer and emerged victorious, figuring out how to integrate my database with word processing to create the book layout. Because she has given countless hours to the project, her name appears as co-author.

It is my hope that the information contained in this volume will not only document women's participation as composers in the world of the classical guitar, but will also assist contemporary guitarists in programming works by women composers, thereby expanding the current classical guitar repertoire. Furthermore, I trust that both performers and audiences throughout the twenty-first century will spend many enjoyable hours playing, performing, and listening to the very rich diversity of music included here.

Janna MacAuslan
July 1997

Abbreviations

A	Alto voice	ob	oboe
a-	alto	orch	orchestra
acc	accordian	org	organ
Arp 2500	Arp synthesizer	perc	percussion
b-	bass	pf	piano
Bari	Baritone voice	pic	piccolo
bsn	bassoon	rec	recorder
c-	contra	S	Soprano voice
cel	celeste	s3	string trio
ch orch	chamber orchestra	s4	string quartet
chor	chorus/choir	sax	saxophone
cl	clarinet	str orch	string orchestra
cmb	cembalo	synth	synthesizer
cont	continuo	T	Tenor voice
cor	english horn	tb	tuba
db	double bass	timb	timbales
elec db	electric bass	timp	timpani
elec keys	electric keyboard	trb	trombone
fl	flute	trp	trumpet
gamba	viola de gamba	vce	voice
gtr	guitar	vib	vibraphone
harm	harmonica	vla	viola
hn	horn	vlc	cello
hp	harp	vln	violin
hpc	harpsichord	wd	wind
keys	keyboard	w ch	wind chime
man	mandolin	wwd	woodwind
mar	marimba	xy	xylophone
mez-S	mezzo Soprano voice		

MUSICAL WORKS BY INSTRUMENTATION

ANTHOLOGY

Fay, Lydia A.

The Spanish Soloist: A Collection of Original Compositions and Arrangements for the Guitar; easy; ms.

Knoop, Mrs.

Le dilettante: A Collection of Choice Pieces for the Guitar; gtr solo; Schatzman and Brulon

Michelson, Sonia

Easy Classic Guitar Solos for Children; easy; Mel Bay

Young Beginners First Repertoire for Classical Guitar; easy; Mel Bay

Walker, Louise

Miniaturen: Zehn kleine Stücke; medium; Heinrichshofen's Verlag

AVANT-GARDE GUITAR

Bruzdowicz, Joanna

Fas et nefas; tape and prepared gtr

Escot, Pozzi

Neyrac lux; 1 player, 3 gtr, (12 string, classical, and electric); 8'; difficult-some quarter tone use, experimental; Publication Contact International

Irman-Allemann, Regina

Drive; quarter tone guitar

Melodie; quarter tone gtr

Lejet, Edith Jacqueline Marie

La voix des voiles; 4'; difficult-quarter tones; Editions Max Eschig

ELECTRIC GUITAR

Anderson, Beth (Barbara Elizabeth)

Peachy Keen-O; org, elec gtr, vib, and perc; ms.

Bailly, Colette

Six etapes; trp, perc, and elec gtr

Bakke, Ruth

A Dance of Death; S, Bari, fl, elec gtr, hp, and perc

Bandt, Rosalie Edith

Variations II, Two Realizations of John Cage's Score; elec gtr, fl, and synth

Bellavance, Ginette (marr. Sauvé)

Match en coordonées; 2 perc, 2 elec gtr, and tape

Diehl, Paula Jespersen

In the Field and Groundwater; sounds, pf ens, elec keys, gtr, elec gtr, elec d-b, and perc; American Music Center Library

Escot, Pozzi

Sands (Symphony No. 5); elec gtr, 5 sax, 4 bass drum, 17 vln, 9 db, and perc; 15'; Publication Contact International

Gudauskas, Giedra

Lithuanian Suite; xy, elec gtr, and pf

Jolas, Betsy

Episode septième, "Nightaway"; 7'; difficult, experimental piece with electronic manipulation; Editions Musicales Alphonse Leduc

Koblenz, Babette

Walking on the Sun; cl, a-sax, trp, pf, elec gtr, and perc; Kodasi

Lejet, Edith Jacqueline Marie

Le journal d'Anne Frank; young girls' chor and ch orch (fl, hp, clavecin, elec gtr, vla, db, and 2 perc); 27'; Billaudot

Lutyens, Elisabeth

Go, Said the Bird, Op. 105; elec gtr and s4; 12'; Olivan Press, Universal Edition, Ltd. (1975)

String Quartet and Electric Guitar; s4 and elec gtr

McKenzie, Sandra

Much Ado about Nothing; man, acc, elec gtr, perc, and pf

Richard III; man, pf, acc, elec gtr, and perc

Musgrave, Thea

Soliloguy I; elec gtr with tape; 9'30"; difficult; Chester, J. and W. Ltd.

Roi, Micheline

Continuances; keys, elec gtr, and perc; 6'; ms.

Schonthal, Ruth

Soundtrack for "A Dark Street"; elec gtr and orch

Shuttleworth, Anne-Marie

Conversations; vce, gtr, and perc

Vierk, Lois

Guitars; 5 miked or elec gtr, 4 pre-recorded gtr, and 1 live gtr; difficult

Weaver, Carol Ann

Algonquin Dawn; elec man, elec gtr, and 2 synth; 20'; difficult; Canadian Music Center

Gathering; chor, elec gtr, perc, and amp pf

Rejoice; chor, elec gtr, and orch

Tower of Babel; a-cap chor, elec gtr, perc, and amp pf

Wiemann, Beth

Fantasy Is a Place Where It Rains; amp gtr and strs (or amp gtr and pf); 17'; in five movements; Nambe Acoma

Wolfe, Julia

Muscle Memory

FLUTE AND GUITAR

Anderson, Avril

Gershwin Suite

Aspen, Kristan

Green Apple Rag; fl and gtr (also available for solo pf and for gtr solo); 5'; medium, ragtime; DearHorse Publications

New Beginnings; 3'30"; medium, tonal; DearHorse Publications

Barnett, Carol

Mythical Journeys; 16'; medium difficult-two movements, quiet, lyrical; ms.

Beecroft, Norma

Tre pezzi brevi; fl and gtr (or hp or pf); 4'; very atonal and difficult; Universal Edition

Birnstein, Renate

Peram; fl, gtr, and vib; Sikorski Verlag

Bodorová, Sylvie

Fairylands Just So

Borràs i Fornell, Teresa

Mont, Op. 104, No. 1; 5'; medium-atonal; ms.

Montgri, mini-sonata, Op. 104, No. 2; 10'; medium-atonal; ms.

Bottelier, Ina

Fête des oiseaux; 5'; medium; Broekmans and van Poppel (1979)

Pavane; medium-tonal; Broekmans and van Poppel (1983)

Brooks, Linnea

Duo for Flute and Guitar; 9 pp; difficult; ms.

Brown, Elizabeth

Augury; 14'; difficult-extended techniques, microtonal, experimental; Quetzal Music

Brusa, Elisbetta

Miniature; ms.

Byrchmore, Ruth M.

In Gest; 10'; ms.

Byrne, Madelyn

Of A Desert Plain; 15 pp; 2 movts, difficult, atonal, but lyrical; ms.

Casson, Margaret

The Cuckoo ("Now the sun is in the west"); fl and gtr (originally vce and hp); G. Goulding (ca 1790)

Clark, Theresa-Ann

Spellings; 5'; medium-meditative, extended techniques, percussive effects; ms.

Cody, Judith Ann

Sonata, Op. 22; 6 pp; medium-rhythmic; Kikimora Publishing

Culbertson, D.C.

Medieval Suite; 5 pp; easy-atonal; ms.

Desportes, Yvonne Berthe Melitta

Bach-annales; fl, gtr, and s4

Six danses pour Syrinx; 14 pp; medium-lyrical, with some rhythmic effects; Billaudot, 1982

Diemer, Emma Lou

There's a Certain Slant of Light, Winter Afternoons

Dinescu, Violeta

Atreju; fl and gtr; 8 pp; difficult-atonal with extended techniques; Astoria Verlag

Dollitz, Grete Franke

Thoughts on Arirang (Korea); 4 pp; medium; ms.

Edell, Therese

38: 3 Sections, 8 Yrs; 5'; medium-lyrical, contemporary; ms.

Erding, Susanne

Musical Moment; fl, gtr, and pantomime

Frajt, Ljudmila

Three Nocturnes for Flute and Guitar, from *Anthology of Classical Guitar Music in Serbia* by Professor Uros Dojcinovic; Ed. Nota-Knjazevac

Gardner, Kay

Innermoods; fl or a-fl and gtr; 3'; easy-medium; Sea Gnomes Music

Gentile, Ada

Quick Moments; 9'; G. Ricordi and Co.

Hankinson, Ann Shrewsbury

Meditation; 12 pp; difficult-moderately modern with soft dissonances; ms.

Hart, Jane Smith

Sonata for Flute and Guitar; 19 pp; medium-Neo Romantic; ms.

Hartmann, Lioba

Birke/Artis/Spaziergans; gtr and F-fl; ms.

Brieghaulof; gtr and F-fl; ms.

Ho, Wai On

Tai Chi

Trio after Spring River in Flowery Moonlight; fl, gtr, and hp

Holmes, Leonie

Colloquium: For Two Flutes and Guitar; 2 fl and gtr; a conversation between the three instruments, unhurried, free style; Waiteata Press

Hoover, Katherine

Canyon Echos, Op. 45; fl and gtr; 18'; difficult-atonal, rhythmically complex; Papagena Press

Izarra, Adina

A dos

Kazandjian-Pearson, Sirvart H.

Duo for Flute and Guitar, Op. 32; Frauenmusikarchiv

Kojima, Yuriko

Music for Alto Flute (or Violin) and Guitar; a-fl and gtr; 10'; ms.

Lambertini, Marta

Eridanus

Gymel

Larsen, Elizabeth (Libby)

Three Pieces for Treble Wind and Guitar: Canti Breve III, Circular Rondo, Prestidigital; 1'50"; medium-1) modal, lyrical; 2) tonal, quiet mood; 3) rhythmic; E.C. Schirmer Music Company, Inc.

Laruelle, Jeanne-Marie

Duettissimo; rec or fl and gtr

Esquisse et toccata

Lauber, Anne

Divertissement; 11 pp; difficult-three movements, dark, atonal; Doberman Music (1979)

Linnemann, Maria Catharina

Ballad of Belfast; ms.

Ballad of County Armagh; ms.

Lynds, Deirdre

John Doe's Running; 6'15"; difficult-light, popular style; Little Piper

MacAuslan, Janna L.

Apryl Toye; 3'; easy to medium-style of Renaissance dances; DearHorse Publications

Bay Bridge Suite; 8'34"; medium-jazz or pop style; DearHorse Publications

MacAuslan, Janna L., with Kristan Aspen

Blochsberg; 5'25"; medium-lyrical, hypnotic; DearHorse Publications

On the Edge; 4'10"; medium-dreamy; DearHorse Publications

Open Door; 3'38"; medium-lyrical; DearHorse Publications

Scottish Suite; 9'; medium-Scottish folk influence; DearHorse Publications

Tangle for Two; 3'51"; medium-tonal tango; DearHorse Publications

'Zona; 4'46"; medium-tonal, mysterious; DearHorse Publications

Markowitz, Judith
Night Breezes; 3'19"; easy-folk-like; ms.

Misurell-Mitchell, Janice
Dream Storm; ms.

Synchromos; ms.

Miyake, Haruna (pseud. Haruna Shibata)
Music for Piccolo, Flute, and Guitar

Morena, Naomi Littlebear
Hearts of Silver; 2 fl and gtr; easy-melodic; DearHorse Publications

Mori, Junko
Autumn Mist; fl (or shakuhachi) and gtr; 7'20"; medium-atonal, impressionist style; ms.

Murdock, Katherine
Triptych for Flute and Guitar; 8'; medium to difficult-atonal, in 3 movements; ms.

O'Leary, Jane
Duo for Flute and Guitar; 7-8'; difficult; Contemporary Music Centre

Obrovská, Jana
Suite in an Old Style; 4 pp; medium; Editio Supraphon

Parker, Alice
Suite; ms.

Patino, Lucia (Chia)
Vagamundeando I

Polin, Claire
Regensburg; ms.

Rapp, Sandy
Sweetwood Aire, from *Life of Shakespeare;* Sandy Rapp Music

Roe, Eileen Betty
Temperaments

Rotaru, Doina
Spiralis III; a-fl and gtr; ms.

Rusche, Marjorie Maxine
Pentagram

Schlünz, Annette
Kammermusik für Flöte und Gitarre; difficult; Bote and Bock
Taubenblaue Schatten haben sich vermischt; Bote and Bock

Schorr, Eva (née Weller)

Mixed Suite vier Sätze; 11'30"; Furore-verlag

Sherman, Elna

Suite No. 1; fl (or a-rec) and gtr (or lute); medium; ms.

Sommer, Silvia

Atardecer for Flute and Guitar

Spampinato, Letizia

Crisalidi; 10 pp; difficult-atonal, advanced, some extended techniques; ms.

Tapia, Gloria

Recreativa III, (dodecafonia); 8'; difficult-12 tone; ms.

Recreativa VI; (originally for fl and pf); ms.

Thomas, Karen P.

Desert Songs; 10'; medium-tonal, semi-popular, rhythmic; ms.

Tower, Joan

Snow Dreams; 9'14"; difficult-modern impressionism, mood evocative; G. Schirmer/AMP

Vorlová , Sláva (née Miroslava Johnová) (pseud. Mira Kord)

Esoterics, Op. 78

Walker, Gwyneth

Etude for Flute and Guitar; 4 pp; medium-lyrical, open, fluid tonality, Bartok-like, originally for flute and piano; Walker Music Publishing

Five Pieces for Flute and Guitar; 15'; difficult-humorous and playful; E.C. Schirmer Music Company, Inc.

Weir, Judith

Gentle Violence for Piccolo and Guitar; pic and gtr; Novello and Co., Ltd.

Wüsthoff-Oppelt, Sabine

Six Miniaturen für Flute and Guitar; medium-tonal, jazzy, popular elements; Lienau, Robert, Musikverlag

Yamashita, Toyoko

Le paradis des enfants (Zyklus für Gitarre and Flöte)

Zimmermann, Margrit

Fantasia: Duetto per flauto e chitarra, Op. 37; ms.

Fantasy for Flute and Guitar, Op. 29; ms.

Zucker, Laurel

The Yearling for Flute and Guitar; difficult-melodic, neo-Romantic; Cantilena Records

GUITAR CONCERTO

Abejo, Sister M. Rosalina, SFCC

Concerto "Recuerdos de Manila" for Guitar and Orchestra (1972)

Archer, Violet

Four Dialogues for Classical Guitar and Chamber Orchestra; gtr and ch orch

Badian, Maya

Guitar Concerto; gtr and orch

Ballou, Esther Williamson

Concerto for Guitar and Chamber Orchestra; gtr and orch; 12'; difficult; American Composers Alliance

Bodorová, Sylvie

Canzone da sonar; gtr and orch

Boyd, Anne Elizabeth

The Voice of the Phoenix; gtr and orch; 25'; Faber Music Ltd.

Boyd, Liona

Concierto baroquissimo; gtr and ch orch; 15'

Songs of My Childhood; gtr and orch; 20'

Calandra, Matilde Tettamanti de

Concerto for Four Guitars and Orchestra; 4 gtr and orch; ASCAP

Concierto para guitarra y orquesta; gtr and orch; Barry Y Cia

Dinescu, Violeta

Fresco; youth orch and gtr ens

Map 67; gtr and ch orch

French, Tania Gabrielle

Concerto for Violin, Guitar, and Orchestra; orch, gtr, and vln; 16'; ms.

Gentile, Ada

Concertante per flauto, chitarra, e orchestra; fl, gtr, and orch; 19'; G. Ricordi and Co.

Shading for Guitar and Chamber Orchestra; gtr and orch; 18'; G. Ricordi and Co.

Izarra, Adina
  Concierto para guitarra y orquesta de cámara; gtr and ch orch

Le Bordays, Christiane
  Concerto de azul; gtr and orch; Bowker

Mari, Pierrette (Anne Valérie)
  Concerto; gtr, perc, and str orch

Obrovská, Jana
  Concerto; 2 gtr and orch
  Concerto meditativo; gtr and orch

Pierrette, Mari
  Concerto; 18'; Billaudot

Ravinale, Irma
  Sinfonia concertante; gtr and orch

Themmen, Ivana Marburger
  Cadenzas, from *Concerto for Guitar and Orchestra;* difficult; ms.
  Concerto for Guitar and Orchestra; gtr and orch; difficult

GUITAR DUO

Anderson, Beth (Barbara Elizabeth)
  Guitar Swale; 7 pp; medium-modal, Satie-like; American Composers
  Alliance

Artzt, Alice
  titles unknown; compositions for 2-3 guitars

Barrell, Joyce Howard
  The Three Inns
  The Two Inns

Borràs i Fornell, Teresa
  Preludio Español, Op. 59; 4'; medium; ms.

Brenet, Thérèse
  Caprice d'une chatte anglaise

Coates, Gloria
  Lunar Loops
  Lunar Loops II; 2 gtr and perc

Coulombe Saint-Marcoux, Micheline

Equation I

Criswick, Mary

Duets; Chester, J. and W. Ltd.

Desportes, Yvonne Berthe Melitta

Ballad des Damoiseaux; 12 pp

Cocktail français; Billaudot

Histoires d'arbres; Billaudot

Pot pourri folk; Billaudot

Dinescu, Violeta

Figuren II; 7 pp; difficult-20th Century, extended techniques; ms.

Herrera, Hilda

Chaya

Hervey, Augusta

Gianetta (Gavotte for Two Guitars); 5 pp; easy-tonal; Boosey and Co. (1898)

Hontos, Margaret

Child's Play; 7 pp; medium-simple, straight-forward tonality; ms.

Kanach, Sharon

ON

Kircher, Irina

Canción und Bossa Nova; 7 pp; medium-traditional with folkloric and popular elements; Verlag Hubertus Nogatz

Konishi, Nagako

Serenade; 2 gtr, tuned differently; 12'; difficult-free notation, explores tone colors produced by the guitars; ms.

Kruisbrink, Annette

Louis XIV; ms.

Kubo, Mayako

Le mie passacaglie; 2 players, 4 gtrs; Breitkopf and Härtel

Linnemann, Maria Catharina

Juliette; Editions Henry Lemoine

The Old Church, theme and variations; ms.

To Sleep, Perchance to Dream; ms.

Marez Oyens, Tera de

Prazsky Hrad (The Prague Castle); 19 pp; difficult-atonal; ms.

Marina, Carmen (pseud. of Carmen Manteca Gioconda)

Counterpoint and Folk; GioMar Editions

Prelude and Fugue on a Theme by Gaspar Sanz; GioMar Editions

Three Pieces: Counterpoint, Dance, and Folk Song; GioMar Editions

Marlow, Janet

Après-vous; 6'; ms.

Obrovská, Jana

Due musici; 5 pp; medium; Editions Orphée

Oribello, Juanita

Are We In The Grass; 3 pp; medium, Bluegrass, flat-picking style; ms.

Pratten, Madame Sydney (née Catherina Josepha Pelzer)

Div. 4 Duets (2 G.)

Div. 4 Pieces (2 G.)

Div. Danish March (2 G.)

Div. Three Duets

Presti, Ida

Bagatelle

Danse d'Avila; 5 pp; med to difficult; Ricordi

Espagne

Etude; Ricordi

Etude

Etude fantasque; 6 pp; medium; Les Cahiers de la Guitare #12

La hongroise (Hommage à Béla Bartók)

Prelude No. 1; 12 pp; med to difficult; Ricordi

Ravinale, Irma

Jontly

Rodríguez, Marcela

Senderos que se bifurcan; 17 pp; medium-various styles; ms.

Roi, Micheline

Algunos; 8'; difficult-atonal with some extended techniques; ms.

Sommer, Silvia

Canción para desear una buenas noches

Para dos buenos amigos

van Schaijk-Lambermont, Herma

Competition; ms.

von Zieritz, Grete

Danza

Wallach, Joelle

Music for Manda (for student and teacher); 4'; easy-tonal, fugal, plaintive; American Composers Alliance

Yamashita, Tokoyo

Toccata und Bolero für 2 Gitarren

Zivkovic, Mirjana

Diptych; from *Antologia of Classical Guitar Music in Serbia* by Prof. Uros Dojcinovic; Ed. Nota-Knjazevac

GUITAR ENSEMBLE

Cecconi-Botella, Monic (Monique Gabrielle)

Alpha; 6 gtr and 4 perc

Criswick, Mary

Ragtime for Guitar Ensemble; Chappell and Co., Ltd.

Simpkin's Selection; easy; Fentone Music

Desportes, Yvonne Berthe Melitta

Saltarelle; 12 gtr

Euteneuer-Rohrer, Ursula Henrietta

Klanggewebe; gtr ens, trb, acc, db, and perc

Izarra, Adina

Dos movimientos para quinteto guitarra y cuarteto de cuerdas; 5 gtr and s4

Konishi, Nagako

Estranger; 2 a-gtr, 3 regular gtr, bass guitar, and elec contra bass gtr; 12'; ms.

Leone, Mae Grace

titles unknown; guitar ensemble pieces

Lutyens, Elisabeth

Anerca, Op. 77; speaker and 10 gtr; Olivan Press, Universal Edition, Ltd., (1975)

Meier, Margaret S.

Rejoicing, recessional from *The RATAGM Suite*; 5 gtr or gtr ens; 2'30"; medium-tonal, melodic, simple harmonies; ms.

Reich, Amy
Nursery Rhyme; multiple gtr

Richer, Jeannine (also Janine)
En ce temps-la; 12 gtr

Rite; 20 gtr

Yamashita, Toyoko
Ameisenmarsch für Gitarre-chor; gtr ens

GUITAR QUARTET

Calcagno, Elsa
Madrigal; 7 pp; medium; ms.

Epstein, Marti
For Guitars and Cello; 4 gtr and vlc; ms.

Finzi, Graciane
Libre-Parcours;

Gentile, Ada
Rarefatte aggregazione; 8'; G. Ricordi and Co.

Herrera, Hilda
Introducción y chaya

Marina, Carmen (pseud. of Carmen Manteca Gioconda)
Fugue; GioMar Editions

Roe, Eileen Betty
Omega Suite

Uyttenhove, Yolande
Stèle pour Aliénor d'Aquitaine, Op. 58; 4 gtr

GUITAR SOLO

Abreu, Zequinha
Não me tóques (Don't Touch Me), chorinho; 2 pp; medium-tonal, rhythmic; Irmãos Vitale editores

Os pintinhos no terreiro (Chickens in the Dirt), chôro-sapéca; 2 pp; medium-tonal, rhythmic; Irmãos Vitale editores

Tico-Tico no fubá (Bird in the Wheat), chôro-sapéca; 2 pp; medium-tonal, rhythmic; Irmãos Vitale editores

Alexander, Elizabeth

Diminutives; 5'; Seafarer Press

Alexander, Leni

Meralo

Almenar, Mariade

Soirée; 8 pp; Ediziones Musicales

Anderson, Ruth M.

Cards (Whist, Hearts, Baccarat); 10'; difficult-atonal; ms.

Anido, Maria Luisa

Aire de Vidalita; 1 p; medium, tonal, Romantic; Bèrben Editore

Aire norteño; Korn

Baile norteño (Dance of the North Argentine Indians); also published with two other pieces as *Pout pourri de pericones;* Casa Nuñez (1940)

Bailecito

Barcarola; Ricordi Americana

Canción de cuna, from *Album di musiche per chitarra;* 2 pp; medium, tonal, Romantic; Bèrben Editore (1953)

Canción del Yucatan; Korn

Canción No. 3; Bèrben Editore

Canto de la llanura, from *Impresiones argentinas;* Korn

Catamarqueña, from *Impresiones argentinas;* Korn

Chacarera

De mi tierra, from *Pout pourri de pericones;* Casa Nuñez (1940)

El misachico, from *Impresiones argentinas;* Korn

Gato; Casa Nuñez, 1939

Gris y mar; 14 pp; medium, nostalgic arpeggios; Union Musical Espanõla editores

Impresiones argentinas; a collection of nine pieces; Korn

Lejanía (preludio No. 1), from the series, *Preludi nostalgici;* Edizioni Ricordi (1971)

Melancolía (preludio)

Pout pourri de pericones: Baile norteño, De mi tierra, and Ritmo popular; Casa Nuñez

Preludio

Preludio campero No. 3, from *Album di musiche per chitarra*; 2 pp; medium, tonal; Bèrben Editore

Triste No. 1, from *Impresiones argentinas*; 1 p; medium, tonal, melanchoy; Korn

Anton, Susana (née Mendoza)

Ensayo; Editorial Argentina de Compositores, N 115

Archer, Violet

Fantasy on Blanche comme la neige

Ayers, Lydia

Etude de tempéré; difficult-microtonal, played on fretboard; ms.

Azuma, Cristina

A Toy; Guitar Solo Publications

Bakke, Ruth

Capricho nocturno; 4'; difficult-lightly atonal; Norsk Musikkinformasion

Barklund, Irma L.

Pieces for Guitar

Barrell, Joyce Howard

Eight Studies for Guitar, Op. 31; 8 pp; easy-tonal; MSM

Four Soliloquies, Op. 64; 8 pp; medium-atonal; Anglian Edition

Light Studies, Op. 31

Shapes, Op. 72

Beat, Janet

Arabesque, scenes from Jordan; 6'; Furore-verlag

Bertin, Elisa

Tres composiciones: 1. Cucuca (vals), 2. Mazurca, 3. Zamba; easy; Ricordi Americana

Birnstein, Renate

Quasi fantasia

Blood, Esta

If; 3'; medium-almost tonal, contemporary; Guitar Foundation of America

Bodorová, Sylvie

Baltic miniatures

Sostar Mange

Bofill, Anna

Suite de Tamanrasset; 11'; atonal, based on architectural works; Clivis Publications

Borràs i Fornell, Teresa

Cinco danzas, Op. 7; 12 pp; medium, contemporary treatment of flamenco themes; Casa Beethoven Publicacions

Danza catalana; 1 p; easy-tonal; ms.

Estudio; 1 p; easy, tonal; ms.

Mesto (Sorrowful), Op. 58; 2 pp; medium; ms.

Tiento, Op. 125; 3 pp; medium, flamenco-like; ms.

Borroff, Edith

Sonata for Guitar; 14'; American Composers Alliance

Boyd, Liona

Aria di Portonova; 3'

Asturiana; 5'14"

Brazilian Rag

Cantarell, from anthology, *Liona Boyd, First Lady of the Guitar;* 4 pp; medium-arpeggios and tremolo elements; Hansen House, Mid Continental Music

Carnival; 4 pp; medium-tonal; Hal Leonard Publishing Corp.

Christmas Dreams; 3'30"

Danza de las mariposas de Mexico

Ensueño; 5 pp; medium-tonal, romantic; Hal Leonard Publishing Corp.

Fallingbrook Suite: 1. Samba, 2. Waltz, 3. Rag

Fantasy on a Romantic Theme; 4'

Habañera; 4'30"

Llanto de gaviota; medium

Lullaby for My Love; 6'

Madrileña; 4'

Momento eterno; 6'

My Land of Hiawatha (three movements); 13'

Parranda; 5 pp; medium-tonal; Hal Leonard Publishing Corp.

Preludio poetica; 4'30"

Serenade for the Seasons: Autumn, Winter, Spring, Summer; 15'

Shadows of the Wind (In memory of Lenny Breau), from anthology, *Favorite Solos for Classical Guitar*; 4'; medium-tremolo piece; Hal Leonard Publishing Corp.

Siesta en la floresta; 4'

The Children's Waltz; 4'

Boyd, Liona, with Richard Fortin

Fallingbrook Rag, in anthology, *Favorite Solos for Classical Guitar*; 5 pp; medium-tonal, ragtime; Hal Leonard Publishing Corp.

Braase, Albertine

Thème varié pour la guitarre, dédié a Mlle. H. Amnitzboll

Braase, Sophie

Thème varié pour la guitarre, dédié a Mlle. Marguerite de Serene

Brondi, Maria (Marie) Rita

Melocia del Sannio; 1 p; Chiappino

Studio; 3 pp; Chiappino

Studio (Biblioteca del chitarrista); 2 pp; Chiappino

Burston, Maggie

Poem

Caceres L. de Pastor, Carmen

Cori Cadenay for Guitar; Ricordi Americana

Perlaschallay; Ricordi Americana

Calandra, Matilde Tettamanti de

Aires de mi tierra; 3 pp; medium-tonal, derivative of aires from Brazil; Ricordi Americana

Pequeña serie para guitarra: Marcha, Cancion de cuna (Cradle Song), Ronda; 4 pp; medium-nostalgic; Ricordi Americana

Tres preludios; 4 pp; medium-I: tonal, pensive, II: bright and lively, III: arpeggios/chords alternating; Barry Y Cia

Zamba; 2 pp; medium-Flamenco rhythmic dance; Barry Y Cia

Calcagno, Elsa

Me parece estar soñando; 2 pp; medium-tonal and dreamlike; Ricordi Americana

Siete improvisaciones para guitarra

Sonatina; written for Nelly Menotti and Luis Costa; 3 movements, 11 pp; medium-I: tonal and lyrical, II: expressive, III: rhythmic; Randolph

Carvalho, Dinorá (Dinorá Gontijo de Carvalho Murici)

Pobre cega; 2 pp; medium-tonal; Irmãos Vitale editores

Catunda, Eunice

Two Serestas

Chacon, Meme (pseud. of Remedios Chacon Bellido)

Concierto capricho en Do menor (Album #5); 10 pp; medium-difficult, tonal; Ediciones Musicales

Vol. 1, Malagueña, Soleares, and Seguidillas; Spanish Music Center

Vol. 2, Tarandas and Alegrias; Spanish Music Center

Vol. 3, Bulerias, and Sevillanas; Spanish Music Center

Vol. 4, Fandangos, Tientos and Tunguillos (Zapateado); Spanish Music Center

Vol. 5, Murcianas and Caracoles; Spanish Music Center

Chazarreta, Ana Mercedes de Monroy

Piecitas fáciles para guitarra; Ricordi Americana

Christian, Meg

Window Paynes; 4 pp; medium-tonal; Thumbelina Music, BMI

Cody, Judith Ann

City and Country Themes in G Major; Kikimora Publishing

Classical Guitar; Kikimora Publishing

Concert Etudes, Ops. 11, 13, 14, 15, 18; Kikimora Publishing

Dances, Op. 8; Kikimora Publishing

Etude No. 1; Kikimora Publishing

Firelights in C (major); Kikimora Publishing

Firelights in G (major); Kikimora Publishing

Nocturne, Op. 9; Kikimora Publishing

Cory, Eleanor

Phases; 8'; difficult; Phantom Press (Soundspell Productions)

Criswick, Mary

Another Ten for Guitar; Breitkopf and Härtel

First Melody (3 vols.); easy; Fentone Music

Teacher and I (Vols. 1 and 2); easy; Fentone Music

Ten for Guitar; Breitkopf and Härtel

Culbertson, D.C.

Five Twelve-Tone Pieces for Guitar; 2 pp; easy-twelve tone teaching pieces; ms.

Currier, Marilyn Kind

Sonata for Guitar

Davis, Jan

First Guitar Sonata

Intermezzo

Third Guitar Sonata

Davis, Yolanda

Campiando recuerdos; Casa Nuñez

Hágase a un lao

Degenhardt, Annette

A Double Jig for You and Me; 4'08"; Edition AD

An Air in Clare; 3'55"; Edition AD

Au cimetière le Py (In the Py cemetery); 3'43"; Edition AD

Chopinesque (Waltz in A minor); 3'57"; Edition AD

Communiqué to Mark Knopfler; 3'33"; Edition AD

Es geht auch weiter (Tomorrow Is Another Day); 4'31"; Edition AD

Es geht eine dunkle Wolk'-Thema und Variation (A Dark Cloud Loureth from the Sky); 2'49"; Edition AD

Farewell to Connaught; 2'06"; Edition AD

Gebrannte Mandeln (Waltz in G major); 3'17"; Edition AD

HeidieH (Waltz in D major); 3'16"; Edition AD

Heurige Musette (Waltz in E minor); 3'19"; Edition AD

Hörst Du zu, Atahualpa Yupanqui? (Waltz in G Major); 2'36"; Edition AD

Intakt; 4'46"; Edition AD

Leben (Life); 3'37"; Edition AD

Leipzig '84; 3'44"; Edition AD

Lied für die Indianer (Song for the Indians); 3'26"; Edition AD

Marginal; 3'18"; Edition AD

Musette mélancholique (Waltz in A minor); 4'19"; Edition AD

Nach zwei Flaschen Wein (Waltz in G major); 3'; Edition AD

Nachspürend

Narzissen auf Spitzen (Waltz in E major); 3'12"; Edition AD

Nicht eingebracht, nicht wilderfühlt (Neither Committed, nor Taking Off); 3'30"; Edition AD

Nicht ganz einfach (Waltz in D major); 3'26"; Edition AD

Noch nicht alles verspielt (Still Kicking); 2'36"; Edition AD

Requiem; 3'02"; Edition AD

Sandino Will Win; 3'02"; Edition AD

Schachteltanz im Spreizschritt (Waltz in D major); 2'24"; Edition AD

Strasse der Zikaden

Sunrise in Clare

Those Days

To Winnie and Nelson Mandela; 3'01"; Edition AD

Tombeau à Andres Segovia

Über einen Walzer (Waltz in E minor); 2'35"; Edition AD

Und zieht dahin

Unentschieden (Changeable); 1'33"; Edition AD

Unstet

Voller Hoffnung

Walzer in a-moll (Waltz in A minor); 3'30"; Edition AD

Wehmut in d-moll (Waltz in D minor); 3'31"; Edition AD

Weit ins Land (Far into the Country); 3'14"; Edition AD

Zwischentöne (Halftones); 2'37"; Edition AD

Desportes, Yvonne Berthe Melitta

En Schumanitant; Billaudot

Guitare Mozartzienne; 12'; easy-medium, Mozart-like; Billaudot

Modes d'antan; 6 pp; easy-medium. modal studies; Billaudot

Play Bach, Dances; 8 pp; easy-medium, in the style of Bach; Billaudot

Stücke for Gitarre Solo; Billaudot

Diakvnishvili, Mzisavar Zakharevna

Andante expressivo allegro molto

Diemer, Emma Lou

Bellsong; originally for carillon; difficult; Seesaw Music Corp.

Echo Space (for Peter Madlem); difficult-20th century atonality; Seesaw Music Corp.

Dinescu, Violeta

Parra Quitarra; 7 pp; difficult-atonal; Astoria Verlag

Dollitz, Grete Franke
Stringed Pioneers

Dorigny Denoyers, Mme
Romance sur la mort de Mazet; Reproduction, Minkoff (1976)

Duchesne, Geneviere
Pièces faciles pour guitare, Bd. 1; easy; Durand and Cie.

Duncan, Eve
Buddha Fantasy; 6'; medium-snare drum effect-atonal; ms.
Isis; 9'; medium-atonal, with snare drum effect; ms.

Eiríksdóttir, Karólina
Whence This Calm?; 14'

Epstein, Marti
The Parting Glass (written for David Tanenbaum); ms.

Erding, Susanne
Labirinto del sole

Farre de Prat, Carmen
Billiken (vals)
Cantos argentinos
El gato santiagueño
Martita
Pinina
Souvenir e una melodia

Ferrari, Gabriella (née Colombari de Montegre)
A une fiancée; Schirmer

Finzi, Graciane
Non si move una foglia; Durand and Cie.

Fleischer, Tsippi
To The Fruit Of My Land; Israel Music Institute

Frotta, Judith
Fantasie pour la guitare sur le duo de Mr. Paer: quel sepolocro che recechindo; (ca. 1825)

Furgeri, Bianca Maria
Trasparenze

Gabriel, Mary Ann Virginia, (married George E. March)
Hoila! Hoila!; Boosey and Hawkes

Gabus, Monique

Stèle pour une jeune indienne; 5'; medium; Editions Henry Lemoine

Garcia, Olimpiades

Grand minuetto; 2 pp; medium-tonal in A; Union Musical Espanõla Editores

La fuga del zapatero (Motivo espanõl No. 2); 3 pp; easy-medium, tonal in A; Union Musical Espanõla Editores

Garcia, Rosa Ascot

Española; fingered by R. Sainz de la Maza; 2 pp; medium, tonal, Romantic; Union Musical Española Editores

Gardner, Kay

Seven Modal Improvisations; any instrument; 5' each; Sea Gnomes Music

Travelin' (Minstrel I); gtr solo or fl and gtr; medium, guitar in dadabd tuning; Sea Gnomes Music

Gartenlaub, Odette

Ponctuations; Rideau Rouge

Gentile, Ada

Petite pièce; 7'; G. Ricordi and Co.

Gil del Bosque, Rosa

Evocución romántica; 7 pp; Union Musical Espanõla editores

Gileno, Jean Anthony

Austerity

Giteck, Janice

Puja: Songs to the Divine Mother; 15'; ms.

Giuliani-Guglielmi, Emilia

Belliniana No. 3; difficult-tonal 19th century style; G. Ricordi and Co.

Belliniana No. 4; difficult-tonal 19th century style; G. Ricordi and Co.

Belliniana, Op. 2 (includes Bellinianas Nos. 1-6); difficult-tonal 19th century style; Ricordi, Schott

Six Preludes, Op. 46; medium studies; Schott (1928), B. Schott's Söhne, Weinberger (Vienna)

Variazioni per chitarra, Op. 5 (theme by Rossini); medium-tonal 19th century style; G. Ricordi and Co.

Variazioni su un tema di Mercadante, Op. 9; difficult, tonal 19th century style; Bèrben Edizioni musicali

Giuranna, Elena Barbara

Incipit; 3 pp; medium; Bèrben Edizioni musicali

Gonzaga, Chiquinha (Francisca Hedwigwes Neves Gonzaga)

O Corta-Jaca; 3 pp; medium, lively poplular style; Montacute Publishing Co.

Grétry, Angelique-Dorothée-Lucile (Lucille, Lucie)

titles unknown in *Recueil de musique arrangée pour le cistre ou guitarre allemande contenant les plus jolies ariettes avec accompagnement, et des airs variés...*par M. Pollet l'aine; gtr or lyre

Grigsby, Beverly (née Pinsky)

Movements for Guitar: Prelude, Serenade, Dance; 10'; difficult-atonal, 1: extended techniques, 2: lyrical, 3: rhythmic, neo-romantic; ms.

Gubaidulina, Sofia Asgatovna

Serenade, from *The Russian Collection,* Vol. V; 1 p; difficult--Neo-Romantic with simple, spiritual quality; Editions Orphée

Gumert, Lynn

Prisms; 5 pp; medium-evocative atmosphere, tonal, lyrical and Neo-Romantic; ms.

Guraieb Kuri, Rosa

Impresiones for Guitar

Hara, Kazuko

Preludio, Aria e Toccata; Casa de la Guitarra

Harting-Ware, Lynn

Fantasy and Ricercare; 3 pp; medium-evokes earlier times; Acoma Company

Réverie and March; 5 pp; Acoma Company

Hartmann, Lioba

Gitarrenstücke; 10 string gtr; ms.

Havlik, Branka

Two Burlesques, from *Compositions of Yugoslav Authors for Classical Guitar, Album No. 1;* Ed. Nota-Knjazevac

Hayden, Carrie V. (née C.V. Sterns) (married W. L. Hayden)

Darkies Dance, in *The Guitar in America Collection;* 2 pp; easy-almost rag-like; Belwin Mills, originally C.V. Stearns

Reverie, in *The Guitar in America Collection;* 2 pp; easy to medium-lyrical; Belwin Mills, originally C.V. Stearns

Helmuth, Mara

Stream Collisions; moves from tonality to atonality

Henkel, Kathy

River Sky (based on poem by Lynn Harting Ware); 8 pp; medium-lyrical, a mood piece; Acoma Company

Ho, Wai On

Distance

Melody

Study on Thirds

Tremolo

Hovda, Eleanor

Lady Astor

Izarra, Adina

Desde una ventana con Loros; ms.

Dos jornadas

Folias de España

Silencios

Jeppsson, Kerstin Maria

Vocazione per chitarra solo, ded to Magnus Andersson; 7 pp; difficult-atonal, rhythmically complex; Edition Suecia

Jirackova, Marta (Martha)

Fantasia on Otakar Jeremias' theme, Op. 27

Joyce, Fiona

Piece No. 1; easy-medium; Guitar International

Kanach, Sharon

Die Altero

Kelley, Mary M.

Shard

Kolb, Barbara

Introduction and Allegra; Boosey and Hawkes

Three Lullabies; gtr, with some humming on the part of the guitarist; 7'30"; difficult-experimental; Boosey and Hawkes

Koptagel, Yuksel

Fossel Suite; gtr (or pf); Bote and Bock

Tamzara (Turkish Dance); gtr (or pf); Bote and Bock

Kruisbrink, Annette

60+; ms.

Faon; ms.

Harmony; ms.

Lara, Maria Teresa

Noche de Rhonda, from the anthology, *Music of Mexico for Acoustic Guitar;* 1 p; easy; Mel Bay

Larsen, Elizabeth (Libby)

Argyle Sketches; four pieces for guitar solo; E.C. Schirmer Music Company, Inc.

Istar fantasia; ms.

Tango; medium-difficult; ms.

Laruelle, Jeanne-Marie

El andaluz

Pieces

Prelude

Valse romantique

Lathrop, Gayle Posselt

Guitar Preludes; ms.

Lauber, Anne

Arabesque; 5 pp; difficult-dark moody, Impressionistic atonality; Doberman Music

Lauro, Natalia

Suite al estilo del preclásico; G. Zanibon

Leite, Clarisse

Suite Imperial; 7 pp; medium-three movts, much chromatisism; ms.

Lejet, Edith Jacqueline Marie

Balance, from *Trois Figures du Zodiaque;* 6'; one of three figures of the zodiac, conceived as a set with Gémeaux and Lion; Editions Transatlantiques

Gémeaux, from *Trois Figures du Zodiaque;* 5'30"; one of three figures of the Zodiac, conceived as a set with Balance and Lion; Editions Amphion

Lion, from *Trois Figures du Zodiaque;* 3'30; difficult-primitive, driving, Stravinsky-like, conceived as a set with Gémeaux and Balance; Editions Max Eschig

Lejeune-Bonnier, Elaine

Trois legends

Lenzi Mozzani, Carmen

Canto triste; Bèrben Editore

León, Tania Justina

Paisanos semos! (We's Hillbilies!); 4'30"; difficult-atonal, with rhythmic variety; Peer/Southern Music Publishing Co., Inc.

Levin, Rami Yona

Ambages; 12'; difficult-atonal, 12-tone parts, mysterious chords; ms.

Linnemann, Maria Catharina

Aus dem Schweigen; ms.

Ballad of County Down; easy-arpeggios; Musical New Services, Ltd.

Ballade pour Christine et Richard; ms.

Der Clown; Musical New Services, Ltd.

Gitarrengeschichten (Guitar Stories), Vol. I and II; solo suites; G. Ricordi & Co.

Guitar Pieces and Rounds for Guitar Beginners G. Ricordi & Co.

His Lady Alison; easy to medium; ms.

If My Fingers Could Dance; VDMK Manuskriptearchiv

Just for My Guitar, Musical New Services, Ltd.

Lady Claire; 1 p; easy-dreamy; Musical New Services, Ltd.

Leichte Folklorestücke; easy-folklore pieces; G. Ricordi & Co.

Lisa; 1 p; easy-dreamy, arpeggios, excellent student piece; ms.

Murmures (Whisperings); 1'; easy-dreamy, recorded with 11 more unpublished solos on Recaptured Moments CD; Daminus Records

Song of the Wild Rose; tremolo; ms.

Sparrow; G. Ricordi & Co.

Suite for Lovers G. Ricordi & Co.

Vagabond's Ragtime; 1 p; easy-ragtime, excellent student piece; ms.

Linnet, Anne

Quatuor brutale, 6 dances

Luff, Enid

Today and Tomorrow

Luizi, Maria Thereza

Eu e você, chorinho Brasileiro; 2 pp; easy to medium; Ricordi Brasileira

Lutyens, Elisabeth

Romanza, Op. 121; 9'; difficult; Olivan Press, Universal Ed., Ltd.

The Dying of the Sun, Op. 73; 6'30"; difficult-atonal, 12-tone, and tone clusters, introspective; Olivan Press, Universal Ed., Ltd.

MacAuslan, Janna L.

De mi corazón; 3'30"; medium-romantic; DearHorse Publications

Tremolo for Kristan; 2 pp; medium to difficult-tremolo, romantic; DearHorse Publications

Zambra; 3'; medium-Flamenco Arabic style; DearHorse Publications

Madriguera, Paquita Rodon

Capuestre d'Istui

Enyorant la meva terra

Humorada; 3 pp; easy to medium-tonal; Columbia Music Co.

L'aplec del l'Ernita

La boda India

Pastoral

Serenata aragonesa

Maguiña, Alicia

Jose Maria (Peruvian Creole Waltz) (arranged by Charles Postelwate); 2 pp; medium-Peruvian creole waltz style; Soundboard (Spring 1987)

Mamlok, Ursula

Five Intermezzi; 6'; difficult-soft, lyrical atonality; C.F. Peters

Marcus, Bunita

Apogee One; 8'; difficult-atonal, rhythmically complex; ms.

Maresca, Chiara

Choros I; difficult; ms.

Terra dalle fitte nebbie e dai fulgidi tramonti che screziano il corso del lago...; 8'; difficult-20th C. style, with extended techniques, including the guitar as a perc instrument; Edipan Musical Edition

Marez Oyens, Tera de

Hall of Mirrors; 8'; difficult-atonal; Donemus

Sequence; difficult; La Corda Editions

Valalan, Springtal; 6'-7'; difficult-atonal; Furore-Verlag

Mari, Pierrette (Anne Valérie)

Espagnolette

Pastels egrenes

Marina, Carmen (pseud. of Carmen Manteca Gioconda)

Choral; GioMar Editions

Primera impressión americana; GioMar Editions

Romanza; GioMar Editions

Sombras y luces; GioMar Editions

Sonata in A Major; GioMar Editions

Sonatina; GioMar Editions

Song of Sorrow on Marichu's Death (elegy); GioMar Editions

Suite No. 1, "Seagulls"; GioMar Editions

Suite No. 2, "White Snow and the Seven Dwarfs"; GioMar Editions

Suite No. 3, "Goya" or "Suite Borbonica"; GioMar Editions

Suite sobre una fabula infantil (Suite on a Fairy Tale); GioMar Editions

Three Pieces: 1. Nocturnal, 2. Dialogue, 3. Rag; GioMar Editions

Toccata on a Popular Spanish Song; GioMar Editions

Tonada; GioMar Editions

Tremoleando; tremolo study; GioMar Editions

Two Pieces: 1. Tonada, 2. Canto sin palabras; GioMar Editions

Zapateado clásico; easy-folk dance, lyrical; GioMar Editions

Markowitz, Judith

Morana; 3'35"; easy to medium-Flamenco, middle eastern mode; ms.

Marlow, Janet

Atmos Clock; 10 string gtr; easy to medium; ms.

Atmospheres; easy to medium; Marizzo Music

Dusk; 10 string gtr; easy to medium; Marizzo Music

Mozart's Spring/Sor; 10 string gtr; easy to medium; Marizzo Music

Ocean/Sky; 10 string gtr; easy to medium; Marizzo Music

The Four Directions: North, East, South, West; 10 string gtr; easy to medium; Marizzo Music

Martegani de Roca, Luisa

Estilo

Vidalita

Zamba

Mell, Eidylia

Andante

Tema variado

Michelson, Sonia

Fantasy

Silver Skating

Starry Night

Miyake, Haruna (pseud. Haruna Shibata)

Sonnet for Solo Guitar; 6 pp; difficult-atonal, experimental, some improv; Casa de la Guitarra

Montero Ayala, Delia

Tremolita: estudio en tremolo; Ricordi

Mori, Junko

An April Idyll; 5'; ms.

Meditation; 7'; ms.

Song in the Songless; 8'; ms.

Twilight; 7'; medium-atonal, impressionist quality; ms.

Moscovitz, Julianne

Guitar Suite in Colors

Tuesday Afternoon in October

Murakumo, Ayako

Prelude

Murdock, Katherine

Three Movements for Guitar; 5'; medium-atonal harmony; ms.

Naito, Akemi

Secret Guitar

Nazarova, Tatiana Borisovna

Romans, kolybelnaya, naigrish

Nogues, Clara

Musica para el collita; 3 pp; easy-tonal. excellent student pieces; Editions Henry Lemoine

Nunn, Ruth

Moods for Guitar; Novello and Co., Ltd.

O'Leary, Jane

Four Pieces for Guitar; 8'; difficult-atonal with impressionist mood; Contemporary Music Centre

Obrovská, Jana

Four Images of Japan; Editions Henry Lemoine

Guitare

Hommage à Béla Bartók, dedicated to and fingered by Milan Zelenka; 4'15"; difficult-atonal, with Bartók-like timbres; Editions Max Eschig

Hommage à choral gothique, fingered by Milan Zelenka; 4 pp; medium-with harmonics and open chord structure; Editions Orphée

Hommage à Utamaro

Passacaglia and Toccata; 5 pp; difficult-atonal; Editio Supraphon

Preludia pro kytaru; 11 pp; difficult-atonal; Editio Supraphon

Sonata; Otto Harrassowitz

Olcott-Bickford, Vahdah (née Ethel Lucretia Olcott)

Album Originale for Guitar, Op. 133

Beggar's Tale

Caprice characteristique; 3 pp; Carl Fischer, Inc. (1905 and 1915)

Choice Selections: Beauty Dream, Day Dreams; 1 p; Geo. Stannard, (1909).

Day Dreams (reverie), Op. 11; 2 pp; easy

Eventide, Op. 18; 1 p.

Gladness, Song without Words, Op. 24; easy; H.F. Odell and Co. (1913)

Guitar Solos and Duets, including *Gladness*; 2 pp; H.F. Odell and Co.

Heart of Joy (waltz), Op. 26; 1 p.

Jeanette (capricietto); Carl Fischer, Inc. (1918)

Knight and Lady Fair (Dance ancienne); Carl Fischer, Inc. (1919)

Lullaby (Cradle Song); Nicomde Editions

Manniken Dance (Danse du mannequin); Carl Fischer, Inc. (1919)

November, An Autumn Impression for the Guitar; Carl Fischer, Inc. (1921)

On A Summer's Day; 1 p.

On the Wings of Morpheus (lullaby); 1 p.

Select Solos for Guitar composed and arr. by Ethel Lucretia Olcott-Bickford; pub. for author by L. W. Heffelfinger Sheet Music, Geo. J. Barkel Co. (1905)

Valse, No. 9; Walter Norwood (1911)

Valse petite; 1 p.

Olive, Vivienne

Text IV; 3'; difficult-three short pieces, 1: dodecaphony, 2: bi-tonality, 3: whole tone; Furore-verlag

Tides of a Current Flowing; 10'; medium-a "lied" for guitar, sets poem of Walt Whitman to music without using the text; Furore-verlag

Oribello, Juanita

Alana's Song; 1 p; medium; ms.

April 7th; 2 pp; medium; ms.

Elena; ms.

EPOGM 1; 6 pp; medium-3 sections, 2 pages each; ms.

Meditations (Bach-style); 3 pp; medium-baroque style; ms.

Prelude I; ms.

There Will Come A Time; 2 pp; medium; ms.

Osawa, Kazuko

Nén; 7'; medium to difficult; Casa de la Guitarra

Ozaita Marques, Maria Luisa

Fantasia and Fugueta for Guitar; ms.

Preludio, danza con tres variaciones, y fanatsia; 8 pp; difficult-twelve tone; ms.

Pascual Navas, Maria Esperanza

Suite antigua

Triptico incaico

Patterson, Andra

Involution

Paulian, Athenais

Airs et variations/Chantés par Madame Catalani, Op. 1; 8 pp; medium; N. Simrock, Pl. No. 2529.

Pereira da Silva, Adelaide

Ponteio No. 1; Ricordi

Peyrot, Fernande

Petite Suite for Guitar; Genf, Menestrel (1954)

Philiba, Nicole

Inventionen for Guitar; 1'20"; medium

Quartre Inventions for Guitar; 1'20"; medium-tonal, romantic, lyrical; Editions Henry Lemoine

Sequences, Vol. 1, Sequences I; 2 pp; medium; Billaudot

Sequences, Vol. 2, Sequences II and III; 3 pp; medium; Billaudot

Sequences, Vol. 3, Sequences IV and V; 3 pp; medium; Billaudot

Pierce, Alexandra

Serenade, on Zander's Cobweb Photo; 12'; difficult-atonal, frequent mood changes; Guitar Foundation of America

Pires de Campos, Lina

Ponteio e toccatina; medium-lyrical, romantic; Irmãos Vitale editores

Prelúdios; medium-lyrical, romantic; Musicalia S/A/ Cultura Musical

Pires Dos Reis, Hilda

Studies Nos. 1 and 2

Polin, Claire

Rainstance; 3'15"; medium-atonal, modern; ms.

Pratten, Madame Sydney (née Catherina Josepha Pelzer)

Caprice for the Guitar; reprinted in *Journal of the Japan Guitar Society*, Vol. 1, No. 3, 1983; 5'; medium; originally published in the composer's home in London in the 19th century.

Div. 4 Pieces

Div. 8 Pieces (L. Schulz)

Div. 8 Pieces (L. Schulz), dedicated to Josiah Andrew Hudleston Esq. and Mrs. Hudleston

Div. A Sunbeam

Div. Air and Brilliant with Variations, dedicated to the Duchess of Hamilton

Div. Air by Mozart with Variations, ded. to Miss Catherine Carr

Div. Air with Variations, dedicated to Miss G. Hanbury Tracy

Div. Calliope

Div. Clouds, Rain and Sunshine

Div. College Hornpipe, dedicated to Lady Pakenham

Div. Coquette

Div. D. of Cambridge's Grand March, dedicated to Miss Butt

Div. Dance Fantastique

Div. Dance of the Witches

Div. Dreaming of Thee

Div. Evening Song

Div. Eventide

Div. Farewell to the Old Year

Div. Favorite Airs, dedicated to Miss Dent

Div. Gitana

Div. Home Sweet Home with Variations

Div. Hungarian March

Div. La donna e mobile, ma Normandie, dedicated to Lady Magnay

Div. Le adieux (Sor)

Div. Lord Raglan's March, dedicated to Lady John Somerset

Div. Mand

Div. March of the Fairies

Div. Melange on Scotch Airs

Div. Moonlight

Div. Oh! Susannah, with Variations, dedicated to the Duchess of Sutherland

Div. on American Airs, dedicated to Constance L. Gower

Div. on Irish Airs, dedicated to Lady Grace Vandeleur

Div. on Portuguese Airs, dedicated to Miss Sarah Carr

Div. on Scotch Air, dedicated to Miss Fanny Moore

Div. on Scotch Airs, dedicated to Mrs. Richard Tothill

Div. on Welch Airs, dedicated to Miss Emma Atcherly

Div. Paganini's Carnaval de Venise, dedicated to Miss Carr

Div. Peasant's Dance

Div. Portuguese and French, dedicated to Miss Hughes

Div. Preludes

Div. Preludes and Pieces

Div. Rambling Thoughts

Div. Reverie, dedicated to Mrs. Tothill

Div. Sacred Selections, dedicated to Mrs. Carr

Div. Sadness

Div. Sea Saw

Div. Selections

Div. Serenade, dedicated to Miss Millicent F. van Notten Pole

Div. Spanish Dance

Div. Tears and Scherzo, dedicated to Mrs. Francis Koe

Div. Three Marches, dedicated to Viscontess Valentina

Div. Treue Liebe

Div. Twilight

Div. Two Marches, dedicated to Miss Hammnond

Div. Two Original Melodies, dedicated to Miss Went

Div. Valse espagnole, dedicated to Miss Dunkin

Div. Various, dedicated to Mrs. Coulson

Div. Various, dedicated to Miss Louisa Montagu

Div. Various, dedicated to Mrs. Landers

Div. Various, dedicated to Mrs. Robertson

Div. Villikins

Div. Violet

Div. Wandering Thoughts

Div. Woodland and Stream

First Divertimento, dedicated to Lady John Somerset

Preobrajenska, Vera Nicolaevna

Rondino

Sonatina

Presti, Ida

Dance rythmique; 2 pp; medium; Ricordi

Etude à ma mère

Etude du Martin; 4 pp; medium; Columbia Music Co.

Etude No. 1; solo (or duet?)

Etude No. 2

Hommage à Manuel Ponce

Prélude (Hommage à Bach)

Prélude pour Alexandre

Segovia

Six Etudes; 11 pp; easy-medium; Editions Max Eschig

Price, Deon Nielson

Alma Jubilo; ms.

Procaccini, Teresa

Cinque pezzi incaici, Op. 60; 10 pp; medium-simply tonality,
folk-like; Zanibon

Sei pezzi incaici, Op. 61; ms.

Sei studi, Op. 63; ms.

Six Studi, Op. 61(?); Carisch S.p.a.

Ravinale, Irma

Improvisazione per chitarra solo; 10 pp; difficult-atonal; Bèrben Edizioni musicali

Invenzione

Sombras

Rehnqvist, Karin Birgitta

Band; Stims Informationcentral för Svensk Musik

Richer, Jeannine (also Janine)

Piège 6; 4 pp; difficult, aleatoric, experimental; Editions Musicales Transatlantiques

Rives for Guitar; Editions Musicales Transatlantiques

Rickard, Sylvia

Suite

Rodríguez, Marcela

El paso del tiempo (in four movements)

Son mis recuerdos Madre

Tristeza gaucha

Rodriguez Arenas, Elba

A la luz de la luna (estilo)

Alma gaucho (estilo)

Ausencia (zamacueca)

De tardecita (estilo)

Flores del campo (zamba)

Roe, Eileen Betty

Larcombe's Fancy, five solos; 4 pp; easy-medium

Short Sonata; 6 pp; medium-tonal, neo-romantic; Thames Publishing

Sonatina dolorosa; 5 pp; easy-tonal; Thames Publishing

Summer Suite; 3 pp; easy; Thames Publishing

Rogatis, Teresa De

Alba sul mare (Dawn at Sea) (Studio arpeggiato)

Balletto; in anthology, *Opere scelte per chitarra;* 11 pp; medium-impressionistic; Bèrben Edizioni musicali

Berceuse; Venturi

Canto arabo; published in magazine, *La Chitarra* (1934)

Fantasia araba

Fuochi fatui (Studio di ottave); in Bèrben anthology; medium

Gavotta della bambola; published in the music magazine, *Il Plettro* (1920)

Mormorio della foresta; reprinted in Bèrben anthology; medium-tonal, ABA form; Vizzari

Soirée Madrilène; in Bèrben anthology; medium

Sonatina (quasi una fantasia); in Bèrben anthology; medium

Studio sul tremolo; dedicated to Gregory Newton

Tarantella diabolica (Studio in 6/8)

Vespro sul fiume (Studio da concerto); Edizioni Curci

Romero, Elena

Tres de junio nocturne

Two Movements Temáticos; gtr or hp

Ruff-Stoehr, Herta Maria Klara

Menuet

Sagreras, Clelia

Chalita (zamba); Casa Nuñez

Flor de Ceibo (zamacueca); Casa Nuñez

La torcacita (zamba); Casa Nuñez

Salvador, Matilde

Homenatge A Mistral; 11 pp; medium-difficult, neo-Romantic, semi-popular style, impressionist arpeggios; Editions Henry Lemoine

Sandler, Felicia Ann Barbara

Coming Home; 10'; difficult; American Music Center Library

São Marcos, Maria Livia

Divertimento (Eleven Easy Pieces); 11 pp; Irmãos Vitale editores

Saparoff, Andrea

Seria en re; 5 pp; medium, atonal, three movements, contrasting cluster effects; Waggamissimo Music, ASCAP, 1983

Schilling, Betty Jean

Rainfall Night; Crying Creek Publishers

Strivation; Crying Creek Publishers

Schönfelder, Ilse

Sechs Stüke, from *Anthology Gitarre 7*; 9 pp; difficult-6 short pieces; mostly atonal, diverse moods; Verlag Neue Musik, Berlin

Schonthal, Ruth

Fantasia in a Nostalgic Mood; 6'; difficult; Fine Arts Music

Fantasy-Variations Upon a Jewish Liturgical Theme; two versions: Tamberello, editor (difficult), R. Deame, editor (easier); difficult-Neo-Romantic; ms.

Scliar, Esther (Ester)

Etude No. 1

Sepúlveda, Maria Luisa

titles unknown; guitar solos

Serrano Redonnet, Ana

titles unknown; guitar solos

Shore, Clare

Cool Spring Meditations; 10'; E.C. Schirmer Music Company, Inc.

Sinde-Ramallal, Clara

Barmi aire de Milonga; Ricordi

Prelude No. 1; Ricordi

Singer, Jeanne

Arietta; 3'30"; ms.

Sommer, Silvia

Recuerdos de... for Guitar

Sonntag, Brunhilde

Akrostichon for Guitar Solo

Spampinato, Letizia

Delta; 3 pp; difficult-atonal; ms.

Diacromia; 7 pp; difficult-atonal; ms.

Spiegel, Laurie

An Earlier Time

Steinburg, Carolyn

Three Pieces for Prepared Guitar; Rocky Press

Strutt, Dorothy

Grey Light

Sulpizi, Mira (Pratesi)

Aire e danza nuove; G. Ricordi and Co.

Ballatelle; also for fl and gtr; G. Ricordi and Co.

Eight Medieval Songs

Szeghy, Iris

A Minute-Fugue; 1'; ms.

Suite into Pocket; 7'; Music Fund/archives

Szekely, Katalin

Miniaturen for Guitar; ms.

Pièce avec interludes for guitar; ms.

Szeto, Caroline

Three Pieces for Guitar

Tann, Hilary

A Sad Pavane Forbidding Mourning; 4'45"; difficult-atonal, interspersed with neo-Renaissance, lute-like passages; ms.

Tapia, Gloria

Aria de la amistad; ms.

Dos piezas de concerto; ms.

Suite juvenil para guitarra, Op. 19A; four movements; ms.

Tate, Phyllis

A Sad Humoresque; 2 pp; easy to medium; Oxford University Press, Music Department

Seascape; 2 pp; medium; Oxford University Press, Music Department

Thomas, Karen P.

Rhapsodic Ignition; ms.

Torres, Ana

1001 caras; difficult; atonal, minimalist, virtuosic; Guitar Review (Spring, 1994)

Tower, Joan

Clocks; 9'07"; difficult; virtuosic, flamenco rhythms, vague tonality, percussive; G. Schirmer/AMP

Relojas; difficult, same piece as Clocks?

Urreta, Alicia

Estudio I and II

van Appledorn, Mary Jeanne

Postcards to John; difficult-evocative; ms.

van Schaijk-Lambermont, Herma

Contrasts; ms.

Velasquez, Consuelo

Bésame mucho; 2 pp; Peer International Corporation

Verhaalen, Sister Marion

Samba

Viard, M. (Mme. or M. de Viard)

titles unknown in *Recueil de romances, chansons et vaudeville arrangés pour la guitarre,* dédiés à la Reine par...; Benaut (1780s?)

Vigneron-Ramackers, Josée (Christiane) (pseud. Jo Delande)

Variations sur Harbouya

Variations sur un cramignon liegeois, Op. 16

Vito-Delvaux, Berthe di

Histoires pour guitare, Op. 139; Schott

Waldo, Elizabeth

Bossa californiana; 1 p; easy; Mizteca Music, Guitar Solo Pub.

Walker, Gwyneth

Rondo lyrico; 5'30"; medium-lyrical; Walker Music Publishing

Six Studies for Guitar (for Alice Artzt); 13'; medium to difficult; E.C. Schirmer Music Company, Inc.

Sonatina; 6'; Walker Music Publishing

Variations; 7'20"; medium-lyrical; Walker Music Publishing

Walker, Louise

Brasilianisch; Heinrichshofen's Verlag

Collection

Etude, C-dur; V. Hladky

Etude, Chromatisch (with Marsch nach einer Tiroler Melodie); V. Hladky

Etude, E-Dur; V. Hladky

Gaucho; medium; Heinrichshofen's Verlag

Kleine Romanze; medium; Heinrichshofen's Verlag

Marsch nach einer Tiroler Melodie; easy; Heinrichshofen's Verlag

Tanzlied; easy to medium; Heinrichshofen's Verlag

Variationen uber ein Spanisches Lied; V. Hladky

Warren , Betsy (Warren-Davis) (pseud. Betsy Frost)

The Blue Goat

Yamashita, Toyoko

Kleine Märchen für Gitarre

Kleine Stücke nach Altjapanishche Volksleider für Gitarre; (1983)

Sech Miniaturen aus einem italienischen Bilderbuch; (1986)

Sonate für Gitarre solo

Zaerr, Laura

Rondo caprice; 5'; difficult-tonal, freely chromatic, melodic; ms.

Zaidel-Rudolph, Jeanne

Tango for Tim; ms.

Zaripova, Naila Gatinovna

Quartetino

Ziffrin, Marilyn Jane

Incantation and Dance; 8'; difficult-basically tonal with Russian modes, some atonality, evocative; ms.

Rhapsody; 6 pp; difficult-basically tonal with Russian modes, some atonality, evocative; Editions Orphée

Souvenir-Homenaje a Andrés Segoviu; 12 pp; Editions Orphée

Three Movements for Guitar; 12'; difficult; basically tonal with Russian modes, some atonality, evocative; ms.

Zimmermann, Margrit

Pezzi brevi; 2 pp; ms.

Pezzi brevi for Guitar, Op. 30 (I. Strada, II. Pagoda); 3 pp; ms.

Zubeldia, Emiliana de (pseud. Emily Bydwealth)

Capricho basko

Paisaje basko

GUITAR TRIO

Barrell, Joyce Howard

Strata, Op. 40

Beat, Janet

Joie de vivre; 3 gtr, bass gtr, and perc; 15'; Scottish Music Information centre

Borràs i Fornell, Teresa

Garberes (Shocks); 2-3 pp; medium, polytonal; ms.

Criswick, Mary

Guitar Trios; Chester, J. and W. Ltd.

Desportes, Yvonne Berthe Melitta
  Partita en La (five movements); guitar trio, or gtr and pf or hpc; 23 pp; easy-medium, based on Baroque dance movements

Dinescu, Violeta
  Figuren III; 11 pp; difficult-atonal with extended techniques; ms.

Hara, Kazuko
  Introduction and Allegro for Guitar Trio

Prado, Almeira
  Livre pour six cordes; Editions Max Eschig

Silverman, Faye-Ellen
  Three guitars; 13'; Seesaw Music Corp

von Zieritz, Grete
  Danza for guitar trio; 7pp; Editions Orphée

Yamashita, Toyoko
  Ameisenmarsch für 3 Gitarren
  Hepaihoi for three guitars

HARP AND GUITAR

Coulthard, Jean
  Music on a Scottish Folk Song; vln, hp, and gtr

Desportes, Yvonne Berthe Melitta
  Les cordes reint; 2 gtr and hp
  Les menestriers du ciel; gtr, fl, and hp

Sepúlveda, Maria Luisa
  Pieces for Guitar and Harp

KEYBOARD AND GUITAR

Calcagno, Elsa
  Pieces for piano and guitar; pf and gtr

Oliveros, Pauline
  Time Let Me Play and Be Golden in the Mercy of His Means; hpc and gtr; Oliveros Foundation

Pratten, Madame Sydney (née Catherina Josepha Pelzer)

Div. Absence, dedicated to Senorita Dona Bernarda Turnbull; pf and gtr

Div. Duo; pf and gtr

German March; pf and gtr

Samter, Alice

Hundert Takte; pf and gtr; 5'; VDMK manuskriptearchiv

Hundert Takte; cmb and gtr; 4'; VDMK manuskriptearchiv

Silsbee, Ann Loomis

Glyphs; hpc and gtr; 17'; ms.

Stoll, Helene Marianne

Sonate für Gitarre und Cembalo, Op. 37; cmb and gtr; 11'; Furore-Verlag

Wolf, [L.], Anna (née Mrasek)

Thema avec Variations arangé pour Cluvecin & Guitarre, dedie a Mme Jacobine de Schoeps; T. Mollo (#1652) (1804)

Yamashita, Toyoko

Canción y danza clásica für Gitarre und Klavier; pf and gtr

Sonate für Gitarre und Klavier; pf and gtr

Zimmermann, Margrit

Visione, Op. 32 for Guitar and Piano; pf and gtr; ms.

LARGE ENSEMBLE

Alsted, Birgitte

Espressione emotionale; gtr, fl, cl, perc, pno, vln, and vlc

Berstand, Ragnhild

Mellom for Og Etter; gtr, cl in b, perc I and II, vln I, vln II, vla, and vcl; 16 pp; difficult-extended techniques, Webern-like; Norsk Mussikkinformasion

Bofill, Anna

Septet de set sous; fl, cl, gtr, pf, vln, and vlc; 11'; atonal, based on architectural works; ms.

Bouchard, Linda

Rocking Glances; fl, ob, vln, vla, vlc, man, gtr, and perc; ms.

Brandman, Margaret Susan

The Optimum Number; sax, trp, trb, gtr, pf, bass, and perc; 5'; Furore

Cory, Eleanor

Octagons; fl, cl, bsn, pf, vib, gtr, vln, and vlc; American Composers Alliance

Gaertner, Katarzyna

Pop Mass; Polskie Wydawn Muzyczne

Konishi, Nagako

Ode for the Eleven; fl, cl, b-cl, bsn, trb, 2 marimba, perc, ob, and gtr; 15'; ms.

Lambertini, Marta

Anonimo Italiano; 2 fl, gtr, vln, vla, and vlc

Antígona; vla, 2 cl, man, gtr, and pf

Lee, Hope

M-Nabri; fl, cl, man, gtr, hp, vla, cb, and mari; ms.

Liter, Monia (Hixon: Monica)

Mediterranean Suite; perc, gtr, hp, and strs; Boosey

Lutyens, Elisabeth

Catena, Op. 44; S, T, and instruments 1131, 2120, perc, hp, cel, pf, man, gtr, and strs; 12'30"; L. Schott

O saisons, O chateaux, Op. 13; S, man, gtr, hp, and str orch; Mills Music

Quincunx; S, Bari, perc, 7 perc, pf, gtr, man, hp, and strs; Mills Music

Marez Oyens, Tera de

Divertimento; descant recorder, s-recorder, timb, perc (Orff), gtrs, vl (fiddle), and tenor gamba; Donemus

McKenzie, Sandra

Peer Gynt; b-ob, 3 cl, acoustic gtr, perc, and str

Mori, Junko

Nightfall; gtr, fl, 2 vln, vla, and vlc (or db); 12'20"; ms.

Musgrave, Thea

Soliloguy II; gtr, fl, 2 ob, bsn, and strs; Chester, J. and W. Ltd,

Pascual Navas, Maria Esperanza

La ñusta Korihuanca; s4, ob, viol, female vce, caja (drum), and gtr

Ptaszynska, Marta

Improvisations; 3333, 4331, perc, cel, hp, pf, gtr, and strs; 10'; Polskie Wydawnictwo Muzyczne

Ravinale, Irma

Dialoghi; vla, gtr, and orch

Rotaru, Doina

Ceasuri (Clocks); cl, bsn, vla, vlc, gtr, pf, and perc

Runa; fl, ob & ob d'amore, gtr, cel, and hpd

Schieve, Catherine

String Figures; pf, hpc, hp, 2 gtr, 2 vln, 2 vlc, and d-b

Shaffer, Jeanne E.

Heart of Dixie; strs, fl, ob, cl, trp, trb, gtr, and perc; ms.

Shore, Clare

Trinity; fl (pic), bsn, trb, gtr, perc, pf, vln, vla, and vlc; 20'; E.C. Schirmer Music Company, Inc.

Wegener-Frensel, Emmy Heil

Rapsodie; 2 sax, 4441, timb, perc, 2 hp, cel, 2 gtr, and strs; 8'; Donemus Amsterdam

Whitehead, Gillian

Music for Christmas; fl, cl, vln, vlc, bsn, gtr, pf or cel, and marimba

Wilkins, Margaret Lucy

Rêve, réveil, révélation, réverbérations; a-fl, cl, b cl, bsn, vib, mar, gtr, hp, 4 vln, vla, vlc, db, synth (DX7 ?)

METHOD

Artzt, Alice

The Art of Practicing; 25 pp; medium; Musical New Services, Ltd. (1978)

Chacon, Meme (pseud. of Remedios Chacon Bellido)

Metodo y ejercicios de Francisco Tarrega III-VI

Cottin, Madeleine

Methode complete de guitare: Contenent un procede rationnel et tres simple pour la formation de tons les accords; easy-tonal studies; Joumade, M. (1909)

Criswick, Mary

Guitar Tutor for Young Children; easy; Breitkopf and Härtel

Ford, Ann (married Thicknesse)

Lessons and Instructions for Playing on the Guitar; 9 pp

Gabetti, Flora

Guitare mon amie; Bèrben Editore

Methods pour debutantes; Schott

Godla, Mary Ann, with Fred Nance

Music Through the Guitar Series; 18 vols.; easy

Primer for the Classic Guitar; easy; Ashley Dealers Service, Inc.

Up To Date Method for Classic Guitar, Book I; easy; Ashley Dealers Service, Inc.

Kukuck, Felicitas (née Kestner)

Spiel mit auf deiner Gitarre--ein Lehr und Speilbuch (Join in and Play, a Guitar School); easy; Möseler Verlag

MacAuslan, Janna L.

Technical Exercises for Strength and Coordination, (Classical Guitar); 10 pp; medium-difficult; DearHorse Publications

Michelson, Sonia

New Dimensions in Classical Guitar for Children; easy; Mel Bay

Olcott-Bickford, Vahdah (née Ethel Lucretia Olcott)

Advanced Course for the Guitar by Vahdah Olcott-Bickford; Oliver Ditson Co. (1924)

Method for Classic Guitar; 120 pp; easy to medium; Peer International Corp. (1964)

The Olcott-Bickford Guitar Method, Op. 85; Oliver Ditson Co. (1921)

Polasek, Barbara

Gitarre Im Gruppenunterricht; easy to medium

Pratten, Madame Sydney (née Catherina Josepha Pelzer)

Guitar Tutor; Boosey and Co. (1881)

Instructions for the Guitar tuned in E major

Learning the Guitar, Simplified, 13th edition; Williams, J., and Pelzer, G. (1900)

Rogatis, Teresa De

Il Maestro e l'allievo: Ricreazioni per principianti di chitarra con accompagnamento dell'insegnante; Edizioni Curci

Metodo per chitarra; Edizioni Curci

Primi passi; Edizioni Curci

São Marcos, Maria Livia

Complément à la technique de la guitare

Einfuhrung in das klassische Gitarrenspeil; 31 pp; easy to medium

Erganzung zur Gitarrentechnick III

Initiation à la guitare classique

Sheer, Anita

Introduction to the Flamenco Guitar

Stanley, Ruth

Starting the Guitar, Book 1 (for Children); Musical New Services, Ltd.

Walker, Louise

Das Tagliche Training; Heinrichshofen's Verlag

Der junge Gitarre-soloist; Heinrichshofen's Verlag

Für den Anfang im Gitarrenspiel; Heinrichshofen's Verlag

Taglische Training für den Anfang, (Vol. 1-6)

MULTI-MEDIA AND GUITAR

Anderson, Beth (Barbara Elizabeth)

Hallophone: vce, sax, gtr, tapes, visuals, and dancers; ms.

Capdeville, Constança

Esboços para um Stabat Mater; fl, tpt, gtr, hp, vln, vla, vlc, pf, tape, lights, dancers

Irman-Allemann, Regina

Lied an Sophie die Henkersmaid, das Mondschaf, Tapetenblume; woman's vce, pf, perc, gtr, fl or pic, and transparencies

PERCUSSION AND GUITAR

Coates, Gloria

Blue Monday; gtr and perc

Lam Man Lee, Violet

Tieh Meng

Rosas Fernandes, Maria Helena

Territorio e ocas

RECORDER AND GUITAR

Ansink, Caroline
Storms; a-rec and 3 gtr

Gambarini, Costanza, with Gruseppe Cambarini
Sonatinas; G. Ricordi and Co.

Gumert, Lynn
Nothing But Flowers and Songs of Sorrow...; t-rec and gtr; 11'30";
medium-Neo Romantic

Kurimoto, Yoko
June End Songs; a-rec and gtr; difficult-atonal, extended techniques,
Zen-like mood; ms.

Lehnstaedt, Lu
*Lustige musik für zwei Blockflöten in C oder anderne
Melodieninstrumente und Gitarre;* gtr and 2 rec in C; Schneider

Roe, Eileen Betty
Seven Tunes, from the *Cecil Harpe Collection;* descant rec and gtr;
Novello and Co., Ltd.

Szönyi, Erzsebet
Twenty Hungarian Folksongs; 2 rec and gtr

Tate, Phyllis
Light Pieces; Oxford University Press, Music Department

Wilkins, Margaret Lucy
Aspects of Night

REEDS AND GUITAR

Ballou, Esther Williamson
Dialogues; ob, pn, and gtr, also ob and gtr; medium-difficult; ms.

Barklund, Irma L.
Mediterranea; pf, ob, and gtr

Desportes, Yvonne Berthe Melitta
L'horloge jazzante; a-sax and gtr; medium-clock-like with jazz feel;
Billaudot

Dring, Madeleine (married Roger Lord)

Dance Gaya; wwd ens and gtr, or pf and ob, also 2 pf

Lutyens, Elisabeth

Deroulement, Op. 145; ob and gtr; 10'30"; Olivan Press, Universal Edition, Ltd.

Marina, Carmen (pseud. of Carmen Manteca Gioconda)

Jazz Duet; cl and gtr; GioMar Editions

Price, Deon Nielsen

Mesurée; soprano sax or cl and gtr; ms.

Strutt, Dorothy

Piece on Three; ob and gtr

SMALL ENSEMBLE

Agudelo Murguia, Graciela

Cancrizante; vln, gtr, vib, pf, and trb

Anderson, Beth (Barbara Elizabeth)

Little Trio; fl, gtr, and vla; 3'; American Composers Alliance

Anderson, Olive Jennie Paxton

My Love's an Arbutus; fl, cl, and gtr (or string trio)

Blood, Esta

Cycle; fl, cl, pf, (movement one) and fl, cl, and gtr (movement two)

Bofill, Anna

Quartet; gtr, hpc, pf, and perc; 9'; atonal, based on architecture; ms.

Briggs, Nancy Louise

Celtica; gtr, fl, vlc, and perc

Buchanan, Dorothy Quita

Echoes and Reflections; cl, gtr, vln, and vlc

Ciobanu, Maia

Prelude; cl, gtr, and trb

Coltrane, Alice McCleod

Bliss: The Eternal Now; pf, hp, and gtr

Cory, Eleanor

Fantasy for Flute, Guitar and Percussion; fl, gtr, and perc; difficult; American Composers Alliance

Coulthard, Jean

The Bird of Dawning Singeth All Night Long; fl, vla, and gtr

Desportes, Yvonne Berthe Melitta

Valse des libéllules et des papillons; fl, vla, gtr, and vlc; 10 pp; medium

Di Lotti, Silvana

A Solo; clar, vln, gtr, man, perc

Duncan, Eve

Raffaello; gtr, ob, and vla; 8'; ms.

Erding, Susanne

El sueño; fl, cl or vla, and gtr

Even-Or (Ben-Or), Mary

Dreams; gtr, fl, and cl

Fine, Vivian

Canciones y danzas; fl, gtr, and vlc; Catamount Facsimile Editions

Franklin, Mary Elizabeth

A Far Away Land; fl, gtr, hp, vla, and marimba

Gardner, Kay

Crystal Bells; fl, vlc, and gtr or hp; 6'30"; easy to medium; Sea Gnomes Music

Lunamuse; fl, vlc, gtr, small perc, and audience participation; 9'; easy to medium-meditative; Sea Gnomes Music

Romance; fl, vla, and gtr or hp; 3'30"; easy to medium-tonal and lyrical; Sea Gnomes Music

Sundancer; fl, vla, perc, and gtr or pf; 6'; medium; Sea Gnomes Music

Touching Souls; a-fl, gtr, and hand drums; 5'40"; easy to medium; Sea Gnomes Music

Hardin, Miss (same as Hardin(g), Elizabeth?)

titles unknown in *The Musical Magazine: Compleat pocket companion for the year 1767[-1772]* consisting of songs and airs for the German flute, violin, guittar[sic] and harpsichord; 6 vols; T. Bennett

Hawley, Carolyn Jean (née Bowen)

Auccassin et Nicollet; narr, gtr, fl, and vlc

Quartet No. 2; ob, gtr, vlc, and hpc

Hays, Sorrel Doris Ernestine

Junture Dance, from *Music for Young People;* rec, harm, triangle, autoharp, and gtr; easy; ms.

Hoover, Katherine

Two Dances for Flute, Oboe, and Guitar; fl, ob, and gtr; American Music Center

Kojima, Yuriko

Lunar Distance; fl, cl, vib, and gtr; 8'; ms.

Kurimoto, Yoko

A Plan of 4x4; fl, gtr, and vlc; ms.

LaChartre, Nicole Marie

Essa II; hp, hpc, gtr, and zarb

Lind, Jenny (Johanna Maria)

Serenading Polka; vln, gtr, and pf; Oliver Ditson Co.

Linnemann, Maria Catharina

Come August and September; fl, cl, vlc, and gtr; ms.

Lomon, Ruth

Shapes; vln, vlc, gtr, and pf; ms.

Marbe, Myriam

Cyclus; fl, gtr, and perc; ms.

Marcus, Bunita

1975; Arp 2500, a-sax, b-cl, gtr, and steel dr; ms.

Marina, Carmen (pseud. of Carmen Manteca Gioconda)

Trio; gtr, fl, and vlc; GioMar Editions

Marshall, Pamela J.

Through the Mist; fl, vln, and gtr; 10-12'; difficult-atonal, but lyrical; Spindrift Music Company

Meneely-Kyder, Sarah Suderley

Buzz; resonating bells, tubular bells, kalimba, and gtr

Mertens, Dolores

Pieces; hp, gtr, pf, and har

Moretto, Nelly

Composition No. 7; fl, vla, b-cl, and gtr

Musgrave, Thea

Sonata for Three; gtr, fl, and vln; 6'45"; difficult, mild atonality, some neo-Romanticism, fun; Novello and Co., Ltd.

Noda, Eva (Saito)

Tanka; fl, ob, and gtr; medium, neo-Romantic with modal and tonal qualities; ms.

Nowak, Alison

   Quintet; fl, vln, bsn, gtr, and pf; facsimile at NNACA, 1973

Obrovská, Jana

   Bisbiglii e gridi; b-cl, gtr, and pf

   Musica per tre; vln, gtr, and acc

Oribello, Juanita

   Flowers on My Dial; a-rec, vlc, and gtr; 4 pp; medium; ms.

Ravinale, Irma

   Serenata; gtr, fl, and vla

Schloss, Myrna

   Guitar Varia; gtr, hpc, and synth

   Thirteenth Summer; fl, gtr, and vlc; four movements

Schmidt, Mia

   Lilith for Two Violas, Two Guitars, and Percussion; 2 vla, 2 gtr, and perc; 12'; difficult; Contemporary Music Adesso

Schorr, Eva (née Weller)

   Trio for Flute, Viola, and Guitar in Andenken a A. Diabelli; fl, vla, and gtr

Shafer, Sharon Guertin

   Le désert; 2 fl, vlc, gtr, and hpc; 4-5'; medium-tonal, melodic, sparse, mediative; ms.

Skirving, W. (a lady)

   Miss Margt Hamilton's Quickstep, for the Pianoforte, Guitar and German-flute...The Whim, or Miss Agnes Graham's Favourite; pf, gtr, and "german-flute"; Muir Wood and Co. (G. Walker)

Sommer, Silvia

   Trio for Flute, Guitar and Contrabass; fl, gtr, and db

Strutt, Dorothy

   Quartet on Haiku; fl, cl, gtr, and vln; Chas. Ford?

Thome, Diane

   Stepping Inward; ob or Eng hn, vla, hp, gtr, and man; 10'; Acoma-Nambe

van Epen-de Groot, Else Antonia

   Trio for Flute, Viola and Guitar; fl, vla, and gtr

von Zieritz, Grete

   Tanzsuite; gtr or hp, cl, bsn, and perc

Weaver, Carol Ann

Procession; man, gtr, and pf; 8'

Wylie, Ruth Shaw

Terrae Incognitae, Op. 34; fl, vla, gtr, pf, and perc; 15'; difficult; H. Branch, 1977

Three Inscapes, Op. 26; fl, vla, gtr, pf, and perc; 10'; difficult; H. Branch, 1977

Yamashita, Toyoko

An dem Marchenbuch "Kosmos"; gtr, pf, fl, vln, and vlc

Zaerr, Laura

Pentanomos (suite in five movements); hp, gtr, and rec; 7'; medium-tonally based, freely chromatic; ms.

STRINGS AND GUITAR

Beat, Janet

Convergencies; db and gtr; 5'50"; Scottish Music Information Centre

Bobrow, Sanchie

Our Town; vln and gtr

Bofill, Anna

Variazioni su tre temi di Anna Bon Di Venezia; gtr, vla, and vlc; 15'; ms.

Byrchmore, Ruth M.

Hare and the Tortoise; vla and gtr; 12'; difficult-20th C. techniques, atonal; ms.

Conrad, Laurie M.

Two Pieces; vla and gtr

Di Lotti, Silvana

Duo in eco; vln and gtr

French, Tania Gabrielle

Harbors of Light; vln and gtr; 16'; medium-difficult-neo-Romantic; ms.

Three Landscapes; vln and gtr, transcribed for fl and gtr; 6'30"; medium, lyrical; ms.

Godla, Mary Ann

Collection of Eight Short Pieces; gtr, 2 vln, vla, and vlc; easy

Concerto Primer; gtr and string ens; easy

Ho, Wai On

3.10 am; speaker, vla, and gtr

Kolb, Barbara

Umbrian Colours; vln and gtr; Boosey and Hawkes

Kubo, Mayako

Auf den Saiten; gtr and s4

Larsen, Elizabeth (Libby)

Cajun Set; gtr, vln, vla, and vlc; three pieces; E.C. Schirmer Music Company, Inc.

Lauber, Anne

Cantate 1; gtr and s4; ms.

Lutyens, Elisabeth

Nocturnes, Op. 30; vln, vlc, and gtr; 6'; Schott (1955)

Marez Oyens, Tera de

Pearls and Strings; vlc and gtr; difficult-aleatory parts; Donemus

Marina, Carmen (pseud. of Carmen Manteca Gioconda)

Duet; vln and gtr; GioMar Editions

Six Bagatelles; vla and gtr; GioMar Editions

Mell, Eidylia

Sonata; vln and gtr

Mori, Junko

Spring Dawn; vln or vla and gtr; 12'; ms.

Obrovská, Jana

Capriccios; vln and gtr

Oribello, Juanita

Linda's Cello II; vlc and gtr; ms.

Piechowska, Alina (also Piechowska-Pascal)

Trois fresques; vlc and gtr

Ravinale, Irma

Sequentia; gtr and s4

Saint John, Kathleen Louise

Rhapsody; vln and gtr

Ulehla, Ludmila

Six Silhouettes; gtr and s4

Vorlová , Sláva (née Miroslava Johnová) (pseud. Mira Kord)
Sonata lirica da tre, Op. 62; vln, vla, and gtr

Waldo, Elisabeth
El gran quivira; gtr, db, and s4; ms.

Zimmermann, Margrit
Duetto for Cello and Guitar, Op. 26; vlc and gtr; ms.

TAPE AND GUITAR

Beat, Janet
A Willow Swept by Rain; 12' 08"; Scottish Music Information Centre

Fereyra, Beatriz
Passacaille déboîtée pour un lutin; tape and gtr or lute

Hall, Helen
Vortices; fl, gtr, and tape

Ho, Wai On
Tango Concertino; 2 channel tape and gtr

Leite, Vânia Dantas
Te quero verde; computer tape, gtr, and berimbau (musical bow); electronic merengue

THEATRE MUSIC

Bobrow, Sanchie
Beauty and the Beast (after La Fontaine); vln, 2 gtr, 3 rec, and perc

UNKNOWN INSTRUMENTS

Baroni Basile, Adrian (Andreana)
titles unknown; none of her works have survived

Berthe (Bierthe), Mme (née Offhuis)
titles unknown; guitar solos and duets

Constant, Rosalie de
titles unknown; pieces and arrangements

Fracker, Cora Robins
titles unknown

Marchisio, Barbara
titles unknown

Mounsey, Elizabeth
titles unknown

Walker, Louise
Argentinishiche Weise (triste)

UNUSUAL INSTRUMENTS AND GUITAR

Cecconi-Botella, Monic (Monique Gabrielle)
D'ailleurs; 2 Ondes Martenot, elec gtr, and perc

Hovda, Eleanor
Ondes doubles II; gtr and Ondes Martenot

Spiegel, Laurie
Song Without Words; gtr and man

VOICE AND GUITAR

Alain, Marie Claire
Les chansons espiègles; Schott

Alemany, Susana F. de
Five Villancicos Comentados; vce, gtr, rec, and perc; G. Ricordi/G. Schirmer, Inc. (US)

Anderson, Beth (Barbara Elizabeth)
He Says He's Got; ms.

Bakke, Ruth
Hor Alle Som Torster; (text: *The Bible*, Isaiah 56, John 6);5'; difficult-atonal, dark; Norsk Musikkinformasion

Prayer; S, gtr, and org; 6 pp; difficult-atonal, dark; Norsk Musikkinformasion

Barker, Laura

Seven Romances

Barnett, Carol

Cinco poemas de Becquer; mix-chor, rec, gtr, and wind chimes; ms.

Voices (song cycle); (text: Nancy Cox); S and gtr; 22 pp; style-lyrical, evocative, six movts, one solo movt each for voice and guitar; ms.

Bauld, Alison

Humpty Dumpty; T , fl, and gtr

One Pearl; S or counter-T, gtr, and maracas; Novello and Co., Ltd. (1973)

Baumgarten, Chris

Hallo, Du: A Collection of Literary Chansons, Songs and Lieder; vce, gtr, and pf; Henschel (1971)

Beat, Janet

Cat's Cradle for the Nemuri-Neko; female vce and gtr or clarsech or medieval hp; 4'48"; Scottish Music Information Centre

The Leaves of My Brain; S or T and gtr; 6'; Scottish Music Information Centre

Beecroft, Norma

Rasas II; A, fl, hp, gtr, elec org or pf, 2 perc, and 4-channel tape; Canadian Music Center (1974)

Blood, Esta

Five Armenian Folksongs; S, gtr, and fl or cl; 10'; easy-medium, in folk style; Frank E. Warren Music Service

Blum, Irm (Irma?)

Fantastische Kinderwelt; pf, vce, rec or vla, and gtr; Noetzel, Locarno

Bobrow, Sanchie

As You Like It; gtr, rec, vces, and vln

Bofill, Anna

Canço de primavera; mez-S and gtr; 12'; difficult-atonal, geometrical, inspired by the composers architectural works, or on the physical principles of nature; ms.

Bouchard, Linda

A Christmas pot-pourri; S, fl, vln, 2 gtr, pf, and perc; ms.

OCAMOW; Bari, gtr, vlc, and perc; 40'; Canadian Music Center

Boyd, Anne Elizabeth

The Rose Garden; gtrs, various instruments, vce, and ch; 70'; Faber Music Ltd.

Brondi, Maria (Marie) Rita

Romance au rouet; vce and gtr

Byrchmore, Ruth M.

After Lorca; 2 gtr with orator; 22'; text by F. Garcia Lorca in Spanish; ms.

Color y fragancia; gtr and S; 16'; text by F. Garcia Lorca in Spanish; ms.

Into the Silent Lands; gtr and S; 17'; text by S. Cowie in English; ms.

Lady of Silences; gtr with orator, text by T.S. Eliot; 10'; difficult-20th century techniques, impressionist, dark; ms.

Campagne, Conny

Guido Gezelle; chor, recs, gtrs, ob, and cl

Carr-Boyd, Ann Kirsten

Catch 75; S, fl, and gtr

Folk Songs 76: Folk Songs from France, Greece, Mongolia and Canada

Carroll, Nancy

When I am Dying

Casson, Margaret

Noon, rondo; vce and gtr or pf; Cobbold (ca. 1800)/Durham Cathedral Library ms.

Catunda, Eunice

Negrinho do pastoreis; 3 vce, gtr, fl, and perc

Chance, Nancy Laird

Dark Song; S, 2 fl, 2 cl, 2 hn, hp, gtr, pf, and 5 perc; Seesaw Music Corp.

Cherbourg, Mlle

Premier recueil de chansons avec accompagnement de guitarre et six menuets en duo pour deux guitarres; vce and 1 or 2 gtr; 15 pp; Bailleaux

Clingan, Judith Ann

Images, for the film, *Into the Darkest Night*; mez-S, fl, cl, and gtr

Cohen, Marcia (née Spilky)

Shir shel shirim; S, ob, gtr, vib, and 2 perc

Contamine, Mlle de

title unknown, volume of airs with guitar accompaniment

Cory, Eleanor

Aria viva; T, fl, ob, Eng hn, bsn, and gtr; American Composers Alliance

Coulthard, Jean

Three Shakespeare Sonnets; S, strs, gtr or vlc solo, and 8 vlc

Three Shakespeare Sonnets; A, gtr, and strs

Cuervas, Matilde

El vita (Canto popular andalúz), in *Guitar Review* #16; 1 p; easy

Davidson, Tina

Graffiti; S, elec gtr, fl, and pf; ms.

Davis, Jean Reynolds (Mrs. H. Warren, Jr.)

Adoremus; S, A, and gtr

De Freitas, Elvira Manuela Fernandez

Andaluzia, Op. 20; text by Lorca

Dia, (Countess) Beatrice de

A Chantar m'er de so qu'eu no volria; vce and gtr, arranged; Friedrich Gennrich

Dianda, Hilda Fanny

Canciones, 3, gtr, vib, and 3 perc; text by Rafael Alberti; Edición Heliográfica/Editorial Argentina de Musíca

Dinescu, Violeta

Epadi; mez-S and gtr

Erendira; chamber opera with gtr

Dockhorn, Lotte

Schalk und Scheaz; Leuchart and Co.

Dollitz, Grete Franke

Song Cycle--A Love Story

Songs for Erika with a Guitar

Eiríksdóttir, Karólína

Some Days; S, fl, cl, vlc, gtr, and hpc; 12'15" text: Thorsteinn frá Hamri;

Erding, Susanne

Moritaten I-III; mez-S and gtr or pf

Fedele, Diacenta

Scelta di villanelle napolitane bellissime con alcune ottave siciliane nove, con le sue intavolature di guitarra alla spagniola; Francesco Grossi (1628)

Fernandez, Teresita

Bola de nieve

Canta pajarito

Ismaelillo

La gaviota

Pinares de Mayari

Rondas

Tia jutia

Finzi, Graciane

Univers de lumière; S, orators, s4, cl, hpc, pf, bandoneon, gtr, and tape

Fleischer, Tsippi

Mein Volk; mez-S and gtr; ms.

Forman, Joanne

Lorca Songs; S and gtr

French, Tania Gabrielle

Oread; solo voices, chor, gtr, and ch orch; 35'; text by Williams, Whitman, Lowell, Sandburg, Crane; ms.

Fritz, Sherilyn Gail

Travel Songs; S, Bari, and gtr

Galli (Gallo?), (signora) Caterina

titles unknown in *Duets or canzonets for 2 voices, guitars or 2 german flutes and a bass compos'd by sigr. Fomelli, Hasse and the most eminent Italian masters* [Nos. I-X]; J. Walsh (c.1755-62)

Gardner, Kay

Changing; mez-S and gtr; Sea Gnomes Music

Song of our Coming; mez-S and gtr; Sea Gnomes Music

Thirteen Songs; mez-S and gtr; Sea Gnomes Music

Three Mother Songs; mez-S and gtr; 3' each; Sea Gnomes Music

Two Sapphic Songs; medium vce, and gtr; 3' each; Sea Gnomes Music

Genty, Mlle

Ile Receuil de chanson avec un accompagnement de guitarre par musique & par tablature; 21 pp; de La Chevardière (1761)

Receuil de chanson avec un accompagnement de guitarre; 20 pp; gravé par Mlle Vendôme

Geyer, Marianne

titles unknown; songs with guitar accompaniment

Gibbs, Prue

The French Revolution; 2 vce, fl, cl, gtr, pf, dr, and vlc

Gideon, Miriam

Little Ivory Fingers Pulled By Strings; mez-S and gtr

Gifford, Helen Margaret

As Dew in Aprille; boy vce or S, and gtr or hp

Gileno, Jean Anthony

The Rustic Alleluia, chor, org, and gtr

Giteck, Janice

Eight Sandbars on the Takano River; 5 women's vce, fl, bsn, and gtr; 13'; text by G. Snyder; ms.

Grétry, Angelique-Dorotheé-Lucile (Lucille, Lucie)

titles unknown in *Etrennes chantantes ou choix des plus nouvelles ariettes, romances et vaudevilles avec accompagnement de guitarre;* Goujon fils (1787)

Griffes-Kortering, Lois

The Owl and the Pussy-cat; S, gtr, and vln; medium; ms.

Grigsby, Beverly (née Pinsky)

Dialogue; T and gtr

Love Songs; T and gtr

Gumert, Lynn

The Night Lies Poised; S, a-fl, and gtr; 10'30"; difficult-lyrical;

Hawley, Carolyn Jean (née Bowen)

Sonnets to Orpheus; Bar, gtr, fl, pf, and strs

Hilderley, Jeriann G

Jeritree's House of Many Colours; vce, perc, vlc, gtr, and wooden fl

Ho, Wai On

Song Cycle; high vce and gtr or pf; poems by MacNiece

Wisdom; high vce and gtr

Holm, Kristin

Lossna; S, pf, hn, and gtr; 8'; difficult-modern extended techniques, text: Sten Hagliden; Norsk Musikkinformasion

Hölszky, Adriana

Sonett für Frauenstimme und zwei Gitarren; 2 gtr and woman's vce; Astoria Verlag

Hovda, Eleanor

Match; vce, gongs, fl, and gtr

Some of Us, Most of the Time; vce, gtr, fl, and perc

Hunkins, Eusebia Simpson

Appalachian Mass; S, chor, hpc or org, and gtr or lute; Carl Fischer, Inc.

Izarra, Adina

Margarita; vce, fl, and gtr

Janárceková, Viera

Der Goldene Mantel

Kinkle, Johanna (née Mockel)

title unknown

Kolb, Barbara

Chansons bas; vce, gtr or hp, and 7 perc; difficult; Carl Fischer, Inc.

Looking For Claudio; S, and ch ensemble including gtr; difficult-experimental; Boosey and Hawkes

Songs Before an Adieu; fl, a-fl, gtr, and vce; difficult; Boosey and Hawkes

The Sentences; S and gtr; text by Pinsky; Boosey and Hawkes

Konishi, Nagako

Vase for Lamentation; 2 S, gtr, and pf; 12'; difficult-aleatoric, sparce, experimental, dialog between guitar and voices; ms.

Krzanowska, Grazyna

Postlude; mez-S, fl, gtr, vln, and vlc

Kukuck, Felicitas (née Kestner)

Das Märchen vom dicken fetten Pfannekuchen (The Story of the Fat Pancake); chor and gtr; medium; Möseler Verlag

Die Brücke (The Bridge); vce, rec, and gtr or lute; medium; Robert Lienau, Musikverlag

Die Wiehnachtgeschichte in Liedern (The Christmas Story in Song); medium; Möseler Verlag

Ich hab die Nacht geträumet; girl's vce and gtr; easy; Möseler Verlag

Liebslieder (Ten Love Songs for Soprano and Guitar); S and gtr; medium, lyrics by Margret Johannsen; Möseler Verlag

Kuntze, Lilia Magarita Vazquez

titles unknown

Kurakina (Kourakin), Natal'ya Ivanova (Princess)

Celui que plait le mieux (Romance, Accompt. par Gatayes); vce and gtr or lyre; (melody only by Kurakina) Boieldieu, (c. 1815)

Deh non partir mio dolce amore and *La notte non riposo*; #33 in *Journal d'airs italiens, français et russes*, par I.B. Hainglaise, Année I; Chez l'aut, et Gerstenburg et Dittmar (1796)

Romance de Florian; #13 in *Journal d'airs italiens, français et russes* par I. B. Hainglaise, Année I; vce and 1 or 2 gtr; Chez l'aut, et Gerstenberg et Dittmar (1796)

T'amo tanto e tanto t'amo; #31 in *Journal d'airs italiens, français et russes* par I. B. Hainglaise, Année I; Chez l'aut, et Gerstenberg et Dittmar (1796)

Lagerhiem-Romare, Marcit

Anna Snackskrin

Barndomsjulen

Da Tar Jag Min Gitarr

De Kan Aldrig Fang a Mej

Fran Grandenock Glantom; 6 song cycle

Karlek por Telefon

Lat Tustraden Tala

Livets Forstra Dag

Mor, Du Ar Mig Nara

Rollita

Sensommar

Lambertini, Marta

Tre canti d'amore; S, fl, and gtr; Editorial Argentina de Compositores

Larsen, Elizabeth (Libby)

Three More Rilke Songs; S, fl, gtr, and hp; ms.

Three Rilke Songs; T and gtr, also S, fl, gtr, and hp; E.C. Schirmer Music Company, Inc.

Lewin, Olive

Daniel; ch, gtr, and perc

Run Moses; ch and gtr

Linnet, Anne

Som Sand der Forsvinder; vce and 2 gtr

Luff, Enid

Metres and Images; Bari, cl, gtr, and perc; Primavera

Spring Bereaved; Bari and gtr; song cycle; Primavera

Lutyens, Elisabeth

By All These, Op. 120; S and gtr

Infidelio, Op. 29; S, T, and 7 instruments; opera in 7 scenes; Olivan (1954)

Marez Oyens, Tera de

De Kapitein is jarig; unknown instrumentation; opera for children

Takadon; vce, ww, brass, perc, gtr, str, and pf; De Toots, 1978

The Narrow Path; S, fl, and 2 gtr; 15-20'; forthcoming

Marina, Carmen (pseud. of Carmen Manteca Gioconda)

Adivinanze de la guitar; GioMar Editions

Canción incrédula; GioMar Editions

Dos canciones de Navidad; GioMar Editions

Endechas a la mar; text: Gerardo Diego; GioMar Editions

Five Children Songs; text: Rachel Field; GioMar Editions

Four American Songs; text: Rachel Field; GioMar Editions

Four Songs; text: Miguel de Unamuno; GioMar Editions

God's Vacation; text: Carmen Marina; GioMar Editions

La vida es sueño; GioMar Editions

Los pastores de Belen; text: Lope de Vega; GioMar Editions

Lyric; GioMar Editions

Madre la mi madre; text: Miquel de Cervantes; GioMar Editions

Segovia; GioMar Editions

Six Capricces; text: F. Garcia Lorca; GioMar Editions

Song of Segismundo; text: Calderon de La Barca; GioMar Editions

Songs; text: Spanish poets; GioMar Editions

Songs of Life and Hope; text: R. Alberti; GioMar Editions

Songs to Sing; album of 12 songs in English and Spanish; GioMar Editions

Sunday Morning in New England; GioMar Editions

The Four Little Foxes; text: Lew Sarett; GioMar Editions

Three Enchanted Cities: Granada, Córdoba, Sevilla; Mez-S, fl, vlc, and gtr; GioMar Editions

Tiromichanta; GioMar Editions

Tres Anas; GioMar Editions

Two cantos de cuna; text: Carmen Marina; GioMar Editions

Two Songs; text: J. Ferran and Carmen Marina; GioMar Editions

Two Songs; text: R. Montesinos; GioMar Editions

Two Songs for Georgia: The Red Eye; Take Away the Moon; text: B. Dekle; GioMar Editions

Where are you from?; GioMar Editions

Y despues de todo que; GioMar Editions

You are my man, aren't you; GioMar Editions

Marlow, Janet

Life Crossings; vce, 10-string gtr; easy-medium; Marizzo Music

Mountains of New Mexico; 10-string gtr; easy-medium; Marizzo Music

Rain Language; vce, 10-string gtr, and koto; easy-medium; Marizzo Music

Martins, Maria de Lourdes (Clara da Silva)

Soneto; Bari and gtr

Matveyeva, Novella (Hixon: Matveyevna)

A Soldier Road Through the Forest

Following the Gypsies

Foot-prints

Gypsy-Woman

How Long Our Journey Is

Little Star

Missouri

Red Indian Song

Road Song

Sorceress

The Adriatic Sea

The Homeless Brownie

The Horizon

The Little Ship

The Organ-Grinder

titles unknown; songs with guitar accompaniment

We Dance This Song

Mazourova, Jarmila

Come; S and gtr

Meister, Leila

Ancrens; British Broadcasting Company Library

Chansons sur texts

Mell, Eidylia

Dos enemigos

Por los caminos

Una gentil dama

Ven muerte tan escondida

Mendoza, Anne Elizabeth

Hey Betty Martin; vce, pf or gtr, perc, and fl a bec, ad lib; 10'; Faber Music Ltd.

Meneely-Kyder, Sarah Suderley

Everywoman: A Morality Tale; w-vces, mix-ch, 15 small and toy instruments, gtr, and pf; oratorio text: N.F-H. Meneely

Five Systems; w-vces, resonating bells, tubular chimes, kalima and gtr

Moscovitz, Julienne

Once There Was A Worm

Musgrave, Thea

Five Love Songs; S or T and gtr; 10'; Chester, J. and W. Ltd.

Sir Patrick Spens; T and gtr; 7'; Chester, J. and W. Ltd.

Obrovská, Jana

Canzoni in stilo antiquo; A and gtr

Five Songs

Olcott-Bickford, Vahdah (née Ethel Lucretia Olcott)

In A Rare Garden, Op. 27, No. 1

Nectar; printed in *Guitar Review,* #24, 1960; 1 p

Oribello, Juanita

Absorbing Interlude; S and gtr; 4 pp; medium; ms.

Ozaita Marques, Maria Luisa

El militar y la señora; ms.

El quitasol; ms.

Homenaje a Goya; S and gtr; ms.

Patino, Lucia (Chia)

Tulipan; vce, fl, gtr, vln, and vlc

Paull, Barberi

Three Lullabies; mez-S, gtr, and elec keys or pf

Phillips, Karen Ann

titles unknown; ms.

Polin, Claire

Music for the Prince of Wales; vce and vlc or gtr; ms.

Wind Songs; S and gtr; 10-11'; medium atonal, ms.

Porter, Debra

Spanish Dream; S, fl, gtr, and pf; 3'; medium-Romantic style; ms.

Pradell, Leila

Song Cycle of Protest for Vietnam; S, gtr, and pf

Pratten, Madame Sydney (née Catherina Josepha Pelzer)

Four Italian Songs (dedicated to Miss Chichester)

Four Swiss Songs (dedicated to Miss Harriet Wilberfore Bird)

Selection of Ewer's Gems of German Songs (dedicated to Miss Jane L.E. Wilson)

Six Scotch Songs (dedicated to Miss Elphinston)

Six Songs (dedicated to Lady Agneta Yorke)

Six Songs (dedicated to Lady Dinorben)

Six Songs (dedicated to Lady Victoria Wellesley)

Song for the Guitar

Songs of Nations (dedicated to Duchess of Wellington)

Three French Songs (dedicated to Lady John Somerset)

Three Italian Songs (dedicated to Contess Ferrers)

Three Neapolitan Songs (dedicated to Miss Stapleston)

Twelve Songs and Duets (dedicated to Mary and Albinia Brodrick)

Procaccini, Teresa

Chanson; ms.

Five Chansons, Op. 59; ms.

Tre canti popolari, Op. 77; vce, chor, fl, gtr, and small orch; ms.

Puget, Loise (Loisa, Luisa, Louise, Louisa) (married name: Lemoine)

Baiser de la promise; vce and gtr or pf; L. Schott

Chanson andalouse; vce, man, and pf or gtr; Editions Henry Lemoine and Cie

Fleurette; Heugel & Cie

Je t'aime; vce and gtr or pf; Williams

Je veux t'aimer; vce and gtr or pf; Williams

Veritable amour; Williams

Rainier, Priaulx

Dance of the Rain; T or S and gtr; L. Schott

Ubunzima (Misfortune); S or T and gtr; Zulu text; Schott and Co, Ltd

Reichardt, Lousie (Luise)

Zwölf Gesänge mit Begleitung der Gitarre; Förster

Rezende, Marisa

title unknown; vce, rec, and gtr

Roe, Eileen Betty

Circle Beguiled; 3 vce and gtr

Firstlings; high vce, wwd, and gtr; text: Rita Ford; Thames Publishing

Men Were Deceivers Ever; Bari and gtr

Musical Moments; Bari and gtr

Roster, Danielle

Anweisung an Sisyphos; 4 pp; difficult-atonal; ms.

In Uralten Seen für vox and gitarre; ms.

Natur; 25 pp; difficult-atonal; ms.

Rubin, Anna

Dangerous Lullabies; Bari, a-sax, vlc, gtr, perc, pf, sampler and toy pf; ms.

Saariaho, Kaija

Adjö; S, fl, and gtr; Jasemusiikki Ky

Ju Lägre Solen for Soprano, Flute, and Guitar

Sagreras, Clelia

Dolor oculto; Casa Nuñez

Saint John, Kathleen Louise

Go Find a New Lover

Trois poèmes; S and gtr

Samuel, Rhian

Three Songs with Guitar; Andresier Editions

Saporiti, Teresa

Airs with Guitar

Schmidt, Mia

Die gestundete Zeit; mez-S and gtr; 6'; difficult; extended techniques, avant-garde; Contemporary Music Adesso

Scott, Lady John (Alicia Ann)

Annie Laurie; facsimile of 1850 ed

Sepúlveda, Maria Luisa

Cancionero chileno

Serrano Redonnet, Ana

Arreos

Bagualas de chaya

Coplas

Danza

El maule

El misachico

La generala

Lamento

Melisma de la soledad

Quebrodeñas; vce, fl, ob, cl, bsn, gtr, and caja india (small drum)

Songs

Vidala Aymará

Yo sé lo que estoy cantando

Shaffer, Jeanne E.

Juniper Shoes; S, gtr, fl, and vln; 7'; medium to difficult; ms.

Shatal, Miriam

Four Ballads with English Text

Shore, Clare

Grave Numbers; medium vce and gtr; 20'; text: Blanche Farley; E.C. Schirmer Music Company, Inc.

Silverman, Faye-Ellen

In Shadow; three songs and two interludes; S, cl, and gtr; 6'30"; Seesaw Music Corp.

Simcoe, Joan

And You, Muses; w-chor, fl, and gtr; text: M. Bernard (translation of poetry by Sappho); easy-modal, lyrical; ms.

Spampinato, Letizia

Eclissi; S and gtr; 5 pp; difficult-atonal; ms.

Stilman-Lasansky, Julia (Ada Julia)

Cantares del la madre joven, Cantata No. 2; S, fl, amp gtr, vln, vla, vlc, and glock; text: Tagore; American Composers Alliance

Sullivan, Marion Dix

The Blue Juniata

Swain, Freda

The Harvester's Song

Szeghy, Iris

To You; text: *Song of Solomon, The Bible,* in Latin and Slovak; S, T, fl, vlc, gtr, and triangle; 15'; Music Fund Archives

Szekely, Katalin

Missa Esztergom; S and gtr orch; ms.

Tate, Phyllis

St. Martha and the Dragon, sur un texte de Chas. Cauley; narr, S or T solo, chor, child chor, and ch orch, ob, Eng hn, hp, pf, harmonium or org, gtr, timb, 2 perc, strs, and tape; 42'; Oxford U. Press

The Pride of Lions; vces, narr, gtr, recs, and perc (amplified and non-amplified); 25'; a story with musical accompaniment; Oxford University Press

Trois chansons tristes; S and gtr; 8'; Oxford University Press

Two Ballads; mez-S and gtr; Oxford University Press

Thompson, Caroline Lorraine

To Paint a Portrait of a Bird; vce, fls, and gtr

Thorkelsdóttir, Mist Barbara

Dance; 13'; Iceland Music Information Centre

Urreta, Alicia

Hasta aquí la memoria; S, pf, perc, gtr, and str orch

Van der Mark, Maria (née de Jong)

Langs die Stroompie in die Berge

Reenvuel

van Epen-de Groot, Else Antonia

Een dag uit het leven van...; mixed chor, T, Bari, orch: 2131, 2330, 2 perc, hp, strs, and combo: perc, pf, gtr, and db; Donemus

Vargas, Eva

Von Zeit zu Zeit

Wenn Gott is Will

Vieu, Jane

Sous la brume; vce, gtr, and man

Volkstein, Pauline

Twenty Songs with Guitar Accompaniment

Waldo, Elisabeth

Ballad of Lola Montez; S, gtr, and pf; ms.

Balsa Boat; T, gtr, and pf; ms.

Indian Lullaby; S, gtr, and pf; ms.

Making Chicha; S, gtr, and pf; ms.

Mexican-California Children's Song Cycle; S, gtr, and pf; ms.

Suychusca; Bari, gtr, and pf; ms.

Wa-Sho-Sho---Lullaby; S, gtr, and pf; ms.

Walker, Gwyneth

As A Branch In May; medium vce and gtr (also chor and pf); E.C. Schirmer Music Company, Inc.

Songs for Baritone and Guitar; Bari and gtr; 13'; medium difficult; E.C. Schirmer Music Company, Inc.

Songs for Voice and Guitar; Walker Music Publishing

Three Songs for Tres Voces (on a poem by W.B. Yates); T, Counter-T, Bari, and gtr; 9'; difficult; E.C. Schirmer Music Company, Inc.

Weigl, Vally

The Drums of War; medium vce and gtr; American Composers Alliance

Whitehead, Gillian

Murduk; S, fl, cl, vln or vla, vlc, gtr, hps or pf, and perc

Riddles; mez-S, fl, mar, gtr, and hpc (also for w-chor and hp)

Three Songs of Janet Frame; S, fl, ob, cl or b-cl, hrn, trp, gtr, and db

Wilson, Mrs. Cornwall Baron

Water Music: A Collection on National Melodies

Winter, Sister Miriam Theresa (Gloria Frances)

Gold, Incense, and Myrrh; S,A, mixed chor, and gtr; Vanguard Music Corp

I Know a Secret; S, A, w-chor, and gtr; Vanguard Music Corp

Joy is Like the Rain; S, A, w-chor, and gtr; Vanguard Music Corp

Knock, Knock; S, A, w-chor, gtr, and perc; Vanguard Music Corp

Let the Cosmos Ring; Vanguard Music Corp

Men of a Pilgrim People; Vanguard Music Corp

Seasons; S, A, w-chor, gtr, and perc; Vanguard Music Corp

Wong, Hsiung-Zee

Artsongs and Ballads

Yamashita, Toyoko

Das goldene und das silberne Glöchen; S, fl, and gtr

Erinnerung für Sopran und Gitarre; S and gtr

Zaffauk, Theresa

Lieder mit Reglersing der Gitarre

Ziffrin, Marilyn Jane

Drinking Song and Dance, from *Captain Kidd* (opera); B, chor, 2 gtr, S-rec, and perc ens; ms.

Zimmermann, Margrit

Drei Sonetten von Petrarca, Op. 35; vce, fl, and gtr; ms.

Pensieri, Op. 31; T, gtr, and fl; ms.

Zumsteeg, Emilie

Fünf Lieder mit Begleitung der Gitarre

COMPOSER BIOGRAPHIES

Abejo, Sister M. Rosalina, SFCC
Philippine pianist, conductor, composer, and educator, born in 1922. (Cohen; Hixon; Norton/Grove; Olivier, 1988)

Abreu, Zequinha
Brazilian composer. Looking for more information.

Agudelo-Murguia, Graciela
Mexican composer, pianist, singer, and educator, born in 1945. (Cohen; Boenke; Hixon)

Alain, Marie-Claire
French organist, composer, writer on music, and educator, born in St. Germaine-en-Laye, France in 1926. (Cohen; Hixon)

Alemany, Susana F. de
Looking for information about this composer.

Alexander, Elizabeth
USA composer born in the 20th century. She studied composition at the College of Wooster and at Cornell University, where she received her Doctorate of Composition degree. Her principal teachers were Jack Gallagher, Steven Studky, Karel Husa, and Yehudi Wyner. She has received numerous grants and awards, and her works are often performed. She lives in Ithaca, New York. (Composer letter)

Alexander, Leni
German-Chilean composer born in 1924. She writes for film and electronic music media, is an instrumentalist and a music educator. (Cohen; Hixon; Norton/Grove; Olivier, 1988)

Almenar, Mariade
Spanish composer. Looking for more information.

Alsted, Birgitte
Danish composer and violinist, born in 1942. She studied at the Kongelige Danske Musikkonservatorium in Copenhagen and became active in the contemporary music study circle. This led her to an interest in composing, which she began in 1971. As a free-lance violinist and teacher she encourages creativity in children. She has collaborated with actor, producer, and writer Brigitte Kolerus on theatrical performance pieces, often with feminist themes. (Cohen; Hixon; Norton/Grove)

Anderson, Avril
English composer born in 1953. She was educated at Winchester Art College the Royal College of Music (1972-76), where her principal teachers were Humphrey Searle and John Lambert. In 1977 she received a scholarship to the New England Conservatory and also studied privately with David Del Tredici in New York. After returning to England she studied with Jonathan Harvey at Sussex University. In 1987 she and her husband founded the contemporary music ensemble, Sounds Positive. (Cohen; Hixon; Norton/Grove)

Anderson, Beth
USA composer and writer on music topics, born in 1950. She studied in Kentucky, at Mills College, in California, and worked toward a PhD at New York University. Her teachers were John Cage, Terry Riley, Robert Ashley, Helen Lipscomb, Richard Swift, and others. She has taught at the College of New Rochelle and currently teaches at Greenwich House Music School. Winner of many competitions, she has received significant grants and awards. She has written articles on music, primarily for *Ear Magazine*. (Cohen; Composer letter; Le Page, 1983; Norton/Grove)

Anderson, Olive Jennie Paxton
Australian composer born in 1917. (Cohen)

Anderson, Ruth M.
USA composer and retired music professor, Los Angeles Harbor College. (International Congress on Women in Music program, Mexico City, 1984)

Anido, Maria Luisa
Argentine composer born in 1909. She performed guitar duets with Miguel Llobet, established an international carreer as a guitarist, and composed many pieces for the guitar. (Cohen; *Guitar Review*, no. 10 [1949])

Ansink, Caroline
Dutch composer born in 1959. (Cohen; Olivier, 1988)

Anton, Susana (née Mendoza)
Looking for information about this composer.

Archer, Violet Balestreri
Canadian composer born in Montreal in 1913. She studied at McGill Conservatory, and after a period of private study with Bela Bartok, won scholarships which allowed her to study with Paul Hindemith at Yale (1948-49). She received her MMus in 1950, and taught at North Texas State College and at the University of Oklahoma (1953-61), when she became chair of the theory and composition department of the University of Alberta. She has won many prestigious awards and is a prolific composer. (Boenke; Cohen; Hixon; Norton/Grove)

Artzt, Alice (Josephine)
USA guitarist and composer, born in 1943. She studied guitar with Ida Presti, Alexander Lagoya, and Julian Bream and composition with Darius Milhaud. She has an established career as an internationally touring guitarist. (Hixon; Summerfield)

Aspen, Kristan
USA flutist and composer, born in 1948 in Maine. After receiving a BS in sociology from Oberlin College, she toured nationally with the feminist folk quartet, the Izquierda Ensemble (1976-80) and then with the Musica Femina Flute Guitar Duo (1984-present). She has made one recording with the Izquierda Ensemble, and four

recordings with Musica Femina. (Boenke; Hixon)

Ayers, Lydia
USA composer, 20th century, birthdate unknown. She composes with microtonal systems such as Partch, Indian, and Asian scales, utilizing extended vocal and woodwind techniques. She has been affiliated with the Center for Electronic Music (NY) and the University of Illinois. Earlier research took her to Spain and Tunisia. Her works have received numerous performances. (Music Alaska Women program, 1993)

Azuma, Cristina
Brazilian guitarist, recording artist, and composer, born in 1965. She graduated from the University of São Paulo and received her PhD in musicology from the Sorbonne. She performs worldwide as a soloist and in chamber ensembles. (*GSP Catalog*, July 1996)

Badian, Maya
Romanian composer born in 1945. She is a member of the Union of Romanian Composers. (Cohen; Hixon; Norton/Grove)

Bailly, Collette
French pianist and electronic music composer, born in Lyons in 1930. (Boenke; Cohen; Hixon)

Bakke, Ruth
Norwegian organ recitalist and composer, born in Bergen in 1947. She studied at the Universities of Bergen and Oslo and in the USA at the University of Redlands, CA and Washington State University. She is a member of the Society of Norwegian Composers. (Cohen; Hixon; Norton/Grove)

Ballou, Esther Williamson
USA composer, pianist, and music educator (1915-1973). She went to Bennington College, Mills College, and Juilliard. Principal teachers were Otto Luening and Wallingford Reiger. She taught at Juilliard, Catholic University, and at American University in Washington, D.C. (1955-73). Her scores are in the American University library collection. (Boenke; Cohen; Hixon; Jape; Olivier, 1988; Norton/Grove)

Bandt, Rosalie Edith
Australian composer and music educator, born in 1951. Her musical education has been very international, including Monash University, with further studies in Illinois and California, at Schola Cantorum, Basel, and in France and Germany. She taught at Latrobe University (1978-80). (Cohen; Hixon)

Barker, Laura Wilson
English composer, violinist, and teacher, born in Thirkleby, Yorkshire (1819-1905). She taught at York School for the Blind. She married playwright Tom Taylor, and wrote music for his plays. In 1880, when she was widowed, she retired to Coleshill to concentrate on songwriting. (Cohen; Hixon)

Barklund, Irma L.
Swedish composer, organist, pianist, recorder player, and music educator, born in 1909 in Dala-Jarna. She studied literature and art history before taking organ and piano at the Conservatory of Stockholm. In 1960 she was certified in church music and began composition studies with H. Lindroth and Werner Wolf Glaser. She has taught since 1948 at the Community Music School in Vasteras. (Boenke; Cohen; Hixon)

Barnett, Carol Edith
USA composer and pianist, born in Dubuque, Iowa in 1949. She studied piano with Bernard Weiser and composition with Dominick Argento and Paul Fetler, receiving both her bachelor's and master's degrees from the University of Minnesota. She has received commissions from the Minnesota Composers' Commissioning Program and the Minnesota Music Teachers' Association. (Boenke; Cohen; Hixon; Zaimont, 1991)

Baroni Basile, Andriana (Andreana)
Italian singer, guitarist, lutenist, harpist, lyre player, and composer. She was born near Naples ca. 1580, and died in 1640. Called by Monteverdi in 1610, she was employed at the court of the Duke of Mantua until 1616. She also sang at the courts of Venice and Naples, accompanied by her daughters, Eleanora and Caterina, who were both singers. None of her works are known to have survived. (Cohen; Hixon)

Barrell, Joyce Howard
English composer, teacher, guitarist, organist, violinist and pianist (1917-1989). She was educated at Leichester University and taught from 1965 at the Suffolk Rural Music School. (Boenke; Cohen; Hixon; Norton/Grove)

Bauld, Alison
Australian actress, composer, writer, lecturer, and music educator. Born in 1944, she studied acting at the National Institute for Dramatic Art and composition at the University of Sydney, receiving the Sydney Moss Scholarship to study composition with Elizabeth Lutyens. She has taught at York University since 1971. (Cohen; Hixon; Olivier, 1988; Norton/Grove)

Baumgarten, Chris
German conductor, composer, music educator, and writer on music, born in Berlin in 1910. She attended the Charlottenburg Musikhockschule (1937-41) and conducted choirs until 1947. From 1948 to 1961, she lectured at the German Theatre Institute in Weimar and at the Theatre School in Leipzig. She taught singing to actors from her own voice studio. (Cohen; Hixon)

Beat, Janet Eveline
Scottish composer, lecturer, and

music critic, born in 1937 in Streetly. She graduated from Birmingham University in 1962 and received the University's Cunningham award. She has taught at the Royal Scottish Academy of Music and Drama in Glasgow and been a music critic for several newspapers. (Boenke; Cohen; Hixon; Norton/Grove)

Beecroft, Norma Marian
Canadian composer, flutist, and pianist, born in 1934 in Oshawa, Ontario, Canada. She studied at the Toronto Conservatory (1950-58), at Tanglewood, Darmstadt, and the Academy of St. Cecilia in Rome. Electronic music studies were at the University of Toronto and in New York at the Electronic Music Studio with Davidovsky in 1964. Beecroft has received numerous scholarships, grants, and awards. She is a script writer for the Canadian Broadcasting Corporation, a producer for the National Music Department, and Director of the Association of Composers, Authors, and Publishers of Canada. (Boenke; Cohen; Hixon; Norton/Grove; Pan American Union, Vol. 17)

Bellavance, Ginette (marr. Sauvé)
Canadian composer born in 1946 in Québec. She received the MMus in composition from the University of Montreal and later studied at the University of Québec. She has composed for films. (Cohen; Hixon)

Ben-Or, Mary

See **Even-Or, Mary**

Berstand, Ragnhild
Looking for information about this composer.

Berthe (Bierthe) (née Offhuis)
Possibly Belgian composer born ca. 1750. It is said that she composed for and played the theorbo, lute, mandolin, and guitar. None of her guitar works are known to have survived. (Cohen; Hixon)

Bertin, Elisa
Looking for information about this composer.

Bickford, Vahdah Olcott
See **Olcott-Bickford, Vahdah**

Birnstein, Renate
German composer, violinist, and pianist, born in 1946 in Hamburg. She studied at the Hochschule für Musik and received her diploma in composition and piano in 1973. She studied composition with Diether de la Motte and Gyorgy Ligeti. From 1973 to 1980 she lectured at the Hochschule in Lübeck and also has taught at the Hochschule in Hamburg. She won the Prix de Rome in 1983 and studied in Rome for one year. (Cohen; Hixon; Norton/Grove; Olivier, 1988)

Blood, Esta
Born in New York in 1933, Esta Blood is a composer, pianist, and teacher of piano. She attended the Manhattan School of Music (1942-47), then studied with

Malke Gottlieb and Anita Meyer in Schenectady. She studied composition with Henry Brant, Vivian Fine, and Louis Calabro. (Boenke; Cohen; Hixon)

Blum, Irm (Irma?)
Looking for information about this composer.

Bobrow, Sanchie
USA composer, violinist, writer on music, and music educator, born in 1960. Her undergraduate degree is from Douglass College, Rutgers (1981). She studied at the Aaron Copland School, receiving her MA in composition in 1983. She then taught at the Copland School and has been a studio musician and film music composer. (Cohen; Hixon)

Bodorová, Sylvie
Czech composer born in 1954. At the Bratislava Conservatory she studied composition and piano, then, in 1979, graduated from the Janacek Academy of Arts and Music in Brno. Her principal composition teachers include Juraj Pospisil, Ctirad Kohoutek, and Franco Donatoni. She lives in Prague and lectures at the Institute of Music Theory and History of the Czechoslovak Academy of Sciences. (Cohen; Hixon; Norton/Grove)

Bofill Levi, Anna
Spanish composer, pianist, and architect, born in 1944. She received her doctorate in architecture from the University of Barcelona in 1974. Earlier she had studied music theory and piano with J. Albareda at the Caminals Academy (1950-59), and composition with J. Cercós, Josep Mestres-Quadreny, and Xavier Montsalvatge (1960-61). She also studied electronic music at the Laboratorio Phonos in Barcelona. (Cohen; Hixon; Norton/Grove; Olivier, 1988)

Borràs i Fornell, Teresa
Spanish composer born in 1930. She studied on scholarship in Italy. Her primary composition teacher was Rudolf Halffter. (Cohen)

Borroff, Edith
USA composer, musicologist, pianist, music educator, and music administrator. Edith was born into a musical family in New York in 1925. Her mother, Marie Christine Bergersen, was a pianist, and her father was a tenor. She studied at the American University where she received both her BMus and her MMus in composition (1948). Because of the prejudice faced by women in composition at that time, she changed directions and went into musicology and music history. She received her PhD in history of music from the University of Michigan under Louise Cuyler in 1958. She taught at Hillsdale College, MI, (1958-62), where she was also Associate Dean for interdisciplinary studies. From 1962 to 1966 she was a professor at the University of Wisconsin and at Eastern Michigan University. In 1973 she

became a professor of music at SUNY Binghamton. She has received many grants including an Andrew Mellon postdoctoral award. She has authored several books on music history. (Boenke; Cohen; Hixon; Norton/Grove)

Bottelier, Ina
Possibly English 20th-century composer. (Cohen; Hixon)

Bouchard, Linda
Canadian composer born in Québec in 1957. She is a flutist, conductor, poet, and music educator. She studied composition with Henry Brant, Vivian Fine, Ursula Mamlock, and Elias Tanenbaum. Her conducting studies were with Henry Brant, Neely Bruce, and Arthur Weisberg. Flute studies were with Samuel Baron, Linda Chesis, Sue Ann Kahn, Alain Marion, Harvey Sollberger, and Ransom Wilson. Her BA is from Bennington College (1979) and her MA in composition is from the Manhattan School of Music (1982). She has taught flute and music appreciation in high schools in Québec, and was a teaching assistant at Bennington College in 1978 while studying there. (Cohen; Hixon)

Boyd, Anne Elizabeth
Australian composer born in Sydney in 1946. She is a flutist, composer, pianist, lecturer, recorder player, music educator, and music editor. She studied flute at the New South Wales Conservatorium of Music from 1960 to 1963, received her BA in composition from the University of Sydney in 1966, and received her PhD from York University in England in 1972. (Helleu; Le Page, 1988; Norton/Grove)

Boyd, Liona
Canadian/English guitarist, recording artist, and composer, born in 1950 in London. In 1975 she became a naturalized Canadian citizen. She studied guitar with Eli Kassner in Toronto and with Alexander Lagoya in Paris. She attended the University of Toronto. Her Carnegie Recital Hall debut was in 1975. She has recorded often and continues to tour extensively. (Cohen; Hixon; Summerfield, 1991)

Braase, Albertine
Danish composer, 19th-20th century. (Cohen; Hixon)

Braase, Sophie
Danish composer, 20th century. (Cohen; Hixon)

Brandman, Margaret Susan
Australian composer, born in 1951. She plays guitar, accordian, clarinet, drums, and piano. She received her diploma from the Sydney Conservatory and her BMus from Sydney University, where she studied composition with Peter Sculthorpe. Since 1977 she has written a column on keyboard matters for the *Journal of Australian Music and Musicians*. Brandman is an active writer and producer of radio programs. (Boenke; Cohen; Hixon)

Brenet, Thérèse
French composer and organist, born in 1935. She studied with Darius Milhaud and Jean Rivier. She received a piano diploma from the Conservatoire de Reims and graduated with distinction from the Conservatoire National Supérieur de Paris. She won the Prix de Rome in 1965 and has been a professor at the Paris Conservatory since 1970. (Boenke; Cohen; Hixon; Norton/Grove)

Briggs, Nancy Louise
USA composer and pianist, born in 1950. Her BA is from the University of California, Berkeley in 1971. She studied at the Royal Conservatory of Music at The Hague, Netherlands for a year following her graduation. From 1977 to 1980 she studied electronic music and recording at the Center for Contemporary Music at Mills College. Her doctoral studies were at University of California in San Diego. In 1980 she won a scholarship to the Aspen Music Festival. (Cohen; Hixon)

Brondi, Maria Rita
Italian composer, guitarist, and writer born in Rimini in 1884. She concertized throughout Europe, wrote for the guitar, and wrote a book entitled, *Il liuto e la chitarra. Richerche storiche sulla loro origine e sul loro sviluppo. (The Lute and the Guitar. Historical Research on Their Origin and on Their Development)* Torino: Fratelli Bocca Editori, 1926. (Bone;

Cohen; Hixon; McCutcheon; *Guitar Review*, no. 11 [1950])

Brooks, Linnea
USA composer, popular song writer, and pianist, born in Oakland, California in 1950. She graduated from Marylhurst College in 1991 with her Bachelor of Music degree in composition. Awards include BMI Songwriter Showcase, American Song Festival Awards, and selection for the Oregon On Tour program sponsored by the Oregon Arts Commission. She currently directs a local choir, teaches privately, and performs as a soloist and with a Portland, Oregon band called Loose Women. (Composer letter)

Brown, Elizabeth
USA composer and flutist, born in 1953. A graduate of Juilliard, she has performed worldwide and is also an accomplished shakuhachi player. Her music has been performed at Lincoln Center and the Smithsonian, as well as on radio. Her compositions are recorded on the CRI and Harmonia Mundi labels. (National Flute Association convention program, 1996)

Brusa, Elisbetta
Italian composer and music educator, born in 1954. (Cohen; Hixon)

Bruzdowicz, Joanna
Polish composer born in 1943. She attended the Warsaw Lyceum of Music and the Warsaw

Conservatory of Music, before studying with Nadia Boulanger and Oliver Messiaen in Paris. She did further study with Pierre Schaeffer at the Paris Conservatory and received her PhD from the Sorbonne. She is also an arts administrator and recording artist (piano). (Cohen; Hixon; Norton/Grove)

Buchanan, Dorothy Quita
New Zealand composer and teacher, born in 1945. She graduated from the University of Canterbury in 1967, then formed the Centre Sound choral group and the Christchurch music workshops. After receiving a teaching diploma in 1976, she became the first composer-in-schools. She is active as a lecturer, writer, and music director. (Norton/Grove)

Burston, Maggie
Canadian composer, pianist, music educator, and poet, born in England in 1925. She studied piano at the Royal Academy of Music. She taught in Israel (1944-55) before moving to Toronto where she taught in Hebrew schools. She studied harmony, sight singing, and composition at the Royal Conservatory under Gordon Delamont (1968-72); then composition with Dr. Dolin; and solfegge and composition with Nadia Boulanger in 1976. (Cohen; Hixon)

Byrchmore, Ruth M.
British composer, born and educated in Birmingham,

England. She attended Sheffield University (BMus and MMus) and the Royal Academy of Music, graduating with a RAM Diploma of Advanced Studies. In 1991 she received a fellowship and was composer-in-residence at Wells Cathedral School. Currently she teaches at the Royal Academy of Music. (Composer letter)

Byrne, Madelyn
USA composer born in 1963. She is a doctoral student at City University of New York, studying jazz, classical, and contemporary styles. (Composer letter)

Caceres L. de Pastor, Carmen
Looking for information about this composer.

Calandra, Matilde T. de
Spanish or Italian 20th-century composer. (Cohen; Hixon)

Calcagno, Elsa
Argentine composer born in 1910. Elsa Calcagno studied piano at the Conservatorio Nacional de Musica e Arte Escenica. She was President of the Cultural Commission of the Sinfonica Feminina Association. She also founded El Unisono Association and was music critic for the journal, *La Mujer*. Her music criticism has appeared in major South American journals. She is an active composer and performer. (Boenke; Cohen; Hixon)

Campagne, Conny
Dutch composer, pianist, violist,

recorder player, and music educator, born in 1922. She studied her instruments with F. Contrad, J.G.T. Lohmann, and F. Buchtger. She became a Japanese prisoner of war when she was living in Java. In 1946 she returned to Holland and resumed her studies in The Hague where she also taught. (Cohen; Hixon)

Capdeville, Constança
Portuguese composer, teacher, pianist, and percussionist, born in Barcelona in 1937. She studied at the Lisbon Conservatório Nacional, where she won the composition prize in 1962. She has been on the composition faculty of the Universidade Nova and at the Escola Superior de Música in Lisbon. She has written works for stage and screen, in chamber, orchestral, and solo forms. In recent years she has been inspired to write multimedia music theater pieces. (Hixon; Norton/Grove)

Carr-Boyd, Ann Kirsten
Born in Sydney, Australia, in 1938. She is a composer and writer on music. She received her BMus and her MMus (1963) from the University of Sydney. A Sydney Moss Scholarship allowed her to study in London with Peter Racine Fricker (1963-64) and Alexander Goehr (1964-65). She has written extensively. Her article on Australian composers was included in the the *New Grove Dictionary of Music and Musicians*. She has taught at the University of Sydney and

received numerous awards and commissions. (Cohen; composer letter; Hixon; Norton/Grove)

Carroll, Nancy
Looking for information about this composer.

Carvalho, Dinorah de
Brazilian composer, conductor, pianist, and music educator (1905-1980). A child prodigy, she entered the São Paulo Conservatory at the age of six to study piano with Maria Lacaz Machado and Carlino Crescenzo. By 1912 she was beginning to compose, and in 1916 she graduated. A scholarship to study piano with Isidor Philipp in Europe led to success as a concert pianist. Upon returning to Brazil in 1929, she studied composition with Lamberto Baldi and orchestration with Martin Braunwieser and Ernst Mehlich. In 1939 she was appointed federal inspector for advanced music education at the São Paulo Conservatory, and she founded the Women's Orchestra of São Paulo, the first women's orchestra in South America. She has been honored repeatedly by the Brazilian government for her efforts in music education for children, and she was the first woman to be elected to the Brazilian Academy of Music. (Cohen; Hixon; Norton/Grove)

Casson, Margaret
English composer, singer, and harpsichordist, born ca. 1775. It may be that she is the same

person as Miss E. Casson. (Cohen; Hixon; Jackson)

Catunda, Eunice
Brazilian composer and pianist, born in 1915. She studied piano with Oscar Guanabarino and Marieta Lion and composition with Franceschini and Guarnieri. Koellreutter introduced her to 12-tone composition, which she uses with folk elements in her own compositional style. She has taught at the Rio de Janeiro Conservatory and the University of Brasília. (Norton/Grove)

Cecconi-Botella, Monic (Monique Gabrielle)
French pianist and composer, born in Courbevoi in 1936. She studied at the Paris Conservatory with Maurice Duruflé and Jean Rivier. In 1966 she won the First Grand Prix de Rome and in 1978 began teaching at the Paris Conservatory, becoming a professor in 1982. She is known for her work with multi-media arts collaborations. (Boenke; Cohen; Hixon; Norton/Grove)

Chacon, Meme (pseud. of Remedios Chacon Bellido)
Looking for information about this composer.

Chance, Nancy Laird
USA composer born in Ohio in 1931. She studied at Bryn Mawr College and Columbia University, where her teachers were Ussachevsky, Luening, and Chou Wen-Chung. From 1974 to 1978 she lived and taught in

Kenya. (Boenke; Cohen; Hixon; Zaimont, 1991)

Chazarreta, Ana Mercedes de Monroy
Looking for information about this composer.

Cherbourg, Mlle
French composer, 19th century. (Cohen; Hixon; Jackson)

Christian, Meg
USA singer/songwriter, guitarist, and founding member of Olivia Records, one of the first women's music recording companies established in 1973 to produce lesbian feminist artists. In recent years Christian has been devoted to Gurumayi Chidvilasananda and is in charge of Gurumayi's musical programs. Many albums of Meg Christian's songs were released on the Olivia label (1973-86). (*Hotwire*, July 1985; Olivia Records program notes)

Ciobanu, Maia
Romanian composer and pianist, born in Bucharest in 1952. She was educated at the George Enescu Music Academy and Ciprian Porumbescu Conservatory. She then taught at the Enescu Academy (1975-76). (Cohen; Hixon)

Clark, Theresa Ann
African American musician and composer, born in 1953. She performed with an early 1970s feminist rock/jazz fusion band called Hysteria, based in Washington, D.C. She relocated

to Seattle and in 1986 graduated *summa cum laude* with a BFA in music from Cornish College for the Arts. In 1988 she recorded *In Here By Turns*, an album of music and poetry with Carletta Wilson, poet. In 1997 she will graduate from the University of Washington Medical School. (Boenke; Composer letter; Hixon)

Clingan, Judith Ann
Australian composer and teacher, born in 1945. She studied recorder, bassoon, voice, and composition at the Canberra School of Music. Further studies in voice and conducting were at the Kodaly Institute of Music in Kecskemet, Hungary. She founded and composes for the Canberra Children's Choir. She also founded the Youth Music Society summer music program. (Cohen; Hixon)

Coates, Gloria
USA composer born in 1934. She studied at Columbia University, where she received degrees in dance, theatre, and music. Her MMus degree is from Louisiana State University, and she has done advanced study with Jack Beeson, Otto Luening, and Alexander Tcherepnin. (Norton/Grove)

Cody, Judith Ann
USA composer and lecturer born in 1943. From 1968-1969 she studied Japanese music. She has received awards for her compositions. (Boenke; Cohen; Hixon)

Cohen, Marcia (née Spilky)
USA composer born in 1937. Her education included the University of Michigan, Roosevelt University (BA in education, 1958), De Paul University (composition), and Northwestern University (MMus, 1968). Her principal teachers were Leslie Bassett and Alan Stout. She has been composer-in-residence of the Columbia Dance Troupe and on the faculty of the Young Artists Studios, School of the Art Institute of Chicago. (Cohen; Hixon; Zaimont, 1991)

Coltrane, Alice McCleod
African American composer, harpist, organist, pianist, and percussionist. Born in Detroit in 1937, she married the jazz saxophonist John Coltrane. Her music is described as combining African and Asian mysticism with Western sounds. (Cohen; Hixon; Walker-Hill [uses McLeod])

Conrad, Laurie M.
USA composer, pianist, and music educator born in 1946. Her degrees (BM and MM) are from Ithaca College where she studied with Karel Husa, Malcom Lewis, and George King Driscoll. She has received grants, including Meet the Composer, and is a member of ASCAP. (Cohen; Hixon)

Constant, Rosalie de
Swiss guitarist and composer (1758-1835). She wrote guitar solos and songs with guitar accompaniment which Mme. de

Stael praised to the composer Zingarelli. (Cohen; Hixon)

Contamine, Mlle de
Parisian French composer born ca. 1780. She wrote songs with guitar accompaniment. (Cohen; Hixon)

Cory, Eleanor
USA composer and writer on music, born in 1943. Her BA is from Sarah Lawrence College, her MA is from Harvard Graduate School of Education, her MMus is from the New England Conservatory, and her DMA is from Columbia University. She has taught at Yale, Columbia, Hofstra University, the New England Conservatory, Brooklyn College, Baruch College, and City University of New York. She has been president of the American Composers Alliance, and her music has been recorded on CRI, Advance, Opus One, and Soundspells labels. (Boenke; Cohen; Composer interview; Hixon; Zaimont, 1991)

Cottin, Madeleine
French guitarist, mandolinist, and writer on music, born in 1876. Her death date is not known. She and her brother, Alfred (1863-1926) were active in the Parisian guitar scene. Her *Méthode Complète de Guitare*, published by Jourmade in 1909, was very popular, selling over 150,000 copies in 1914 alone. It was then translated into Spanish and Portuguese. Equally popular was her mandolin method. She took

an active part in the Tarrega centenary in Paris in 1952. (Bone; *Guitar Review*, no. 11 [1950]; Hixon; *Soundboard*, spring 1995)

Coulombe Saint-Marcoux, Micheline
Canadian composer, music educator, and writer on music, born in Québec (1938-1985). She studied at the Ecole Vincent d'Indy under Claude Champagne, receiving a BMus in 1962. At the Montreal Conservatory of Music she studied with Gilles Tremblay and Clermont Pepin. Further studies were with Tony Aubin, Gilbert Amy, and Jean-Pierre Guezec in France. In 1969 she founded and toured with the Groupe Electroacoustique de Paris, whose members came from five countries. She organized conferences, lectured widely, and was the recipient of grants and fellowships. (Boenke; Cohen; Hixon [uses Saint-Marcoux])

Coulthard, Jean
Canadian composer born in 1908. She was educated at the Toronto Conservatory of Music and the Royal College of Music. She studied with some of the leading composers of the 20th century, including Ralph Vaughan Williams, Darius Milhaud, Bela Bartók, and Nadia Boulanger. She has taught at the University of British Columbia since 1947 and has received numerous awards and commissions, including an honorary doctorate. (Boenke; Cohen; Hixon; Norton/Grove)

Criswick, Mary
English guitarist composer, music educator, and singer, born in Southend on Sea, Essex, in 1945. She received her musical education at Bristol University and the Guildhall School of Music in London. She taught guitar at City University and St. Paul's Girls' School until 1974. Since then she has been a singer with Florilegium Musicum de Paris and a writer on music for *Soundboard*. (Cohen; Hixon)

Cuervas, Matilde
Spanish flamenco guitarist and writer on music, born in Seville in 1887. Her death date is unknown. She toured as a soloist, and also as a guitar duo with her husband, the celebrated guitarist, Emilio Pujol. (Bone; Hixon; *Guitar Review*, no. 16 [1954])

Culbertson, D.C. (Dawn)
Contemporary USA composer, lutenist, and writer on music. Her master's degree is from the Peabody Conservatory, and she did post graduate study at Catholic and Columbia Universities. She has written for the national quarterly, *High Performance Review*, and for the *Baltimore Monthly*. She has been a classical radio announcer and is founder of the Baltimore Composers Forum. (*Hot Wire*, March 1987; Music Alaska Women conference program, 1993)

Currier, Marilyn Kind
USA composer, 20th century. (Cohen; Hixon)

Davidson, Tina
USA composer born in 1952. (Cohen says 1954.) She was educated at Bennington College where she studied with Henry Brand, Vivian Fine, and Louis Calabro. In 1978 she studied composition privately with Clifford Taylor. Her piano teachers have included Lionel Nowak, Walther Wollman, H. Schultz-Thierbach (Germany), Karol Kline (Tel-Aviv), and Sylvia Glickman. She has received many grants and awards and since 1981 has been piano lecturer at Drexel University. (Cohen; Hixon)

Davis, Jan
Looking for information about this composer.

Davis, Jean Reynolds
Born in 1927 in Maryland, USA, Ms. Davis is a composer of opera and sacred music, a music educator and administrator, a pianist, and writer on music. She received her BM from the University of Pennsylvania and has received various recognitions, including an ASCAP award. (Boenke; Cohen; Hixon)

Davis, Yolanda
Guitarist and composer, early 20th-century, possibly Argentine. (*Guitar Review*, no. 11 [1950])

De Freitas, Elvira Manuel Fernandez
Portuguese pianist, conductor, and composer, born in Lisbon in 1927. Her father, composer Frederico

de Freitas, was her first teacher. At the Lisbon Conservatory she continued with her father, then with Lourenco V. Cid, Jorge Croner de Vasconelos, Antonio E. da Costa Ferreira, and Fernando Lopes Garcia. She later studied at the Paris Conservatory with Nadia Boulanger and Olivier Messiaen. She was the conductor of the National Orchestra in Lisbon and taught at the Lisbon Conservatory until 1978 when she became professor at the Gregorian Institute. (Cohen; Hixon)

Degenhardt, Annette
Contemporary German composer, born in Mainz. She studied at the Hochschule für Musik und Darstellende Kunst in Frankfurt am Main (1985-90). In 1986 she produced her first LP album of original compositions. Since then she has produced recordings in 1992 and 1994. (Composer letter)

Delande, Jo
See **Vigneron-Ramackers, Josée**

De Rogatis, Teresa
See **Rogatis, Teresa De**

Desportes, Yvonne Berthe Melitta
French composer and music educator, born in Coburg, Saxony (1907-1993). The daughter of composer Emile Desportes, she studied at the Paris Conservatory with Jean and Noel Gallon, Paul Dukas, and Marcel Dupre. She won several prizes including the Prix de Rome in 1932. From 1943 she lectured at the Paris

Conservatory, first in solfége and later in counterpoint and fugue. She also taught piano accompaniment at the Lycee la Fontaine. She was made a Chevalier of the National Order of Merit. (Boenke; Cohen; Hixon; Norton/Grove; Olivier, 1988)

Dia, Countess de
Late 12th-century troubadour, who was married to Guillem of Potiers and was the lover of the troubadour Raimbaut d'Orange. (Cohen; Hixon; Norton/Grove) (Cohen and Norton/Grove use Beatrice de Dia, Contessa.)

Diakvnishvili, Mzisavar Zakharevna
Russian composer born in 1938. She studied composition under A.D. Machavarian at the Tbilisi Conservatory, graduating in 1963. (Cohen; Hixon)

Dianda, Hilda Fanny
Argentine composer, music educator, musicologist, conductor, and writer on music, born in 1925. She studied composition in Buenos Aires with Honorio Siccardi, then took conducting in Venice with Hermann Scherchen. Both the French and Italian governments have awarded her study grants. She taught at the School of Fine Arts of the National University of Cordoba in Argentina (1967-70). She has toured and conducted throughout Latin America and Europe, and participated in many international festivals. (Boenke; Cohen; Hixon; Norton/Grove)

Diehl, Paula Jespersen
Electronic music composer, 20th-century, USA. (Cohen; Hixon)

Diemer, Emma Lou
Born in Kansas City, Missouri, in 1927, she obtained both her BM and her MM degrees at Yale School of Music, where she worked with Richard Donovan and Paul Hindemith. A Fulbright Scholarship in composition and piano allowed her to study at the Royal Conservatory in Brussels (1952-53). She received her PhD in composition (1960) from the Eastman School of Music where her teachers were Bernard Rogers and Howard Hanson. She taught theory and composition at the University of Maryland (1965-70) and at the University of California at Santa Barbara since 1971. She is an organist, pianist, composer, and lecturer and has received many awards and prizes. (Boenke; Cohen; Hixon; Norton/Grove)

Di Lotti, Silvana
Born in Italy in 1942, she first studied music in Turin. After graduation she studied in Salzburg at the International Sommer-Akademie and in Siena, with Luciano Berio and Pierre Boulez at the Accademia Chigiana. Her works have been played at contemporary music festivals in Italy, and she has taught at the Turin Conservatory. (Norton/Grove)

Dinescu, Violeta
Romanian composer, pianist, and writer on music, born in 1953. She studied at the George Enescu Music School and at the Bucharest Conservatory where she received her master's degree in 1978, studying composition under Myriam Marbé. She then taught at the Enescu School (1978-82) before moving to Germany. She has been a lecturer in theory, counterpoint, and harmony at music schools in Heidelberg, Frankfurt, and Bayreuth and has been active in international music festivals and organizations. She is a prolific composer who has received numerous awards, prizes, and commissions worldwide. (Boenke; Cohen; Hixon; Norton/Grove)

Dockhorn, Lotte
German composer of songs, 19th century. (Cohen; Hixon)

Dollitz, Grete Franke
Born in Germany in 1924, she graduated from Hunter College in New York City. She is a music educator, guitarist, and composer. (Hixon; Composer letter)

Dorigny Denoyers, Mme
French composer, 19th century. (Cohen; Hixon)

Dring, Madeleine
English composer (1923-1977). She studied at the Royal College of Music, where her principal teachers were Herbert Howells and Ralph Vaughan Williams. She was an actress, singer, violinist, pianist, librettist, and composer. (Cohen; Hixon)

Duchesne, Geneviere
Looking for information about
this composer.

Duncan, Eve
Australian composer and
guitarist born in 1956. She studied
guitar with Jochen Schubert, then
attended the Melbourne and
Latrobe Universities in music
composition, graduating with
honors in 1990. She has worked
with Keith Humble and
Theodore Dollarhide. In Europe
she studied with Tera de Marez
Oyens and Thomas Christian
David. In 1995 she founded the
Melbourne Composer's League.
Her works have been performed
at major music festivals in
Australia, Switzerland,
Germany, the Netherlands,
Austria, Japan, and Thailand.
Her piece *Buddha Fantasy* has
been recorded on CD by guitarist
Stefan Feingold of Switzerland.
(Norton/Grove)

Edell, Therese
USA composer, singer, and
guitarist, born in 1950. She
studied bassoon at the College-
Conservatory of Music,
University of Cincinnati. Active
in the women's music movement,
she produced an LP in 1978, *From
Women's Faces* (Sea Friends
Records). She toured for many
years, receiving national
recognition in the folk and
lesbian-feminist communities.
(Concert program)

Eiríksdóttir, Karólina
Icelandic composer born in 1951.

She received her undergraduate
degree from Reykjavik College
and her master's degree from the
University of Michigan in 1976.
She teaches at the Reykjavík
College of Music. Her pieces have
been performed in Iceland,
throughout Scandinavia, and in
the USA. (Cohen; Hixon;
Norton/Grove)

Epstein, Marti
Looking for information about
this composer.

Erding, Susanne
German composer born in 1955.
She has won prizes for her
compositions, including opera,
symphonic, and chamber works.
(Cohen; Hixon; Norton/Grove)

Escot, Pozzi
Peruvian American composer,
music theorist, writer on music,
and music educator, born in 1933.
She was educated at Sas-Rosay
Music Academy in Lima, the
Juilliard School of Music (MS
1957), and the Hamburg
Hochschule für Musik (1957-61).
Her composition teachers were
Andrés Sas, William Bergsma,
and Philipp Jarnach. She has
received many grants and
awards, including McDowell
Fellowships and Ford Foundation
grants. She taught at the New
England Conservatory of Music
and has been on the faculty of
Wheaton College since 1972. Her
works have been performed by
major orchestras worldwide.
(Boenke; Cohen; Hixon;
Norton/Grove)

Euteneuer-Rohrer, Ursula Henrietta
German composer, pianist, and music educator born in 1953. She was educated at the Karlsruhe Staatliche Hochschule für Musik, completing composition studies in 1981. She attended the Darmstadt Summer School for New Music several times, and has taught theory and piano at the Gaggenau Music School since 1980. (Cohen; Hixon)

Even-Or (Ben-Or), Mary
Israeli conductor and composer born in 1939. She entered Tel Aviv University to study law, then changed to musicology. She graduated with degrees in composition and conducting from the Rubin Academy of Music and earned her MMus with distinction in composition in 1983. (Cohen; Hixon)

Farre de Prat, Carmen
Looking for information about this composer.

Fay, Lydia A.
Looking for information about this composer.

Fedele, Diacinta, Romana
Italian composer, 17th century. (Cohen; Hixon; Jackson)

Fereyra, Beatriz
Argentine composer born in 1937. She is largely self-taught, but received encouragement from Nadia Boulanger during a stay in Paris (1962-63). She studied electronic and electroacoustic

music at the R.A.I. Sound Studio in Milan. She participated in Pierre Schaeffer's Groupe de Recherches Musicales from 1964 to 1970 in Paris and did further study with Ligeti and Earle Brown at Darmstadt Summer School. Her other studies included music therapy and ethnomusicology. She has conducted seminars at the Paris Conservatory and taught at Dartmouth College. She lives in France where she devotes herself to composition. (Norton/Grove)

Fernandes, Maria Helena Rosas
See **Rosas Fernandes, Maria H.**

Fernandez, Teresita
Cuban singer, guitarist, and composer, born in 1930. She sang her own compositions and accompanied herself on the guitar. She has participated in numerous radio and television performances and has given many concerts in Havana. (Cohen; Hixon)

Ferrari, Gabriella (née Colombari de Montègre)
French-Italian composer (1851-1921). She was a child piano prodigy who studied in Milan and Naples before becoming a student of Charles Gounod and Alfred Apel in France. She and her works were featured on the Leborne and Lamoureux concerts. Cohen; Hixon)

Fine, Vivian
USA composer and pianist, born in 1913. At age five she was

awarded a scholarship to study piano at the Chicago Musical College. From age thirteen she studied under Ruth Crawford Seeger and Adolf Weidig at the American Conservatory. In 1931 she moved to New York to pursue studies with Roger Sessions, Abby Whiteside, and George Szell. For a few years Fine was accompanist and composer for modern dance groups. She taught at New York University, the Juilliard School, State University Teachers' College in Potsdam, Connecticut College of Dance, and Bennington College (1964-88). She was one of the founders of the American Composers Alliance and has been the recipient of prestigious grants and awards, including a Ford Foundation Grant in 1970, an NEA Award in 1974, and a Guggenheim Fellowship in 1980. She has had major commissions and her recorded works are on the CRI label. (Boenke; Cohen; Hixon; Norton/Grove)

Finzi, Graciane

French composer, pianist, and teacher, born in Morocco in 1945. Her early studies were at the Conservatory in Casablanca. Later she attended the Paris Conservatory where her principal teachers were Henri Chellan, Yvonne Desportes, Joseph Bonvenuti, Elsa Barraine, and Tony Aubin. She has taught music in Casablanca and since 1979 at the Paris Conservatory. She organized the music festival at La Défense (1975-80). (Boenke; Cohen; Hixon; Norton/Grove)

Fleischer, Tsippi (Fleischer-Dolgopolsky, Tsipporah)

Israeli composer and music educator born in 1946. Her undergraduate work was at the Rubin Academy of Music in Jerusalem. Her MA in music education is from New York University (1975). She has taught at Tel Aviv College of Music Teachers, at Tel Aviv University (musicology), and since 1984, at Bar Lian University. Israeli TV and radio have broadcast some of her works. (Cohen; Hixon; Norton/Grove)

Ford, Ann (marr. Thicknesse)

English singer, guitarist, viola da gamba and musical glass (glass harmonica) player, composer, and writer on music (1737-1824). (Hixon; Jackson)

Forman, Joanne

USA composer born in Chicago in 1934. She studied at Los Angeles City College, Los Angeles State College, University of California, Merritt College, and the University of New Mexico. Her composition studies were with Carolyn Trojanowski Chean (1953-57). She was director of a theater group, The Migrant Theatre (1966), and vice president of El Centro Cultural y Museo del Barrio from 1973. She co-directed Apple House Gallery (1961-65). She is also a writer, puppeteer, and playwright. (Boenke; Cohen; Hixon)

Fracker, Cora Robins
USA guitarist and composer born
in Iowa in 1849. Her death date is
unknown. She composed for the
piano as well as the guitar.
(Cohen; Hixon)

Frajt, Ludmila
Serbian composer born in 1919.
She studied with Miloje
Milojevic and Josep Slavenski at
the Music Academy of Belgrade,
then worked as an administrator
in TV, radio, and film. In 1961 she
attended the modern music course
in Darmstadt. She has received
prizes for her works and currently
teaches composition at the Music
University of Belgrade. (Cohen;
Hixon; Letter from Professor Uros
Dojcinovic; Norton/Grove)

Franklin, Mary Elizabeth
Looking for information about
this composer.

French, Tania Gabrielle
USA composer and choral
conductor born in 1963. (Cohen;
Hixon)

Fresnel, Emmy Heil
See **Wegener-Fresnel, Emmy**

Fritz, Sherilyn Gail
Canadian composer born in 1957.
She studied at the University of
British Columbia where she
received her BMus and teaching
credentials. Her compositions
have won numerous awards.
(Cohen; Hixon)

Frost, Betsy
See **Warren, Betsy**

Frotta, Judith
Looking for information about
this composer.

Furgeri, Bianca Maria
Italian composer, organist, choral
conductor, pianist, educator, and
writer on music, born in 1935. She
was educated at the Milan and
Padua Conservatories and has
taught since 1962. Her teachers
included G. Giuseppe Piccioli, B.
Coltro, Wolfango della Vecchia,
and G.F. Ghedini. In 1969 she was
appointed professor of harmony
and counterpoint at the Bologna
Conservatory. She is the
recipient of numerous awards and
prizes, and her works have been
performed throughout Europe.
(Cohen; Hixon; Norton/Grove)

Gabetti, Flora
Looking for information about
this composer.

Gabriel, Mary Ann Virginia
English composer and pianist
(1825-1877). Her husband, George
E. March, wrote the librettos for
her operettas. (Cohen; Hixon)

Gabus, Monique
French composer, pianist, and
music educator, born in 1924. She
studied at the Paris Conservatory
where she won prizes in harmony
and composition. She taught at
the Schola Cantorum of Paris
until ill-health forced her to
resign. (Boenke; Cohen; Hixon)

Gaertner, Katarzyna
Polish composer born in 1942. She
received an award from the

Polish Ministry of Culture in 1975. Her songs have been performed at various music festivals. (Cohen; Hixon)

Galli (Gallo?), Caterina (signora)
Italian popular singer who lived in England and performed at Covent Garden in 1797. (Cohen; Jackson)

Gambarini, Costanza
Italian composer, born ca. 1951. (Cohen, Hixon)

Garcia, Olimpiades
Looking for information about this composer.

Garcia Ascot, Rosa
Spanish composer born in Madrid in 1906. She studied piano with Enrique Granados, and piano and composition with Manuel de Falla, for whom she was accompanist at his Paris debut. She was married to Jesús Bal y Gay and lived in Mexico. (Cohen; Hixon)

Gardner, Kay
USA composer, flutist, recording artist, and writer, born in New York in 1941. She studied conducting with Elizabeth Green at the University of Michigan. In 1968 she founded the Norfolk Chamber Consort. She received her MMus from the SUNY, Stony Brook in 1974. Samuel Baron was her principal flute teacher. In 1977 she went to Denver to study conducting with Antonia Brico, and the following year made her

conducting debut at the National Women's Music Festival in Champaign, Illinois. In 1978 she founded the New England Women's Symphony. Since then she has composed opera, researched, written, and lectured about music and healing, and continued to perform at various women's music festivals. (Boenke; Cohen; Composer letter; Hixon; Norton/Grove)

Gartenlaub, Odette
French composer, pianist, music educator, and writer on music, born in 1922. In 1936 at age fourteen she won a first prize in piano from the Paris Conservatory. She studied composition there and won the Prix de Rome in 1948. She has performed as a piano soloist with major orchestras, and has taught at the Paris Conservatory since 1959. (Boenke; Cohen; Hixon)

Gentile, Ada
Italian composer, pianist, and music educator, born in 1947. She studied at the Conservatory of San Pietro a Majella in Naples and the Conservatory of Santa Cecilia in Rome, receiving her graduate degree in composition in 1974. Further studies were with Goffredo Petrassi (1975-76). She has taught at the Conservatories of Trieste, Frosinone, and St. Cecilia. Her works have been performed at international contemporary music festivals and on national and Vatican radio. (Boenke; Cohen; Hixon; Norton/Grove)

Genty, Mlle
French composer, fl. ca. 1760s?
(Cohen; Hixon; Jackson)

Geyer, Marianne
Austrian composer born in 1883.
Her death date is unknown. She
composed songs with guitar
accompaniment and lived in
Berlin. (Cohen; Hixon)

Gibbs, Prue
Australian composer, 20th
century. (Cohen; Hixon)

Gideon, Miriam
USA composer and teacher, born
in 1906. She received her BA from
Boston University in 1926, her
MA in musicology from Columbia
University in 1946, and her
doctorate in sacred music and
composition from Jewish
Theological Seminary of America
in 1970. Her primary composition
teachers were Lazare Saminsky
and Roger Sessions. She has
taught at Brooklyn College
(1944-54), Jewish Theological
Seminary since 1955, City
College, CUNY (1947-55 and
1971-76), and the Manhattan
School of Music since 1967. She
has received numerous awards
and grants. Her works have been
performed by many major
orchestras in the USA, Europe,
and South America. (Boenke;
Cohen; Hixon; Norton/Grove)

Gifford, Helen Margaret
Australian composer, pianist, and
music librarian, born in 1935. She
was educated at the University
of Melbourne Conservatorium,

where she received her MMus in
1958. Her interest in Asian music,
especially India and Polynesia,
can be heard in some of her works.
In 1970 she was composer-in-
residence of the Melbourne
Theatre Company. (Boenke;
Cohen; Hixon; Norton/Grove)

Gil del Bosque, Rosa
Looking for information about
this composer.

Gileno, Jean Anthony
USA composer and music
therapist, born in 1941. She
received her MME from Temple
University in 1973. She studied
with Regina Therese Unsinn for
her PhD. (Cohen; Hixon)

Giteck, Janice
USA composer born in 1946. She
received her BA (1968) and her
MA in composition (1969) from
Mills College. She then attended
the Paris Conservatory. Her
teachers have included Messiaen,
Milhaud, Childs, Subotnick, L.
Klein, C. Jones and L. Cross. She
has taught in Frankfort, Germany
(1970-71); at California State
University, Hayward (1974);
University of California,
Berkeley (1974-76); and the
Cornish Institute in Seattle since
1979. The recipient of many
commissions and awards, she has
also been active as a writer and
radio programmer. (Boenke;
Cohen; Hixon; Norton/Grove)

Giuliani-Guglielmi, Emilia
Emilia was born in 1813 in
Vienna, daughter of the famous

Italian guitarist and composer, Mauro Giuliani. She was educated at the convent L'Adorazione di Gesu (1821-26), then married Pietro Guglielmi. Her exact death date is unknown, but there are records of her touring Europe during 1841-44. (Cohen; Hixon; Nolan; Zuth) (Cohen and Hixon use Giuliani-Giulelmi.)

Giuranna, Elena Barbara
Italian composer, harpist, pianist, and music educator, born in 1902. She studied harp at the Conservatory of Palermo, receiving a diploma in 1918. In 1921 she graduated in composition from the Regio Conservatory of Naples. Then she studied piano in Milan with Giorgio Federico Ghedini. Her piano debut was with the Naples Symphonic Orchestra in 1923. She was the first Italian woman composer invited to participate in music festivals in Vienna and Brussels. After 1937 she taught at the St. Cecilia Conservatory in Rome. The recipient of many prizes and awards, she is married to conductor Mario Giuranna. (Boenke; Cohen; Hixon; Norton/Grove)

Godla, Mary Ann
Contemporary USA guitarist, arranger, composer, music educator, and writer on music. (Cohen; Hixon)

Gonzaga, Chiquinha (Francisca Hedwiges Neves Gonzaga)
Brazilian conductor, pianist, and composer of light opera and musicals (1847-1935). She studied piano with E. Alvarez Lobo and Artur Napoleao. In 1885 she became the first woman to conduct a theatre orchestra in Brazil. A prolific composer, she wrote over 2000 works, including scores for 77 plays, often collaborating with famous playwrights of the time. She toured in Europe (1902-10) and set several Portuguese plays to music. Gonzaga's immense popularity began during her lifetime and has continued for many decades. She was also active in the Brazilian anti-slavery movement. (Boenke; Cohen; Hixon; Norton/Grove)

Grétry, Angelique-Dorothée-Lucile (Lucie)
French composer of opera and light-opera (1770-1790). She studied with her father, the composer Andre Ernest Modeste Grétry. At age fourteen she wrote her first opera, which was succcessfully produced at the Comedie-Italienne in Paris. She died soon after her marriage to the composer Pierre Marin du Champcourt. (Cohen; Hixon; Jackson)

Griffes-Kortering, Lois
USA composer born in 1934. She holds a BME degree (1984) from Hope College, Holland, MI. (Composer letter)

Grigsby, Beverly (née Pinsky)
USA composer born in 1928. She began studying medicine at University of Southern

California, then switched to music at the Southern California School of Music and Arts (1947-49). From 1949 to 1951 she was the student of Ernst Krenek. Her diplomas include BA from San Fernando Valley State College in 1961, MA from California State University, Northridge in 1963, and DMA from University of Southern California in 1969. Post-doctoral work was in computer music at Stanford University. Her operas have received performances at international festivals. She is the recipient of many awards and commissions. Since 1969 she has taught at CSU, Northridge, and since retiring in the early 1990s, she has been director of the International Institute for the Study of Women in Music, at CSU. (Cohen; Composer letter; Hixon; Norton/Grove)

Gubaidulina, Sofia Asgatovna
Composer and pianist, born in the former USSR in 1931. She studied at the Kazan Music Academy (1946-49), the Kazan Conservatory (1949-54), and the Moscow Conservatory (1954-63). Her principal composition teachers were Albert Leman, Nidolai Peiko, and Vissarion Shebalin. One of the leading contemporary Soviet composers, she also has been an accompanist for the Moscow Theatre Institute, has composed for several theatre and film projects, and has worked at the Electronic Music Studio in Moscow. In 1975 she formed the improvisation group, Asteya, with two other composers, and in the 1980s became internationally recognized for her compositions. (Boenke; Cohen; Hixon; Norton/Grove [uses Sofiya Gubaydulina]; Ophee)

Gudauskas, Giedra
Lithuanian American composer, pianist, and teacher, born in 1923. She studied voice and piano at Kaunas State Conservatory (1933-40). At Roosevelt University she studied composition with Karel Jirak, receiving a BMus in 1952. In the same year she became a US citizen. Later she studied film scoring and jazz improvisation at the University of California and taught privately. (Cohen; Hixon)

Gumert, Lynn
Looking for information about this composer.

Guraieb Kuri, Rosa
Mexican pianist and composer of Lebanese origin, born in 1931. She studied in Beruit and Mexico City, and at Yale University (1954). Her principal teachers were Carlos Chavez, Gerhart Nuench, Alfonso de Elias, Mario Lavista, and Daniel Catan. As a concert pianist she has appeared with the National Symphony Orchestra of Mexico, and her works have been presented at forums and festivals. (Cohen; Hixon; Norton/Grove)

Hall, Helen
Looking for information about this composer.

Hankinson, Ann Shrewsbury
USA composer born in 1944. She
spent her early childhood in
Pakistan, Burma, and India,
moving to Los Angeles in 1961.
She studied at the University of
Southern California, then
received her MA and PhD from
the University of California at
San Diego. Major teachers include
Henri Lazaroff, Bernard Rands,
Robert Erickson, and Pauline
Oliveros. She taught at the
University of California at Santa
Barbara (1982-84), and currently
teaches at the University of
Utah in Salt Lake City. She
received an NEA grant in 1979.
(Boenke; Hixon)

Hara, Kazuko
Born in Japan in 1935, Kazuko
Hara studied at Teijutsu Daigaku
in Tokyo, Ecole Normale de
Musique in Paris, and the
L'Académie International d'Eté
in Nice. She has been a professor
of music at the Osaka University
of Arts since 1968 and a lecturer at
Tokyo Teijutsu Daigaku since
1970. She has won several prizes
and scholarships. (Boenke;
Cohen; Hixon; Norton/Grove)

**Hardin, Miss (same as Elisabeth
Hardin(g)?)**
English composer, 18th century.
(Cohen; Hixon; Jackson)

Hart, Jane Smith
USA composer and music
administrator, born in 1913. She
received her BS from the
Juilliard School of Music in 1938
and her MA from Columbia

Teachers College in 1958. She
chaired the music department at
the Horace Mann School from
1971 to 1977 and was director of
composer musical productions for
that same institution. She also
chaired the New Rochelle Music
Teachers' Council from 1965 to
1969 and directed the Young
Artists New Rochelle Annual
Concert from 1964 to 1977. (Cohen;
Composer letter; Hixon)

Harting-Ware, Lynn
Canadian guitarist, music writer,
and composer. She received her
BM from the College-
Conservatory of Music,
University of Cincinnati, and her
MM from Kent State University.
Her principal teachers were Eli
Kassner and Clare Callahan.
She is founding editor of *Guitar
Canada* magazine, contributing
writer for many publications, and
as a touring concert guitarist, is
dedicated to establishing a 20th-
century guitar repertory.
(Composer letter)

Hartmann, Liobe
Looking for information about
this composer.

Havlik, Branka
Contemporary composer born in
Belgrade, Serbia. She teaches at
the J. Slavenski Music
Conservatory in Belgrade. (Letter
from Professor Uros Dojcinovic)

**Hawley, Carolyn Jean (née
Bowen)**
USA composer born in 1931. She is
a pianist, conductor, educator,

and writer on music. She received her BA from Hamline University (1954), her MA from Mills College (1958), and also studied at the University of New Mexico (1957). She has taught privately and at Laney College in Oakland, CA. She conducted the Berkeley Community Orchestra and Chorus and founded the Ukiah Symphony Orchestra. (Boenke; Cohen; Hixon)

Hayden, Carrie V. (née C.V. Stearns?)
USA composer of the 19th century. She and her husband, W. L. Hayden, began their own publishing house in Boston. She often published under the name C.V. Stearns, which may have been her maiden name. (Danner)

Hays, Sorrel Doris Ernestine
USA composer, pianist, music educator, and writer on music, born in 1941. Her musical education included BM (1959), University of Chattanooga; artist diploma (1966), Munich Hochschule; and MM (1968), University of Wisconsin, where she studied with Paul Badura-Skoda. Further studies in composition were with Richard Hervig at the University of Iowa (1969). She has been a soloist for many European concerts and has taught at the University of Wisconsin and Cornell College (Iowa). She has won many awards and grants and been recognized for her promotion of women in music. (Cohen; Hixon)

Helmuth, Mara
USA composer born in 1957. She composes primarily for computer, both tape and real-time systems, and occasionally for acoustic instruments. She is Assistant Professor in Composition at the University of Cincinnati, College-Conservatory of Music. She has also taught at Texas A&M and New York University. Her BM and MM are from the University of Illinois and her PhD is from Columbia University. (Norton/Grove)

Henkel, Kathy
A native of Los Angeles, Kathy studied at Califonia State University, Northridge, where she received her BA and MA degrees in music. In recent years she has been a reviewer with the Los Angeles Times, a music researcher with Paramount Pictures, and a script writer and producer for classical radio station KUSC. She also writes program notes for Los Angeles area orchestras and chamber groups. (Music Alaska Women, 1993 conference program)

Herrera, Hilda
Looking for information about this composer.

Hervey, Augusta
Looking for information about this composer.

Hilderley, Jeriann G.
USA composer born in 1937. She is a composer, percussionist, and writer on music. She studied at

Smith College, University of California at Berkeley, and the University of Michigan. Her MA is in both music and art. Her principal teachers were sculptor Joseph Goto, painter Herman Cherry, and composer Denise Hoffman. She directed both a women's theatre group and Sea Wave Records. (Cohen; Hixon)

Ho, Wai On
British composer born in Hong Kong in 1946. She studied Chinese language and literature at the Chinese University of Hong Kong. She received a scholarship to study at the Royal Academy of Music (1966-71), where her composition teacher was James Iliff. After earning advanced degrees she went on to receive her MMus in electronic and contemporary music (1984) from University College, Cardiff. In 1988 she established Inter-Artes, a group which creates cross-cultural arts projects. (Cohen; Hixon; Norton/Grove)

Holm, Kristin
Looking for information about this composer.

Holmes, Leonie
Looking for information about this composer.

Hölszky, Adriana
Romanian composer and pianist, born to Austrian German parents in 1953. She attended the Bucharest Conservatory (1972-75) and studied privately in Germany. Her principal teachers

have included Stefan Niculescu, Milko Kelemen, Günter Louegk, and Erhard Karkoschka. She has received many prizes for composition and has taught at the Stuttgart Musikhochschule (1980-89) and the Darmstadt summer courses. (Cohen; Hixon; Norton/Grove)

Hontos, Margaret
Contemporary USA composer. She holds a master of arts degree in composition from UCLA. She has studied with Aurelio dela Vega, Manuel Enriquez, Ian Krouse, and Paul Reale. She is a member of the International Alliance of Women in Music and the National Association of Composers, USA. She has received awards and commissions. (Composer letter)

Hoover, Katherine
USA composer and flutist, born in 1937. She received her BM in theory from the Eastman School of Music, and her MA in theory from the Manhattan School of Music. She has studied flute with Joseph Mariano and William Kincaid. She has taught at the Manhattan School of Music, the Juilliard School, and at Teacher's College, Columbia University. She has organized music festivals of works by women composers and been a recipient of the National Endowment Composers' Grant, an ASCAP Award, and the prestigious Academy of Arts and Letters 1994 Academy Composition Award. She is an active concert flutist

and recording artist. (Boenke; Cohen; Composer letter; Hixon)

Hovda, Eleanor
USA composer, music educator, choreographer, and dancer, born in 1940. Her undergraduate work was done at Randolph-Macon Women's College in Virginia and American University, where she received her BA in piano in 1963. She studied composition at Yale and at the University of Illinois. Further study was with Stockhausen. Her MFA is from Sarah Lawrence in dance. She studied music composition for dance with Dlugloszewski and dance with Erik Hawkins and Merce Cunningham. She teaches dance at St. Scholastica College and has lectured at Sarah Lawrence College and Wesleyan University. (Cohen; Hixon)

Hunkins, Eusebia Simpson
USA composer, music educator, administrator, and folklorist, born in 1920. (Boenke and Cohen use 1902.) She studied at the Juilliard School. Her major teachers were Darius Milhaud, Ernest Hutcheson, and Ernst von Dohnanyi. She also studied at Aspen, Chautauqua, Tanglewood, and Salzburg and taught at Cornell College. From 1972 to 1974 she was involved in The Musical World of Ohio broadcasts. She is an expert on Appalachian folk music. From 1976 she worked for the National Opera Association as a compiler. (Boenke; Cohen; Hixon)

Irman-Allemann, Regina
Swiss guitarist, percussionist, pianist, music educator, and composer, born in 1957. She studied the guitar at Winterthur Conservatory. Her teachers in new music studies were Roland Moser, Peter Streiff, and Robert Rudisuli. She is self-taught in composition. She received a teacher's diploma in 1982 and has taught guitar at Winterthur. In 1985 she began studying percussion. (Cohen; Hixon; Norton/Grove)

Izarra, Adina
Venezuelan composer born in 1959. She obtained her BA and PhD in composition from York University in England, where she studied from 1983 to 1988, with Vic Hoyland as her principal teacher. Since 1988 she has lived in Caracas where she teaches at the Simón Bolivar University and participates in new music activities. Her works are recorded on Bis Grammophon, MIT Press, and the Venezuelan labels, HM Records and Airo Music. (Composer letter)

Janárceková, Viera
Czech composer born in 1944. She studied at Bratislava Conservatory and later took part in harpsichord masterclasses at the Prague Academy and piano masterclasses in Lucerne. In 1972 she moved to Germany where she was a performer and teacher. Since 1981 she has been a free-lance composer, painter, and performer. (Norton/Grove)

Jeppsson, Kerstin Maria
Swedish composer and conductor,
born in 1948. She studied
conducting, harmony, and
counterpoint at the Conservatory
of Music in Stockholm and
Stockholm University,
graduating in 1973 and 1976
respectively. Her principal
teachers were Erland von Koch,
Maurice Karkoff, Krzysztof
Penderecki, Krzysztof Meyer and
Radwan. (Boenke; Cohen; Hixon)

Jirackova, Marta (Martha)
Czech composer and music
administrator, born in 1932. She
studied at the Prague
Conservatory with Emil Hlobil
and after 1958, with Alois Haba.
She was musical director for
Czechoslovak Radio in Prague. In
1978 she studied new
compositional techniques at the
Janacek Academy of Music. With
conductor Jindra Jindackova, she
founded a vocal touring ensemble
called Laetitlia, which toured
throughout Europe performing
ancient folk songs and medieval
music. (Cohen; Hixon)

Jolas, Betsy
French American composer, music
editor, writer on music, conductor,
pianist, and music educator, born
in 1926. Her BA is from
Bennington College (1946). She
continued music studies at the
Paris Conservatory where her
major teachers were Darius
Milhaud, Olivier Messiaen, and
Simon Plé Caussade. She was the
editor of the French radio-
television periodical, *Ecouter*

aujourd'hui. From 1971 to 1974 she
substituted for Olivier Messiaen
at his course at the Paris
Conservatory and was appointed
to that faculty in 1975. She has
taught at Yale, USC, Mills,
Tanglewood, Berkeley, and San
Diego [State?] University. She is
the recipient of many prestigious
awards and prizes, and her works
have been performed worldwide.
(Boenke; Cohen; Composer letter;
Hixon)

Joyce, Fiona
Looking for information about
this composer.

Kanach, Sharon
USA composer, pianist, and
writer on music. She received her
BA from Bennington College in
1979 and studied computer
programming in Paris at IRCAM
in 1981. Her composition teachers
were Vivian Fine, Otto Luening,
Olivier Messiaen, and Nadia
Boulanger, among others. She
teaches piano and composition
privately. (Cohen; Hixon)

Kazandjian-Pearson, Sirvart H.
Armenian singer and composer,
born in Ethiopia in 1944. She
studied at the National
Conservatory of Erevan (1963-68),
at the Paris Conservatory (1969-
70) with Toni Aubin, and later
took voice in Switzerland at the
Conservatory of Geneva. Her
works have been performed in
Armenia, Europe, and the United
States. She has produced a series
of radio shows on Armenian
music. (Cohen; Hixon)

Kelley, Mary M.
Looking for information about this composer.

Kinkle, Johanna (née Mockel)
German pianist, composer, conductor, poet, and writer on music (1810-1858). She was the daughter of Peter Joseph Mockel, a singing teacher at the Royal Bonn Gymnasium, where she first studied composition with Franz Anton. In 1843 she married the poet Gottfried Kinkel and co-founded a literary society in Bonn called the Maikaeferbund. Encouraged by Felix Mendelssohn to pursue music, she moved to Berlin to study composition with Karl Boehmer and Wilhelm Taubert. Upon returning to Bonn she was involved in chamber music and vocal ensembles until her husband was arrested in 1848 and condemned to death for his political activities. He managed to escape from Spandau prison and the family moved to London. There she became a choir director and wrote librettos, poetry, and essays about music, especially about Chopin, to support her family. She committed suicide in 1858. (Cohen; Hixon)

Kircher, Irina
German guitarist and composer, born in Stuttgart in 1966. She studied guitar at the Hockshule für Music und Darstellende Kunst in Stuttgart under Mario Sicca. She won the "Young Musician of the Year" contest two years in a row, first at age ten. In 1983 she moved to Caracas, Venezuela, to study with Antonio Lauro. Since 1983 she performs regularly in a guitar duo with her husband Alfonso Montes. They live in Germany. (Summerfield, 1991)

Knoop, Mrs.
Looking for information about this composer.

Koblenz, Babette
German composer, author, and publisher, born in 1956. She attended the Musikhochschule in Hamburg (1975-80), and studied composition privately with Gyorgy Ligeti. (Cohen; Hixon)

Kojima, Yuriko
Japanese composer and pianist, born in 1962. She studied composition with Isao Matsushita at Osawa College of Music. She won the Roger Sessions Scholarship to the Boston Conservatory, where she studied under John C. Adams. (Letter from Alejandro Madrid)

Kolb, Barbara
USA composer, clarinetist, and music educator, born in 1939 in Connecticut. She was educated at the Hartt College of Music of the University of Hartford (1957-64). At Tanglewood she studied with Lukas Foss and Gunther Schuller. She studied clarinet with Leon Russianoff, received a fellowship from the McDowell Colony, and was clarinetist with the Hartford Symphony Orchestra (1960-65). She was the first American woman to win the Prix de Rome (1969-1971). Other

awards include a Fulbright (1966) and two Guggenheims (1971 and 1976). She has taught at Brooklyn and Wellesley Colleges, and has been a visiting professor at Temple University and the Eastman School of Music. Her works have been performed by major orchestras, and she has received important commissions. (Boenke; Cohen; Composer letter; Hixon; Norton/Grove)

Konishi, Nagado
Japanese composer born in 1945. She was educated at the Tokyo University of Fine Arts, receiving a graduate degree in 1971. She also took graduate courses at the University of California, Berkeley. She is a member of the Japanese Federation of Composers, International [League of?]Women Composers, and the Federation of Women Composers in Japan. (Cohen; Hixon)

Koptagel, Yuksel
Turkish composer and pianist, born in 1931. She studied music with the Turkish composer Cemal Resit and later in Madrid and Paris with Alexander Tansman, Joaquin Rodrigo, José Cubiles, Lazare Levy, and Tony Aubin. She received a Diplome Superieur from the Paris Conservatory. Her works have been performed at music festivals, and she has appeared as a soloist with many orchestras. (Cohen; Hixon)

Kord, Mira
See **Vorlová, Sláva**

Kruisbrink, Annette
Looking for information about this composer.

Krzanowska, Grazyna
Polish composer, 20th century. (Cohen; Hixon)

Kubo, Mayako
Japanese composer, pianist, and and musicologist, born in 1947. She studied at Osawa College of Music (1966-70). She entered the Vienna Musikhochschule in 1972 to study piano, composition, and electronic music. In 1977 she began studies in musicology at Vienna University. (Cohen; Hixon)

Kukuck, Felicitas (née Kestner)
German composer, flutist, pianist, and music educator, born in 1914. She attended the Hochschule für Musik in Berlin (1935-39). Her teachers were Scheck (flute), Uhde (piano), and Hindemith (composition). (Boenke; Cohen; Hixon)

Kuntze, Lilia Vázquez
Mexican composer, 20th century. (Cohen and Hixon use Vázquez.) Looking for more information.

Kurakina (Kourakin), Natal'ya Ivanova (Princess)
Born in St. Petersburg, former USSR (1766-1831). (Jackson)

Kurimoto, Yoko
Japanese composer born in 1951. Her degree is from the Graduate School of Aichi University of Arts (1976). She studied with Kan Ishii. (Cohen; Hixon)

LaChartre, Nicole Marie

French musicologist, composer, and writer on music, born in 1934. She was educated at the Paris Conservatory, where she won prizes while studying with Milhaud and Jolivet. Other teachers included P. Schaeffer and J. Rivier. Later she studied with Xenakis and Barbaude (computer music). She was involved in the Groupe de Recherches Musicales of ORTF in the late 1960s and early 1970s. Her compositions are inspired by writers of mysticism and spiritual experiences. (Cohen; Hixon; Norton/Grove)

Lagerhiem-Romare, Marcit

Looking for information about this composer.

Lam Man Lee, Violet

Contemporary composer born in Hong Kong. (Cohen; Hixon)

Lambertini, Marta

Argentine composer born in 1937. She graduated from the Universidad Católica Argentina in 1972 and later studied electroacoustic composition at the Centro de Investigaciones de la Ciudad de Buenos Aires. She has won numerous prizes and awards for her work. (Norton/Grove)

Lara, Maria Teresa

Mexican composer born in 1959. She studied with Humberto Hernández Medrano at the Taller de Estudios Polifónicos (1979). In 1982 she began in composition at the National Conservatory of Music with Daniel Catán and Mario Lavista. In 1984 she was awarded a scholarship to study composition at CENIDIM with Federico Ibarra. (Tapia Colman)

Laren, Derek

See **van Epen-de Groot, Elsa**

Larsen, Elizabeth (Libby)

USA composer born in 1950. She was educated at the Univerisity of Minnesota, BA (1971), MA (1974), and PhD (1978). Her composition teachers were Paul Fetler, Dominick Argento, and Eric Stokes. She was co-founder of the Minnesota Composers' Forum, and was composer-in-residence for the Minnesota Orchestra from 1983-85. She has received numerous grants and awards, and her compositions have been widely acclaimed. Major orchestras have programmed her works. (Boenke; Cohen; Hixon; Norton/Grove)

Laruelle, Jeanne-Marie

French composer, organist, and music educator born in 1934. She studied at the Schola Cantorum under Jan Langlais and Gaston Litaize. (Boenke; Cohen; Hixon)

Lathrop, Gayle Posselt

USA composer, guitarist, flutist, teacher, and administrator, born in 1942. She studied at Indiana University and at California State University at Humboldt, where she was later guitar lecturer. She has also taught at the College of the Redwoods. (Boenke; Cohen; Hixon)

Lauber, Anne Marianne
Swiss-Canadian composer, pianist, violinist, conductor, and music educator, born in 1943. She studied in Switzerland at the Ribeaupierre Institute and at the Music Conservatory in Lausanne. In 1967 she emigrated to Canada. At McGill University she took orchestration with Alexandre Brott. She received her MA from the University of Montreal in 1982 and her PhD in 1986. She has studied with Serge Garant and André Prévost. Lauber has been active with many Canadian music organizations including the Orchestre Civique des Jeunes des Montreal (1979-80), the Canadian League of Composers (1980-82), and the Canadian Music Centre (1982-92). She has received major grants from the Swiss and Canadian governments. (Boenke; Cohen; Hixon; Norton/Grove)

Lauro, Natalia
Looking for information about this composer.

Le Bordays, Christiane
French composer, musicologist, guitarist, and pianist, born in 1937. She obtained her bachelor's degree and later worked on a PhD at the Sorbonne. She also studied flamenco guitar and dance, and Spanish folklore, which has influenced her compositions. (Cohen; Hixon)

Lee, Hope
Canadian composer of Chinese origin, born in 1953. She was educated at McGill University in Montreal and at the Staatlich Hockschule für Musik in Freiburg, Germany. Her major teachers have been Bengt Hambraeus, Brian Cherney, and Klaus Huber. She has also studied Chinese traditional music and poetry, and computer music. She was a composer-in-residence in Switzerland and a visiting composition instructor at Queen's University in Kingston. She has been the recipient of numerous awards and commissions and has had works performed at various international music festivals. Since 1979 Lee has researched ancient Chinese poetry, history, and theory, in particiular the philosophy and notation of the ch'in, which is a 7-sting Chinese zither. This research has influenced her own creative voice in her compositions. (Cohen; Composer letter; Hixon)

Lehnstaedt, Lu
Looking for information about this composer.

Leite (Dias Batista), Clarisse
Brazilian composer, professor, and pianist, born in 1917. She studied at the Conservatório Dramático e Musical of São Paulo and won a scholarship to study in France in 1930. She worked for São Paulo educational radio (1932-37) and toured for the State Department of Culture (1937-59). She is a professor at the Academia International de Musica do Rio de Janeiro. (Cohen; Hixon; Norton/Grove)

Leite, Vânia Dantas
Brazilian composer, pianist, conductor, and teacher, born in 1945. She was educated at the Escola Nacional de Música, now part of the University of Rio de Janeiro. Her composition teacher there was Frederico Egger. She later studied electronic music with Per Hartmann in London and composition with Esther Scliar in Paris. She has focused on composing and conducting and has held several teaching positions in Brazil. (Norton/Grove)

Lejet, Edith Jacqueline Marie
French composer and professor of music born in 1941. Her teachers at the Paris Conservatory were Rivier and Jolivet. She taught at the Sorbonne Institute of Musicology (1970-72) and became a titular professor at the Paris Conservatory in 1975. She has won many scholarships and prizes, including the Second Grand Prix de Rome (1968). (Boenke; Cohen; Hixon; Norton/Grove)

Lejeune-Bonner, Elaine
French composer, organist, and music educator, born in 1921. She studied at the Schola Cantorum and the Ecole César Franck in Paris. She is a successful organist and teacher who has won several prizes and awards. (Boenke; Cohen; Hixon)

Lenzi Mozzani, Carmen
Looking for information about this composer.

León, Tania Justina
Cuban-American composer, pianist, music educator, and administrator, born in 1943. She studied at the Carlos Alfredo Peyrellade Conservatory in Havana where she received her BA in 1963. Her MA in music education is from the National Conservatory in Havana. She also holds a BA in accounting from Havana University and both a BS and MS in composition from New York University (1971-73). She was been guest conductor and piano soloist with numerous orchestras. In 1976 she founded the Dance Theatre of Harlem Orchestra, for which she is now music director and conductor. She also co-founded the Brooklyn Philharmonic Community Concert Series. She has received numerous grants and awards including ASCAP and Meet the Composer. She has taught at the Lincoln Center Institute, Brooklyn College, City University of New York, and the Conservatory of Music in Brooklyn. (Cohen; Hixon; Norton/Grove)

Leone, Mae Grace
USA composer, organist, conductor, and writer on music, born in 1931. Her BA, MEd, and PhD degrees are from New York College. She did subsequent study at Adelphi College and Goddard College. (Cohen; Hixon)

Levin, Rami Yona
USA composer, oboist, recorder player, pianist, and music educator, born in 1954. She

received her BA (1975) from Yale University and her MA (1978) from the University of California, San Diego, where she studied with Bernard Rands, Pauline Oliveros, Robert Erickson, and Kenneth Gaburo. She also has studied in New York with Miriam Gideon (1970-71). She was oboist with the Morley Wind Ensemble in London (1979-1980). (Boenke; Cohen; Hixon)

Lewin, Olive
Contemporary Jamaican composer and arts administrator. She was the government Director of Art and Culture. (Cohen; Hixon)

Lind, Jenny (Johanna Maria)
Swedish soprano and composer (1820-1887), who was one of the most famous singers in the 19th century. She also composed songs. (Cohen; Hixon)

Linnemann, Maria Catharina
Dutch guitarist, pianist, violinist, composer, and music educator, born in 1947. She lived in England from 1948 to 1971 and studied at the Royal Academy of Music, London (1966-70). She did further study with Nadia Boulanger, before emigrating to Germany in 1971. In 1973 she began to study the guitar and in 1976 began to compose for the instrument. She teaches at the Youth Music School in Gütersloh, Germany. (Cohen; Hixon)

Linnet, Anne
Danish composer, rock singer, pianist, and saxophonist, born in

1953. Her musical career began in a jazz/soul band, and in 1974 she started an all-woman group, which made several recordings. She graduated from the Conservatory in Århus in 1985, with degrees in education and composition, the first woman to receive a composition degree in Denmark. Her principal teachers were Tage Nielsen and Per Nørgård. (Cohen; Hixon; Norton/Grove)

Liter, Monia (Monica)
USA composer, 20th century. (Cohen; Hixon)

Lomon, Ruth
Canadian American composer, pianist, and music educator, born in 1930. She was educated at the Quebec Conservatory, McGill University, and the New England Conservatory (1951-54). Her principal teachers included Frances Judd Cooke and Witold Lutoslawski. She performed in a piano duo (1971-83) and has received many awards and commissions. (Cohen; Hixon; Norton/Grove)

Luff, Enid
Welsh pianist, composer, music publisher, and writer on music, born in 1935. She studied modern languages in the 1950s and received her MMus (1974) from the University of Wales. She studied with Elizabeth Lutyens, Anthony Payne, and Franco Donatoni and started her own publishing company, Primavera. (Cohen; Hixon; Norton/Grove)

Luizi, Maria Thereza
Looking for information about this composer.

Lutyens, Elisabeth
English composer, violist, and writer on music (1906-1983). The daughter of architect Edwin Lutyens, she studied at the Ecole Normale in Paris under N. de Manziarly (1922-23). She took composition with Harold Darke and viola with Ernest Tomlinson at the Royal Academy of Music (1926-30), then studied privately with George Caussade. By 1939, when her compositions were performed at the ISCM Festival in Warsaw, she was beginnning to receive international recognition. After WWII she introduced twelve-tone music to Great Britain, but did not receive unanimous acclaim for two decades. In the mid-1960s she formed Olivan Press to publish her output of over 2000 works. She also wrote books, including an autobiography and in 1969 was awarded the CBE. (Boenke; Cohen; Hixon; Norton/Grove)

Lynds, Deirdre
Looking for information about this composer.

MacAuslan, Janna (pseud. for Auslam, Janna Lynne)
USA composer born in Dallas, Texas in 1951. She earned her BM (1973) from the University of Texas, El Paso and received her MM in guitar performance (1986) from Lewis and Clark College in Portland, Oregon. With Kristan

Aspen, she founded the Musica Femina Flute Guitar Duo, dedicated to performing the music of women composers. She also performs programs of solo guitar works by women, and is the researcher/compiler of this volume. Musica Femina has lectured and toured nationally on a college circuit since 1984 and has made four recordings. *Heartstreams* (1993) features Janna's and Kristan's own compositions. (Boenke; Hixon)

Madriguera Rodon, Paquita
Spanish composer and pianist, born in 1900. Her first teacher was her mother. She later studied piano under Marshall, and composition with Mas and Serracan at the Granados Music Academy. At the early age of eleven she began concertizing in Spain. In 1919 she gave concerts in New York and California and toured in Central and South America. She married guitarist Andrés Segovia later in her life. (Cohen; Hixon)

Maguiña, Alicia
Popular Peruvian singer and composer of songs, born in 1938. As a child she studied piano and guitar, and at age fourteen she composed the first of over 100 songs. Since 1966 she has worked in a duo with her husband, Carlos Hayre, who is her accompanist and arranger. Maguiña has recorded more than two dozen albums and been honored as Peru's "Best Composer" and "Best Singer of the Year" many times since

1958. Specializing in Creole music from the coast of Peru, she has also researched, recorded, and been recognized for her work to preserve the folk music of the Andean mountains. She has been active in APDAYC, the Peruvian composers organization, serving as president from 1980 to 1984. (*Soundboard*, summer 1987)

Mamlok, Ursula
American composer who was born in Berlin in 1928 and became a US citizen in 1945. She received her BM and MM (1958) from the Manhattan School of Music. She studied piano with Gustav Ernest in Germany and composition with George Szell, Roger Sessions, Stefan Wolpe, and Ralph Shapey in New York. She has won numerous awards including an ASCAP in 1969 and the American Academy of Arts and Letters Award in 1981. She has taught at New York University and the Manhattan School of Music and became an assistant professor at Kingsborough College in 1971. Her works have been performed and recorded by major ensembles. (Boenke; Cohen; Hixon; Norton/Grove)

Marbé, Myriam
Romanian composer, pianist, editor, and music educator, born in 1931. Her first piano teacher was her mother, Angela Marbé. She then studied at the C. Porumbescu Conservatory in Bucharest (1944-54). Myriam worked as a musical editor in a cinematographic studio (1953-54) and since 1960

has taught at the Bucharest Conservatory. She has won several competitions and awards for her compositions, and her works have been performed at international festivals. (Boenke; Cohen; Hixon; Norton/Grove)

Marchisio, Barbara
Italian singer, guitarist, and composer, born in Turin (1833-1919). She taught her sister, Carlotta, who became a famous opera singer. Her compositions were primarily vocal. (Cohen; Hixon)

Marcus, Bunita
USA composer born in 1952. She is a clarinetist, pianist, conductor, and music educator. She received her BM from the University of Wisconsin in 1976 and her PhD from the State University of New York in 1981. Her principal teachers were Franz Loschnigg and Morton Feldman. She is a professor at Brooklyn College. Her works have been performed in Europe and the USA as well as Japan. (Cohen; Hixon)

Maresca, Chiara
Possibly Italian composer, 20th century. Looking for more information. (Cohen; Hixon)

Marez-Oyens, Tera de
Dutch composer, choral conductor, pianist, harpsichordist, violinist, and music educator, born in 1932. She died of cancer August 29, 1996. She studied at the Amsterdam Conservatory, graduating in 1953. Her

composition teachers included Hans Henkemans and for electronic music, Gottfried Koenig. She was a concert pianist, conducted choirs and orchestras, produced radio shows, lectured, and wrote on various music topics. A prolific composer, she wrote over 200 works. Until 1988 she was professor of composition at the Conservatory of Zwolle. (Boenke; Cohen; Hixon; Norton/Grove)

Mari, Pierrette (Anne Valérie)
French musicologist, composer, pianist, and writer on music, born in 1929. She studied at the Nice and Paris Conservatories. When an accident to her right hand forced her to give up instrumental work, she taught herself to write with her left hand and took up composition. She has won awards and prizes for her composing and has also written articles for a number of music journals. (Boenke; Cohen; Hixon)

Marina, Carmen (née Maria del Carmen Mantega Pascual)
Spanish guitarist, singer, and composer born in 1936. (Hixon also cites 1942.) At age sixteen she won a scholarship to study at the Royal Conservatory of Music in Madrid, where her teachers were Sainz de la Maza and Brubeck de Burgos. Her degrees are in classical guitar and composition. At eighteen she was touring North Africa and France. She studied with Segovia at his annual masterclass at Santiago de Compostela, Spain for several years. She has lived in the USA since 1971. After a very successful Carnegie Hall debut she founded the Institute of Guitar Music (1976) with her husband. Besides composing, she has an active teaching, touring, and recording career; has won awards and grants; and has appeared on Spanish American television. (Cohen and Hixon use Carmen Marina, pseud. of Carmen Manteca Gioconda.) (Boenke; Cohen; Hixon; Summerfield, 1991)

Markowitz, Judith
USA composer born in Chicago in 1946. She is a flamenco guitarist and amateur composer who works in the field of artifical intelligence. Her PhD is in linguistics from Northwestern University (1977) and her MS is in computer science/artificial intelligence from De Paul University. (Boenke; Composer letter; Hixon)

Marlow, Janet
USA guitarist and composer, born in 1951. She studied with Leonid Bolotine at the Mannes College of Music and with Narciso Yepes in Spain. She is an expert on the 10-string guitar and is active as a performer and recording artist. She has taught for the Extension Division of the Manhattan School of Music and at New York University. (Composer letter)

Marshall, Pamela J.
USA composer, horn player, and lecturer born in 1954. She holds a

BM in composition from the Eastman School of Music and an MM in composition from Yale (1980). She studied computer music in an MIT workshop in 1979. Her composition teachers were Samuel Alder, Warren Benson, and Joseph Schwantner. Marshall has taught at Yale and at Milton Academy in Massachussetts. She received a MacDowell Colony Fellowship in 1981. (Boenke; Cohen; Hixon)

Martegani de Roca, Luisa
Looking for information about this composer.

Martins, Maria de Lourdes (Clara da Silva)
Portuguese composer and teacher born in 1926. She was educated at the National Conservatory in Lisbon, as well as studying with Harold Genzmer and Karlheinz Stockhausen in Germany. She received an Orff Institute certificate in 1960 and was director of Orff-Schulwerke courses in Lisbon. She also taught composition and music education at the Lisbon Conservatory (1971-78) and has won prizes and awards for her compositions. (Norton/Grove)

Matveyeva, Novella
Russian composer, singer, and poet, born in 1934. She gives concerts, performs on television and makes recordings. (Cohen; Hixon [uses Matveyevna])

Mazourova, Jarmila
Czech composer, cimbalom player, pianist, and recorder player, born in 1941. She graduated from the Janacek Academy of Arts and Music in Brno in 1963. She went on to study at the Conservatory of Brno from which she graduated in 1965. She is a teacher at the Brno School of Music. (Boenke; Cohen; Hixon)

McKenzie, Sandra
Australian composer, 20th century. Looking for more information. (Cohen; Hixon)

Meier, Margaret S.
USA composer, pianist, piano teacher, and music educator, born in 1936. She received her music education degree from the Eastman School of Music in 1958 and her MA and PhD degrees in composition from California State University, Los Angeles. Her principal teachers were Roy Travis, Paul Reale, and Alden Ashforth. (Boenke; Cohen [uses Shelton]; Hixon)

Meister, Leila
Looking for information about this composer.

Mell, Eidylia
Looking for information about this composer.

Mendoza, Anne Elizabeth
English composer and music educator, born in 1914. (Cohen; Helleu; Hixon)

Meneely-Kyder, Sarah Suderley
USA composer, pianist, sitar-player, and writer on music, born

in 1945. She received her BA in theory and piano from Goucher College in 1967. Her MM in composition is from the Peabody Conservatory where she studied with Stefan Grove and Earle Brown. She then went on to Yale University to receive an MMA in 1973. (Cohen; Hixon)

Mertens, Dolores
German guitarist, harpist, pianist, and composer, born in 1932. She started by composing light music and later turned to classical composition. She lives in both Germany and the USA and writes for the Mormon Tabernacle Choir. (Cohen; Hixon)

Michelson, Sonia
USA guitarist, composer, and teacher, born in 1928. She received a BA (1949) from the University of California at Berkeley. She taught in the Chicago area (1973-88), then moved to LA to found the Michelson Classic Guitar Studio where she now teaches. She has written method books for teaching young children the guitar and is a regular contributor to music journals including *Soundboard* and publications of the American String Teachers Association. (Composer letter)

Misurell-Mitchell, Janice
USA composer, flutist, and music educator, born in 1946. Her BA is from Goucher Collerge, her MM from the Peabody Conservatory, and her PhD from Northwestern

University. She has also studied jazz improvisation. Currently she teaches at Northwestern and De Paul Universities in Chicago. (Boenke; Cohen; Hixon)

Miyake, Haruna
(pseud. of Haruna Shibata)
Japanese composer and pianist, born in 1942. At age fourteen she made her piano debut with the Tokyo Symphony Orchestra. She was educated in Tokyo and at the Juilliard School. She studied with V. Pershichetti, and won the Edward Benjamin prize for composition in 1964. (Boenke; Cohen; Hixon; Norton/Grove)

Montero Ayala, Delia
Looking for information about this composer.

Morena, Naomi Littlebear
USA composer, folksinger, guitarist, poet, writer, and recording artist, born in 1950. She founded the Ursa Minor Choir (1974-76) and the Izquierda Ensemble (1976-80), feminist ensembles based in Portland, Oregon. Izquierda was popular nationally with lesbian-feminist audiences, and in 1977 the quartet recorded an LP album, *Quiet Thunder*. Naomi is a self-taught musician and composer. Her works include a rock opera about violence against women. (Boenke; Hixon)

Moretto, Nelly
Argentine composer and pianist born in 1925. She attended the Musical Professorship School,

the Rosario, the Conservatorio Nacional de Musica y Arte Escenico, and the Di Tella Institute of High School Studies in Buenos Aires, before coming to the United States to study at the University of Illinois. (Boenke; Cohen; Hixon)

Mori, Junko
Japanese composer born in 1948. She studied at the Tokyo National University of Arts where she received her BA (1971), her MM (1975) in composition, and another MM (1978) in musicology and solfeggio. Her composition teachers included Tomojiro Ikenouchi, Akio Yashiro, and Teizo Matsumura. She is a founding member of the Japanese Federation of Women Composers. (Boenke; Cohen; Hixon; Norton/Grove)

Moscovitz, Julianne
USA composer, guitarist, and music educator, born in 1951. She studied with William Hoskins at Jacksonville University, and with John Fahey privately. Her BA is from the California State University, Hayward (1972). She was music director for the Berkeley Dance Theatre and Gymnasium (1972-73). (Cohen; Hixon)

Mounsey, Elizabeth
English guitarist, organist, pianist, and composer (1819-1905). She was the organist at St. Peter's Church, Cornhill, from 1834-82. Her sister, Ann

Sheppard Bartholomew, was also an organist and the two composed some works together. In 1883 and 1884 Elizabeth gave public concerts on the guitar. She composed music for all the instruments she played and for voice. (Cohen; Hixon; Norton/Grove)

Murakumo, Ayako
Japanese composer born in 1949. She studied at the Graduate School of Aichi Prefectural University of Arts, graduating in 1982. Her principal teacher was Ishii Kan. She won a composition award from the City of Nagoya in 1985. (Cohen; Hixon)

Murdock, Katherine Ann
Contemporary USA composer and violinist. She received her PhD in composition (1986) from the Eastman School of Music, where her principal teachers were Samuel Adler, Joseph Schwantner, and Warren Benson. She has received numerous commissions, and her works have been performed across the United States, as well as in Canada, France, Switzerland, Taiwan, Russia, Australia, Japan, and Romania. She is currently Associate Professor of music theory and composition at Wichita State University and directs the WSU Contemporary Music Festival. In 1992 she received a Kansas Artist Fellowship in composition from the Kansas Arts Commission. (Boenke; Composer letter; Hixon)

Musgrave, Thea
Scottish composer, conductor, and professor, born in 1928. She studied at Edinburgh University (1947-50), at the Paris Conservatory (1950-52), and privately with Nadia Boulanger and Aaron Copland. She has been a lecturer and visiting professor at universities worldwide. She is the recipient of numerous prestigious awards and grants, including the Koussevitzky Prize, several Guggenheims, and honorary doctorates. Her works are performed by major orchestras in the USA and Europe. She receives many commissions and has written a number of works for her husband, violist Peter Mark. (Boenke; Cohen; Hixon; Norton/Grove)

Naito, Akemi
Japanese composer born in 1956. She graduated from the Toho-Gakuen University Music School in 1978 and the Graduate School in 1980. Her principal teachers were Nobuyoshi Iinuma and Akira Miyoshi. (Cohen; Hixon)

Nazarova, Tatiana Borisovna
Composer, violinist, pianist, and music educator, born in Moscow in 1928. She was educated at the Gnesin Institute of Music in Moscow, and received her degree in 1961. From 1952 to 1959 she was concertmistress and then taught there until 1963. (Cohen; Hixon)

Noda, Eva S. (née Eva Saito)
Japanese American composer, pianist and piano teacher, born in Canada in 1921. She was educated at Columbia University (BS, Music Education), and Union Theological Seminary (Master of Sacred Music). She also holds a certificate from the Dalcroze School in New York. (Boenke; Cohen [uses Saito-Nota (sic)]; Hixon)

Nogues, Clara
Looking for information about this composer.

Nowak, Alison
USA composer born in 1948. She received her BA from Bennington College in 1970 and her MA from Columbia University in 1972. Her principal teachers are Vivian Fine, Lou Calabro, Henry Brant, Mario Davidovsky, Jack Beeson, and Charles Wuorinen. (Boenke; Cohen; Hixon)

Nunn, Ruth
English composer and guitarist born in 1954. (Hixon)

O'Leary, Jane
Irish American composer born in 1946. She received her BA from Vassar College in 1968, her MFA from Princeton in 1971, and her PhD also from Princeton in 1978. She has taught at Swarthmore College, College of Music in Dublin, University College Galway. She has lived in Ireland since 1972 and composes fulltime. She is a member of Aosdana, Ireland's distinguished academy of creative artists and is also director of Concorde, a contemporary chamber ensemble.

She has been chairperson of Ireland's Contemporary Music Centre since 1989. She has received numerous awards and major commissions. (Boenke; Cohen; Composer letter; Hixon; Norton/Grove)

Obrovska, Jana
Czech composer, pianist, and music editor (1930-1987). She studied composition under Miroslav Krejci and Emil Hlobil at the Prague Conservatory (1949-1955). She married the guitarist Milan Zelenka and was an editor at Supraphon publishing house. She was the first woman to enter and win the ORTF Concours International de Guitare composer's competition. Obrovska wrote many guitar pieces, several of which are now part of the standard repertory. (Boenke; Cohen; Hixon; Norton/Grove; Summerfield, 1991)

Olcott-Bickford, Vahdah, (née Ethel Lucretia Olcott)
Born in Norwalk, Ohio (1885-1980), she became known as the Grand Dame of American Guitar. She studied guitar with George Lindsey and Manuel Ferrer. Moving to New York in 1914, she was the first woman in the USA to give classical guitar concerts including one at Town Hall. Later she became the guitar teacher for Cornelia Vanderbilt and her mother, as well as other prominent East Coast families. While in New York, she and her husband, Myron Bickford, took the astrological names

"Vahdah" and "Zarh" at the suggestion of the world-famous astrologer, Evangeline Adams. In 1923 the couple moved to Los Angeles where they founded the American Guitar Society. Olcott-Bickford was one of the most influential American guitarists of the 20th century. She produced over 160 works for the guitar published by Oliver Ditson and Carl Fischer. Most are currently out of print. Her work on behalf of the guitar in the USA is comparable to Segovia's work in Europe and South America. Her sheet music collection is one of the most famous and extensive of any North American guitar music collection. It is housed at California State University, Northridge, in the International Guitar Research Archive. (Hixon [uses Bickford]; Purcell; Soundboard, August 1980; Summerfield, 1991)

Olive, Vivienne
English composer, organist, harpsichordist, and music educator, born in 1950. She was educated at Trinity College of Music and the University of York, where she received her BA (1971) and her PhD (1975). Her principal teachers were Rands, Donatoni, and Haubenstock-Ramati. Further study was done in Germany at the Hochschule in Freiburg with Klaus Huber and Stanislav Heller. She has taught music theory in Nuremberg at the Fachakademie für Musik since 1973. (Boenke; Cohen; Hixon; Norton/Grove)

Oliveros, Pauline
USA composer, conductor, and professor, born in 1932. She received her BA from San Francisco State in 1957 and studied privately with Robert Erikson in San Francisco. She was part of an experimental improvisational group with Morton Subotnick and Ramon Sender, which evolved into the San Fransisco Tape Music Center. In 1966 it was moved to Mills College in Oakland and she became the director. She taught at the University of California, San Diego (1967-81). She now directs the Pauline Oliveros Foundation and Deep Listening Publications. She has received international acclaim, been given honorary degrees, and been awarded numerous prizes, including a Guggenheim in 1973, and an NEA commission. She also performs on the accordian, and has made several recordings of her accordian compositions which include electronic manipulation. (Boenke; Cohen; Hixon; Norton/Grove)

Oribello, Juanita
USA composer, guitarist, and vocalist, born in 1942. She has studied at the San Francisco Conservatory; at California State University, Hayward; and at San Francisco State and Chico State universities. Her major composition teachers have been John Adams and Julian White. She has done extensive guitar study with internationally acclaimed players and teachers including Michael Lorimer, Rey de la Torre, David Tanenbaum, Phillip Rosheger, and Abel Carlevaro. Jazz guitar studies were with Jerry Hahn. She is an active performer who has made numerous radio and television appearances as well as concert performances. (Composer letter)

Osawa, Kazuko
Japanese composer born in 1926. She was educated at the Toyko University of the Arts, where her major teachers were Kozabura Hirai, Minao Shibata, and Naotada Otaka. She has been awarded the Ministry of Education Prize for orchestral composition and the Japanese National Broadcasting Station Prize. (Boenke; Cohen; Hixon)

Ozaita Marques, Maria Luisa
Spanish composer, conductor, harpsichordist, and pianist, born in 1939. (Cohen and Hixon use 1937.) She first studied in Spain and then received a bursary to attend the Conservatory of Copenhagen, where she studied with Isaken (harpsichord) and Thybo (composition). She has also studied in Darnstadt, Nice, Santiago de Compostela, and Granada. She is a performing artist and appears often as a conductor, both in Spain and abroad. She was the founding president of Mujeres en la Música (1988), has lectured extensively about women in music, and co-founded a women's chamber orchestra (1991). (Cohen; Hixon; Norton/Grove)

Parker, Alice
USA composer, conductor, music educator, folklorist, and writer on music, born in 1925. She received a BA from Smith College (1947), and an MS from the Juilliard School of Music (1949). Her principal teachers included Robert Shaw, Julius Herford, and Vincent Persichetti. She taught at the Meadowbrook School and the Aspen Music Festival (1970-71) and lectured at Yale and Northwestern Universities. She was an arranger for the Robert Shaw Chorale (1968-73) and later was artistic director of Melodious Accord. She has received numerous recognitions including an honorary doctorate from Hamilton College in 1979. (Boenke; Cohen; Hixon; Norton/Grove)

Pascual Navas, Maria
Looking for information about this composer.

Patino, Lucia
Looking for information about this composer.

Patterson, Andra
New Zealand composer born in 1964. She studied at Victoria University in Wellington (1982-84) and won the New Zealand Emergent Composers' Award in 1984. (Cohen; Hixon)

Paulian, Athenais
Composer and guitarist, dates unknown. She and her brother, Eugene, were part of the 19th century guitarist-composer circle

of Sor and Aguado in Paris. Both of these famous guitarists dedicated works to her. (*Soundboard*, summer 1991)

Paull, Barberi
USA composer born in 1946. She is also a pianist, conductor, music educator, writer on music, and music administrator, as well as a psychologist and music therapist. She studied at the Manhattan School, the Juilliard School, the Berkshire Music Center at Tanglewood, the Dalcroze School, and the Institute of Vocal Arts. Her principal teachers include Charles Wuorineen, Ludmila Ulehla, Billy Taylor, Elias Tannenbaum, Hall Overton, Vincent Persichetti, and Jacob Druckman. She has studied both classical and jazz piano, holds a master's degree from New York University in psychology, and has also studied music therapy and theatre, which she uses for work with emotionally disturbed children. She directed the Barbari Paull Music Theatre (1972-75), and since 1979 directs the Cavu Music Associates in music management and consultation. She has received many awards, fellowships, and commissions. (Boenke; Cohen; Hixon [uses Paul])

Pereira da Silva, Adelaide
Brazilian composer, pianist, and music educator, born in 1938. Her teachers were N. de Sousa, H. Bruch, O. Lacerda, and C. Guarnieri. She has taught at the Faculdade de Musica Santa

Marcelina and the Faculdade Santa Cecilia in São Paulo. (Cohen; Hixon)

Peyrot, Fernande
Swiss composer and music educator (1888-1978). She studied at the Geneva Conservatory under Jaques-Dalcroze and Bloch and later at the Paris Conservatory under Gedalge and Dukas. She taught at the Jaques-Dalcroze Institute, the L'Ecole de Vaugirard in Paris, and at the L'Ecole Normale de Musique. She was recognized at the Second International Competition and Congress on Women Composers in 1961 in Mannheim. (Boenke; Cohen; Hixon)

Philiba, Nicole
French composer, pianist, and music educator born in 1937. She studied at the Paris Conservatory with Dutilleux, Aubin, Jolivet, and Messiaen, and she has been a professor there herself since 1969. Her works have received many performances in Europe. (Boenke; Cohen; Hixon)

Phillips, Karen Ann
USA composer, violist, pianist, and music educator, born in 1942. She studied piano with Mabel Price and Bomar Cramer in Dallas and with Henry Rauch at the Eastman School of Music. In 1967 she received a BMus from the Juilliard School. She is a concert artist and had her own radio show on WNYC (1975-77). She has received many grants and awards. (Cohen; Hixon)

Piechowska, Alina (Piechowska-Pascal)
Polish composer, pianist, conductor, poet, and music educator, born in 1937. She studied piano with her mother first, then with Leokadia Marcinkiewicz-Urbanowicz and M. Silman at the Vilna Conservatory and composition with W. Rudzinski at the State School of Music in Warsaw (1959-61). During 1971-72 she studied with Nadia Boulanger in Paris. She participates in the Group of Experimental Music in Bourges. (Boenke; Cohen; Hixon)

Pierce, Alexandra
USA composer, pianist, and music educator, born in 1934. She received her BM from the University of Michigan (1955), her MM in performance from New England Conservatory (1958), her MA in music history from Radcliffe (1959), and her PhD in music theory and composition from Brandeis University (1968). She is currently professor of music and movement at the University of Redlands. She is a founding member of Moving Voices, a repertory company that performs music and poetry. She has written over 175 works and has received awards and prizes. (Boenke; Cohen; Composer letter; Hixon)

Pierrette, Mari
Looking for information about this composer.

Pires de Campos, Lina
Brazilian composer, pianist, and music educator, born in 1918. Her father was Angelo Del Vecchio, an Italian luthier. She graduated from the João Gomes de Aruajo Conservatorio and the Instituto Musical Benedetto Marcello in São Paulo. Her principal composition teacher was Camargo Guarnieri. In 1964 she started her own music school and in 1977 received a teacher-of-the-year award from the Music Association of São Paulo. (Cohen; Hixon; Norton/Grove [uses Campos, Lina Pires de])

Pires Dos Reis, Hilda
Brazilian composer, conductor, pianist, and professor, born in 1919. Her doctorate is from the Federal University of Rio de Janeiro, where she was later chair of the composition department. She also taught piano at the Brazilian Conservatory. (Cohen; Hixon)

Polasek, Barbara
Looking for information about this composer.

Polin, Claire
USA composer, flutist, musicologist, music educator, writer on music, and music administrator (1926-1995). She received her BM, MMus (1950), and DMus (1955) from the Philadelphia Conservatory of Music, where her principal teacher was Vincent Persichetti. She studied composition at the Juilliard School with Peter

Mennin, and at Tanglewood with Lukas Foss and Roger Sessions. She studied flute under William Kincaid, with whom she later wrote a five-volume flute method. She was on the faculty of the Philadelphia Conservatory and of Rutgers University (1958-91). She received numerous awards, grants, and commissions. Her works have been played by internationally acclaimed performing groups. (Buenke; Cohen; Hixon; Norton/Grove)

Porter, Debra
USA composer, percussionist, and music educator, born in 1954. She was educated at Reed College. She has been a dance accompanist and taught global music at Lewis and Clark and Marylhurst colleges. Her earlier works were influenced by instrumental sounds from around the world, and her later works are more neo-Romantic. (Composer letter)

Pradell, Leila
USA composer, pianist, and music educator, born in 1932. She received her BM from Boston University and her MM from the New England Conservatory. She studied at Tanglewood with Judd Locke, then went to Paris to work with Nadia Boulanger. She has been a consultant and composer for a Boston school district and has taught in schools in Alaska and Massachusetts. She has also taught at the New England Conservatory. (Cohen; Hixon)

Prado, Almeira
Looking for information about this composer.

Pratten, Madame Sydney (née Catherina Josepha Pelzer)
Catherina was a guitarist and composer, born in Germany in 1821. She died in London in 1895. The daughter of Ferdinand Pelzer, a famous guitarist and teacher, she was a child prodigy who gave concerts on stages in London at an early age. As an adult she taught guitar to London's elite including Queen Victoria's children. She wrote over 200 pieces for the guitar, including a guitar method, which were mostly published by her husband, the flutist Robert Sydney Pratten, in their home in London. (Cohen; Harrison; Hixon; Nolan; Summerfield, 1991)

Preobrajenska, Vera Nicolaevna
Russian American composer, pianist, arranger, editor, writer, and music educator, born in 1926. Her BA (1953) is from San Francisco State University, and her MA (1972) and PhD (1973) are from Bernadean University in Las Vegas. Her composition teachers included Milhaud, Bloch, Sessions, Jacobi, von Dohnanyi, Tcherepnin, and Shostakovich. She has been concert manager for Musical Artists of America, was a lecturer at the University of California, Berkeley, and a member of the faculty at Bernadean University. (Boenke; Cohen; Hixon)

Presti, Ida (née Yvette Ida Montagnon)
Celebrated guitarist, composer, and teacher, born in France (1924-1967). She studied the guitar first with her father then with Emilio Pujol, making her debut at age ten. In 1940 she performed on Paganini's guitar in a concert marking the centenary of his death. She married the guitarist Alexander Lagoya in 1953, and the Presti-Lagoya Guitar Duo became the most famous guitar duo in the world. They performed over 2000 concerts before Ida died unexpectedly from an internal hemorrhage caused by an aneurysm. (Cohen; Hixon; Summerfield, 1991)

Price, Deon Nielson
USA composer, pianist, music educator, and writer on music, born in 1934. She received a BA from Brigham Young University then studied at the Academia Pro Arte in Heidelberg with Erwin Schnieder. Her MM in piano and composition is from the University of Michigan, and her doctorate in piano performance (1977) is from the University of Southern California. Her principal teachers were Leslie Bassett and Samuel Adler. She has taught at many California universities and has performed as pianist throughout the Americas, Europe, and the former Soviet Union. She has received many commissions, and her works have been recorded on a Cambria label. (Boenke; Cohen; Hixon; *IAWM Journal*, June 1996)

Procaccini, Teresa
Italian composer, pianist,
organist, music educator, and
music administrator, born in 1934.
She studied piano, organ, and
composition at the Conservatoria
di Foggia, where her principal
teachers were Achille Lango,
Enzo Masetti, and Virgilio
Mortari. At the Conservatory of
Saint Cecilia in Rome, film music
was her course of study, and she
attended the Accademia
Musicale Chigiana in Siena for
composition. She taught at the
Conservatory di Foggia (1971-73),
is professor of composition at
Saint Cecilia Conservatory in
Rome, and also teaches every
summer at the Ottorino Respighi
Academy of Music in Assisi. She
is a music consultant for the
publishers, Armando Armando in
Rome. (Boenke; Cohen; Hixon;
Norton/Grove)

Ptaszynska, Marta
Polish composer, percussionist,
pianist, music educator, and
writer on music, born in 1943. She
received her MA (1968) from the
Conservatory of Warsaw. She
studied with Nadia Boulanger
(1969-70), and received an artist's
diploma in percussion and theory
from the Cleveland Institute of
Music (1972-74). She has lectured
at the Warsaw Conservatory,
Bennington College, and the
Universities of California at
Berkeley and Santa Barbara. She
has won awards for her
compositions and is a specialist in
contemporary percussion works.
(Boenke; Cohen; Hixon)

Puget, Loïse (Louise-Françoise)
French composer and singer (1810-
1889). She wrote very popular
songs which she performed in
salons and in concert. They were
published in volumes at the rate
of one per year from 1830 to 1845.
In 1842 she married the actor,
Gustave Lemoine, who wrote
many of the texts for her songs.
Later she wrote operettas.
(Cohen; Hixon; Norton/Grove)

Rainier, Priaulx (Ivy Priaulx)
British composer, violinist,
pianist, and music educator, born
in South Africa (1903-1986). She
studied at the South African
College of Music and at the Royal
Academy of Music in London. Her
principal teachers were Roswby
Woof, J.B. McEwen, and Nadia
Boulanger, with whom she
studied in Paris in the 1930s. She
taught at the Royal Academy of
Music (1943-61). She received
many awards and commissions,
including one for a violin concerto
from Yehudi Menuhin. In 1973, on
the occasion of her seventieth
birthday, the BBC broadcast a
retrospective concert of some of
her chamber works. (Boenke;
Cohen; Hixon; Norton/Grove)

Rapp, Sandy
USA singer, songwriter, and
guitarist. She has performed in
the UK as well as New York. Her
debut recording appeared in 1986.
(Composer letter)

Ravinale, Irma
Italian composer, pianist, and
music educator, born in 1937. She

studied at the Conservatory of Saint Cecilia in Rome under A. de Nino and G. Petrassi. She became Chair of composition in 1966, and Director of the Conservatory in 1989. She has won major awards and competitions. (Cohen; Hixon; Norton/Grove)

Rehnqvist, Karin Birgitta
Swedish composer and music educator, born in 1957. She earned a teaching degree (1980) from the Kungliga Musikhögskolan in Stockhom before spending four years studying composition with Brian Ferneyhough, Gunnar Bucht, and others. She was elected to the Society of Swedish Composers in 1985. (Cohen; Hixon; Norton/Grove)

Reich, Amy
Contemporary composer. Looking for information. (Cohen; Hixon)

Reichhardt, Lousie (Luise)
German composer, pianist, and singer (1779-1826). She was the daughter and student of Johann Friedrich Reichardt, who was court conductor for King Frederick the Great of Prussia. Her mother was a pianist, singer, and composer, whose father was the composer Franz Benda. Louise toured with her father for many years until his death. Then she founded a singing school in Hamburg with J.H. Clasing. She also organized and conducted a women's chorus. She composed more than 90 vocal pieces which were very popular in the 19th century. The tragedies of her life included losing her singing voice and the death of her fiancé shortly before they were wed. (Cohen; Hixon; Norton/Grove)

Rezende, Marisa
Looking for information about this composer.

Richer, Jeannine (Janine)
French composer and lecturer, born in 1924. She studied at Rouen and at the Paris Conservatory. Her teachers were Max Deutsch and Arnold Schoenberg. She also studied electronic music with Jean Etienne Marie at the International Center of Music Research. She taught at the Ecole Normale de Musique in Paris until 1972. (Cohen; Hixon)

Rickard, Sylvia
Canadian composer, pianist, music educator, and writer on music, born in 1937. She studied at the Toronto Conservatory; the University of British Columbia, Vancouver; Stanford University; and the University of Grenoble, France. She lived in India and Germany in the 1960s and returned to Canada to study with Jean Coulthard in 1972. She has won prizes and competitions. (Cohen; Hixon)

Rodriguez Arenas, Elba
Looking for information about this composer.

Rodriguez, Marcela
Mexican composer and guitarist, born in 1951. She studied guitar with Leo Brouwer and Abel

Carlevaro. She also studied the lute and vihuela with Javier Hinojosa and is the vihuelist with the Cantar y Tañer ensemble directed by Benjamín Juárez. She studied composition with Maria Antonieta Lozano (1975-79) and formed a theatre group called Sombras Blancas, which uses improvisational music. Her compositions have been performed at music festivals in Cuba. (Norton/Grove; Tapia)

Roe, Eileen Betty

English composer, organist, celllist, singer, conductor, and music educator, born in 1930. She studied piano and cello at the Royal Academy of Music and composition privately with Lennox Berkeley. She has taught at several institutions including the London Academy of Music and Dramatic Art (1968-78). She has been Director of Music at St Helen's Church, Kensington. (Boenke; Cohen; Hixon; Norton/Grove)

Rogatis, Teresa De

Italian composer, guitarist, pianist, and music educator, (1893-1979). She was a child prodigy whose first concert was given in 1902 at age seven. Her father, a gifted though not fully trained guitarist, was her first teacher. She studied at the Conservatorio San Pietro at Majella in Naples under Florestano Rossomandi (piano) and Camillo De Nardis (composition). She graduated in 1915 with diplomas in piano and

composition and began a concert career performing on both piano and guitar. During a tour to Egypt in 1921, she met and married Paolo Feninger, an Egyptian businessman of Swiss origin. Remaining in Cairo until 1963, she raised a family, composed, taught piano and guitar, and helped found a National Conservatory. She returned to Naples in 1963 and took a few devoted students including Stefano Aruta. He became a distinguished guitar teacher, who incorporated the best of her teaching method into his own. Her son, pianist Mario Feninger, established the Teresa De Rogatis Foundation in the USA to publish and distribute her musical works. (Cohen; De Rogatis; Hixon)

Roi, Micheline

Canadian composer born in 1963. She was educated at Queen's University where she studied with Istvan Anhalt and Bruce Pennycook. Her master's degree in composition is from McGill University, where her primary teacher was Bengt Hambraeus. Her works have been performed in Canada, the UK, and South America, as well as broadcast on community radio and the CBC. She has won prizes and received commissions in Canada. (Composer letter)

Romero, Elena

Spanish composer, pianist, and conductor, born in 1923. She studied piano with José Balsa and Frank Marshall, starting her concert career at age twelve. Her composition teachers included Ricardo Lamote de Grignon, Joaquin Turina, Julio Gómez, and Lopez Varela. She attended courses in Baroque keyboard music in Germany, and in Paris her tutor was Salvador Bacarisse. She has had a touring concert career, and is perhaps the first Spanish woman to have conducted large symphony orchestras. Ataúlfo Argenta was her conducting teacher. (Norton/Grove)

Rosas Fernandes, Maria Helena
Brailian composer, pianist, choral conductor, and music educator, born in 1933. She graduated from the Brazilian Conservatory of Music in Rio de Janeiro. She studied composition with Osvaldo Lacerda and José de Almeida Prado, receiving her bachelor's degree from the Escola Superior de Musica Santa Marcelina in São Paulo in 1977. She teaches at Campinas University and has conducted children's choirs at several schools and conservatories. (Cohen [uses Fernandes]; Hixon; Norton/Grove)

Roster, Danielle
Composer and guitarist, born in 1964 in Luxemburg. She studied at the Académie de Musique in Wiltz (1973-84) and the Conservatory of Music in Luxemburg, where her guitar teacher was Nicolas Alphonso. She studied musicology and the history of art in Austria at the

University of Salzburg. She is a also a free-lance musicologist whose specialty is women in music. In 1993 she published a book about Clara Wieck Schumann. (Composer letter)

Rotaru, Doina Marilena
Romanian composer born in 1951. She studied composition at the Bucharest Conservatory under Tibeiu Olah (1970-75) and attended the Darmstadt summer courses in 1984, 1990, and 1992. In 1991 she became professor of harmony at the Bucharest Conservatory. She has had international performances of her works and been awarded several major prizes including first prize at the GEDOK competition in 1994. (Norton/Grove)

Rubin, Anna
USA composer born in 1946. Her BA (1968) is in sociology from Pomona College and her BFA (1975) and MFA (1981) are from California Institute of the Arts. She has studied with Pauline Oliveros, Mel Powell, Leonard Stein, and Morton Subotnick in the USA, and with Ton de Leeuw in the Netherlands. In 1996 she was a graduate fellow in composition at Princeton University. She has received many prizes, grants, and commissions for both instrumental and computer music, and her works have been performed at international festivals and conferences. She also uses her tape collage work, *Sticks and Stones*, in workshops with young

people to promote tolerance and understanding of diversity. (Composer letter; Norton/Grove)

Ruff-Stoehr, Herta Maria Klara
German composer, pianist, organist, violinist, and music educator, born in 1904. She studied at the Music Academy in Stuttgart and at the University of Tubingen. She taught piano and organ in Hechingen. (Boenke; Cohen; Hixon)

Rusche, Marjorie Maxine
USA composer, conductor, pianist, and music administrator, born in 1949. She received her MA in theory and composition (1975) from the University of Minnesota where her principal teachers were D. Argento and P. Fetler. She is an active member of the Minnesota Composer's Forum. (Doerrke; Cohen; Hixon)

Saariaho, Kaija
Finnish composer born in 1952. She studied composition under Paavo Heininen at the Sibelius Academy and received a diploma in 1983 from the Musikhochshule in Freiburg, where her teachers were Brian Ferneyhough and Klaus Huber. She has also studied at the IRCAM computer music center in Paris. Many of her works have been recorded and have received awards. (Cohen; Hixon; Norton/Grove)

Sagreras, Clecia
Looking for information about this composer.

Saint John, Kathleen Louise
USA composer, pianist, piano teacher, and music educator, born in 1942. She attended San Diego State University (1962-66) then went to the Juilliard School of Music where she majored in piano and studied composition with Ania Dorfmann (1966-71). Other teachers included Luciano Berio, Hugo Weisgall, Vincent Persichetti, Hal Overton, Stanley Wolfe, and Norman Grossman. She studied at the Columbia Princeton Electronic Music Center (1968-79) with Vladimir Ussachevshy, Bulent Arel, Mario Davidovsky, and Alice Shields. She is the recipient of numerous awards, grants, and fellowships including five McDowell Colony Residencies. She has performed extensively as a pianist and has received many commissions. (Cohen; Hixon)

Salvador, Matilde
Spanish composer, pianist, and music educator, born in 1918. She studied at the Conservatorio Superior de Musica in Valencia and later taught there. (Cohen; Hixon)

Samter, Alice
German composer, pianist, and music educator, born in 1908. Her major teachers were Else Blatt, Amalie Iwan, and Dr. Starck for piano, Gerhard Wehle for improvisation, and Johannes Pranschke for composition. She studied music education at the Music Academy, Berlin under

Heinrich Martens. Her career was interrupted by World War II, which delayed her performing until after 1945. She taught in Berlin high schools from 1946 to 1970, when she retired to devote herself to composing. (Boenke; Cohen; Hixon; Norton/Grove)

Samuel, Rhian
British composer and music educator, born in 1944. She received her BA (1966) and BMus (1967) from the University of Reading, where she studied under Andrew Byrne. Then she went to the USA to study at Washington University, where she received her MA (1970) and her PhD (1978) working with Robert Wykes and Paul Pisk. She taught at the St. Louis Conservatory (1977-83) until she returned to the UK to teach at the University of Reading. She has won several composition prizes, and is co-editor of the *Norton/Grove Dictionary of Women Composers*. (Cohen; Hixon; Norton/Grove)

Sandler, Felicia Ann Barbara
USA composer and choral conductor, born in 1961. She was educated at the University of the Pacific (BM, 1984), the Catholic University of America (Master of Liturgical Music, 1986), and is currently finishing a doctorate at the University of Michigan. Her composition teachers included Bright Sheng, Andrew Imbrie, Ron Caviani, Stan Beckler, and Gerald Muller. She has received many commissions and her choral works are published by E.C.

Schirmer. (Composer letter; Hixon)

São Marcos, Maria Livia
Brazilian guitarist and composer born in 1942. She studied with her father, Professor Manuel São Marcos. She gave her first recital at age thirteen. She graduated from the Conservatorio Dramatic e Musical in São Paulo and in 1962 gave successful concerts in France and Portugal. She studied with Andrés Segovia in Spain at Santiago de Compostela and Emilio Pujol in Lisbon. Since 1970 she has been professor of guitar at the Conservatory of Music in Geneva. She is a respected teacher and concert/recording artist. (Summerfield, 1991)

Saparoff, Andrea
Contemporary USA composer, conductor and guitarist. She studied at the University of California, Northridge, including post-graduate work in composition, electronic music, and conducting. (Cohen; Hixon)

Saporiti, Teresa
Italian composer and soprano (1763 or 1764-1869). (Hixon)

Schieve, Catherine
USA composer, flutist, and accordionist, born in 1956. Her BM (1978) and MM (1980) are from the University of Texas, and her PhD is from the University of California, San Diego. Her major teachers have been Kenneth Gaburo, Barton McLean, Joseph Schwantner, Bernard Rands,

Eugene Kurtz, and Pauline Oliveros. She is a performer in experimental music and chamber ensembles. (Cohen; Hixon)

Schilling, Betty Jean
Looking for information about this composer.

Schloss, Myrna Frances
Canadian composer, pianist, and music educator, born in 1941. She received her BA, MA, and BM from the University of British Columbia, her MM (1980) from Lewis and Clark College, and her PhD in ethnomusicology from Wesleyan University. Her composition teachers were Alvin Lucier, Vincent McDermott, and Harry Freedman. She has taught piano and music in public schools (1965-82), at the University of British Columbia, and at Wesleyan University. (Boenke; Cohen; Hixon)

Schlünz, Annette
Looking for information about this composer.

Schmidt, Mia
German composer born in 1952. She received a diploma in 1977 from the Fachhochschule in Munich, then studied music history at the University of Tübingen, receiving an MA in 1986. She studied composition under Milko Kelemen, Brian Ferneyhough, Klaus Huber, and Mesias Maiguashca (1981-88). She is a mother, music teacher, and free-lance composer in Freiburg. (Composer letter)

Schönfelder, Ilse
Looking for information about this composer.

Schonthal, Ruth
German American composer, pianist, and music educator, born in 1924. She studied in Berlin at the Stern Conservatory (1929-34), in Stockholm at the Royal Academy (1937-40), and in the USA at Yale University, where she earned an AB (1950). Her teachers were Etthoven in Berlin, Manuel Ponce and Rodolfo Halffter in Mexico City (during WWII), and Paul Hindemith at Yale. She concertized with her own compositions in Europe and Mexico, as well as in New York and London. She has won many awards and commissions and has taught at New York University and Westchester Conservatory. (Cohen; Hixon; Norton/Grove)

Schorr, Eva (née Weller)
German composer, organist, and pianist, born in 1927. She was a child prodigy who studied piano and composition at the State Music Academy in Stuttgart under J.N. David, Hermann Keller, and Anton Nowakowski. Her degrees are in church music (1950) and composition (1951). She has won international prizes. (Boenke; Cohen [uses Schorr-Weiler]; Hixon; Norton/Grove)

Scliar, Esther (Ester)
Brazilian composer, pianist, conductor, and music educator, (1926-1978). She graduated from the Instituto de Bellas Artes in

Porto Alegre in 1945. Her principal composition teachers were Joachim Koellreutter, Claudio Santoro, and Edino Krieger. (Cohen uses Krueger.) In 1952 she founded the Coro da Associacão Juvenil Musical, a children's choir. A recipient of many awards and prizes, she taught music analysis and form at the Instituto Villa-Lobos and the Pró-Arte music school in Rio de Janeiro (1962-75). (Boenke; Cohen; Hixon; Norton/Grove)

Scott, Alicia Ann (Lady John) (née Spottiswoode)
Scottish composer (1810-1900). She wrote drawing room ballads with harp accompaniment, remaining anonymous until 1854, when the first collection of songs appeared bearing her name. Her most famous song, "Annie Laurie," was published in 1938 in *The Vocal Melodies of Scotland*. (Cohen; Norton/Grove; *Soundboard*, August 1976)

Sepúlveda, Maria Luisa
Chilean composer, singer, violist, violinist, pianist, conductor, folklorist, and music educator (1898-1958). (Cohen uses 1959.) At the Conservatorio Nacional de Santiago she earned degrees in piano (1905) and composition (1918), becoming the first woman to graduate in composition in Chile. She taught until 1931 at that same institution and then at the Escuela Vocacional de Educación Artística. She was the recipient of numerous awards and prizes. (Cohen; Hixon;

Norton/Grove)

Serrano Redonnet, Ana
Argentine composer, conductor, arrranger, guitarist, critic, and writer on music, born in 1914. (Cohen says 1916.) She studied the guitar with A. Sinopali and composition with G. Gilardi and J. Pahissa. She was director of a folklore program in Buenos Aires (1941-45) and of "La Musica Nacional," a national radio program in 1947. For a few years she was music critic for *Tribuna*, a daily newspaper. (Cohen; Letter from Plesch)

Shafer, Sharon Guertin
USA soprano, composer, music educator, and writer on music, born in 1943. She was educated at Catholic University where she received her BA (1965). Both her masters (1970) and DMA in vocal performance (1973) are from the University of Maryland. She also studied in France at the American Conservatory at Fontainebleau. Since her New York debut in 1987, she has performed extensively throughout the USA, France, and Germany. Her guitar work was broadcast on Belgrade television in the former Yugoslavia. She is widely published and is Chair of the music program at Trinity College in Washington, D.C. (Composer letter; Hixon)

Shaffer, Jeanne Ellison
USA composer, organist, soprano, choral conductor, music educator, and music administrator, born in 1925. She received her AA in

music from Stephens College (1944); her BM in sacred music, voice, and organ from Samford University, Birmingham (1954); her MM in voice and composition from Birmingham Southern College (1958); and her PhD from George Peabody College, Vanderbilt University (1970). Her principal teachers were Hugh Thomas, Gilbert Tryhall, Newton Standberg, and Betty Louise Lumby. She has taught at the University of Alabama in Tuscaloosa, Birmingham Southern College, Southeastern Bible College, Peabody College, Blair Academy of Music, Union University, and Judson College in Marion, GA. (Cohen; Composer letter; Hixon)

Shatal, Miriam

Dutch Israeli composer born in 1903. Before studying composition with Paul Ben Chaim, Arthur Geldrun, and Chaim Alexander, she received a doctorate in biology. (Cohen; Hixon).

Sheer, Anita

USA composer, pianist, flamenco guitarist, and singer (1935-1996). She was a piano prodigy who performed at Carnegie Hall and won the US Piano Competition before graduating from high school. She studied flamenco guitar with Carlos Montoya in New York, then went to Spain for further study with both singers and guitarists. Her performing career spanned clubs, concert halls, Broadway, and television. (*Acoustic Guitar*, November 1996)

Sherman, Elna

USA composer, pianist, music educator, writer on music, and music administrator (1889-1964). (Cohen; Hixon)

Shore, Clare

USA composer and music educator, born in 1954. She received her BA from Wake Forest University, her MMus in composition from the University of Colorado, and her doctorate from the Juilliard School. Her principal composition teachers were Charles Eain, Cecil Effinger, and David Diamond. She has taught at Fordham University, the Manhattan School of Music, and at the University of Virginia. She received an Irving Berlin Fellowship in 1981. (Boenke; Cohen; Hixon)

Shuttleworth, Anne-Marie

South African composer born in 1961. Her BMus degree is from the University of Witwatersrand (1982). (Cohen; Hixon)

Silsbee, Ann Loomis

USA composer, harpsichordist, pianist, and music educator, born in 1930. She received her AB (1951) from Radcliffe, her MM (1969) from Syracuse University, and her DMA (1978) from Cornell University. Her principal teachers were Irving Fine, Earl George, and Karel Husa. She has taught at State University College in Cortland, NY (1970-71), and at Cornell (1971-73). She undertook additional study in

Paris (1973-74) and in Darmstadt (1964). Her compositions have had international performances and she has won the Burge-Eastman Prize. (Boenke; Cohen; Hixon)

Silverman, Faye-Ellen
USA composer, pianist, music editor, music educator, and writer on music, born in 1947. She attended the Dalcroze School of Music and the Manhattan School of Music, Preparatory Division. Her BA (1968) is from Barnard College, and her MA is from Harvard University where she studied with Leon Kirchner and Lukas Foss. She received her DMA (1974) from Columbia University, was a teaching assistant at Columbia, and has been an editor for *Current Musicology*. She also taught graduate courses at the Peabody Institute of John Hopkins University and directed the Peabody Electronic and Computer Music Center. She has been piano soloist with the Brooklyn Philharmonia, has won prizes and scholarships, and her works have been played on radio and television. (Boenke; Cohen; Hixon)

Simcoe, Joan (also uses Szymko)
USA composer, vocal arranger, and choral conductor, born in 1957. She earned a BS in music education from the University of Illinois in Urbana. She conducted the Seattle Women's Ensemble (1981-91) and took composition and ethnomusicology at the

University of Washington (1986). Since moving to Portland, Oregon in 1993, she has conducted the Aurora Chorus and founded Viriditas Vocal Ensemble to showcase her own compositions. She has received commissions and her work is published by Santa Barbara Music Publishing. (Composer letter)

Sinde Ramallal, Clara
Argentine composer, guitarist, singer, arranger, and music educator, born in 1935. She studied the guitar with Consuelo Mallo Lopez, making her guitar debut in 1945. She also studied voice and composition, making a singing debut in 1952. She toured throughout South America both as a soloist and as a member of the Sinde Ramallal Trio, and she has premiered guitar works by A. Galluzzo, Bianchi Pinero, and Elsa Calcagno. She teaches guitar both privately and in the national music schools, and she has received many prizes and awards. (Cohen; Hixon)

Singer, Jeanne
USA composer, pianist, and piano teacher, born in 1924. Her BA in music is from Barnard College. She studied composition and theory at Columbia University where her teachers included Seth Bingham, William Mitchell, Rudolf Thomas, and Douglas Moore. She studied piano privately with Nadia Reisenberg, her primary musical mentor. Singer holds an artist's diploma from the Guild of Piano

Teachers and an honorary doctorate in music (1984) from the World University. She founded the Long Island Trio in 1969. Her music, in all genres, has won over thirty awards, and she has received many commissions and grants. (Boenke; Cohen; Composer letter; Hixon)

Skirving, W. (a lady)
Looking for more information about this composer. (Jackson)

Sommer, Silvia
Austrian composer and pianist, born in 1944. At the Vienna Musikhochschule she studied piano from age eight under Professor Landa and later under Joseph Dichler. Her composition studies were with Alfred Uhl at the Vienna Music Academy. In Austria and abroad she gives concerts which often include her own compositions. (Cohen; Hixon; Norton/Grove)

Sonntag, Brunhilde
German composer, organist, harpsichordist, and music educator, born in 1936. She studied at the University of Music in Vienna and privately with Professor Kurt Hessenberg. She also studied with Otto Siegl and Gottfried von Einem. In the 1970s she received a doctorate in musicology from the University of Marburg. She has taught at the University of Giessen, the Pädagogische Hochschule in Münster, and since 1981, at the Gesamthochschule in Duisburg. (Cohen; Hixon; Norton/Grove)

Spampinato, Letizia
Italian composer born in 1955. She received a diploma in piano in 1978 and did further study in Palermo and Rome where she was awarded degrees in choral conducting and composition in 1980 and 1985. Her major teachers have been I. Ravinale, F. Donatoni, B. Ferneyhough, E. Sollima, and T. Procaccini. She is currently teaching at the Liceo Musicale V. Bellini in Catania. (Composer letter)

Spiegel, Laurie
USA composer born in 1945. She attended Shimer College and the Juilliard School, where Oscar Ghiglia was her guitar teacher, and she studied lute with Suzanne Bloch and Fritz Rikko. She also studied guitar privately with John Duarte. She received her MA from Brooklyn College (1975). Her principal composition teachers were Jacob Druckman and Emmanuel Ghent (computer music). She has taught at the Aspen Music Festival and Bucks County Community College. She founded the Computer Music Studio at New York University then taught there (1982-83). She has received major awards and grants and has written many articles on music and computers. (Cohen; Hixon; Norton/Grove)

Stanley, Ruth
Looking for information about this composer.

Steinburg, Carolyn
USA composer born in 1956. She

studied at North Texas State and at the Manhattan School of Music, receiving her MM in 1980. She then studied privately for two years with Cathy Berberian at the Accademia Chigiana in Siena, Italy and at the Hochschule für Musik in Freiburg. Her DMA is from the Juilliard School (1989). Her principal teachers were Ludmila Ulehla, Franco Donatoni, Bernard Rands, and Brian Ferneyhough, to whom she was married for five years. She has taught at various schools in New York since 1987. (Norton/Grove)

Stilman-Lasansky, Julia
Argentine American composer and pianist, born in 1935 in Argentina. She studied piano with Roberto Castro (1951-56) and composition with Gilardo Gilardi (1956-58), then attended the University of Maryland, where she received her MM (1968) and DMA (1973). She did post-doctoral studies at Yale in 1974 under Krzysztof Penderecki. Other teachers included Morton Subotnick, Lawrence Moss, and Leon Kirchner. She has lived in the USA since 1964 and has received grants and fellowships. (Boenke; Cohen; Hixon)

Stoll, Helene Marianne
German composer, 20th century. (Boenke; Cohen; Hixon)

Strutt, Dorothy
English composer, pianist, cellist, violinist, and contralto, born in 1941. She is a member of the

Barnard-Strutt-Owen Trio founded in 1972. A self-taught composer, she has written many chamber, piano, and vocal pieces. She gives recitals and lecture demonstrations in schools. (Boenke; Cohen; Hixon)

Sullivan, Marion Dix
USA composer active in the 19th century. Little is known about her life. Her song, "The Blue Juniata," (1844) was the first commercial hit by an American woman composer and was mentioned in Mark Twain's autobiography. (Norton/Grove)

Sulpizi, Mira (Pratesi)
Italian composer born in 1923. She studied composition with Soresina and graduated from the Universita Cattolica del Sacro Cuore in Milan. (Boenke; Cohen; Hixon)

Swain, Freda Mary
English composer, flutist, pianist, violinist, music teacher, and music administrator (1902-1985). She studied at the Royal College of Music and also taught there (1924-40). She received awards and prizes for composition and for piano. (Boenke; Cohen; Hixon).

Szeghy, Iris
Czech composer and music educator, born in 1956. She studied at the Music Academy in Bratislava where she also did her graduate and post-graduate work. She has received scholarships for study outside of Czechoslovakia. She was

resident composer at the Akademie Schloss Solitude in Stuttgart (1992-93) and visiting composer at the University of California, San Diego (1994). In 1995 she received a scholarship to produce an electronic work at the Steim Studio in Amsterdam. She was also a composer-in-residence at the State Opera in Hamburg. Her works have been performed in Europe, America, Australia, and Japan. (Composer letter; Hixon)

Szekely, Katalin
Hungarian composer and music educator, born in 1953. She studied at the Liszt Academy of Music in Budapest and later taught there. Her works have been performed in Hungary, the former Yugoslavia, and Norway. She won a Hungarian prize for young composers in 1981. (Cohen; Hixon)

Szeto, Caroline
Looking for information about this composer.

Szönyi, Erzsébet
Hungarian composer, pianist, choral conductor, music educator, and writer on music, born in 1924, and educated at the Liszt Academy. In 1947 she won a scholarship to the Paris Conservatory where she studied with Nadia Boulanger, Tony Aubin, and Olivier Messiaen. She won the conservatory's composition prize in 1948. She taught at the Liszt Academy in Budapest, becoming the director of the school music faculty in 1960. She was an associate of Zoltan Kodaly, implementing his ideas for music education in schools. An important educator in Hungary, she has lectured widely abroad and has also won prizes for composition. (Cohen; Hixon; Norton/Grove)

Szymko, Joan
See **Simcoe, Joan**

Tann (Presslaff), Hilary
Welsh composer, music editor, and music educator, born in 1947. She first studied with Alun Hoddinott at University College, Cardiff, receiving her BMus with honors in 1968. She did graduate research with Jonathan Harvey at the University of Southampton, was a visiting fellow at Princeton (1972-73), and received her MFA (1975) and PhD (1981) from that same institution, where her principal teacher was J.K. Randall. She was a teaching assistant at Princeton, an assistant professor at Bard College, and is currently a professor at Union College in Schenectady. She was editor of the *Journal of the International League of Women Composers* (1982-88) and on the executive board of that organization. She went to Japan (1990?) to teach at Kansai University and study the shakuhachi and noh performing traditions. She is the recipient of many awards and commissions for her compositions. (Boenke; Cohen; Hixon [uses Presslaff]; Norton/Grove)

Tapia, Gloria
Mexican composer born in Araró, Michoacán. She holds two degrees, in Philosophy and in Spanish Literature from the Centro Cultural Universitario, now called Universidad Iberoamericana. In 1952, she enrolled in the Conservatorio Nacional de Música in Mexico City, studying under Blas Galindo. In 1959, she won the National Prize for Chamber Music offered by the Instituto Nacional de Bellas Artes and the Sociedad de Actores y Compositores. She has served as Assistant Director of the Conservatorio Nacional de Música. (Norton/Grove; Tapia)

Tate, Phyllis
English composer, pianist, and tympanist (1911-1987). She studied composition with Harry Farjeon at the Royal Academy of Music in London (1928-32) and worked as a free-lance composer, receiving commissions from the BBC and music festivals. She also wrote commercial music under the pseudonyms Max Morelle and Janos. (Boenke; Cohen; Hixon; Norton/Grove)

Themmen, Ivana Marburger
USA composer, pianist, accompanist, music educator, and poet, born in 1935. She studied at the New England Conservatory and the Eastman School of Music. She did further study at Tanglewood. Her major teachers were Jean Rosenblum (piano), Carl McKinley, Francis Judd

Cooke, Otto Schulhof, Lukas Foss, and Nichols Flagello. She has given concerts in Scandinavia and in England and has been an accompanist for the American Ballet Theatre. She also taught at Hampton Conservatory (1973-75). Her orchestral pieces have been premiered by the Minnesota Orchestra and the Aspen Music Festival Orchestra. Some of her works have been recorded on First Edition, Grenadilla, and Opus One labels. Her guitar concerto was commissioned by Sharon Isbin and premiered by Ms. Isbin with the St. Louis Symphony. (Boenke; Cohen; Hixon)

Thomas, Karen P.
USA composer, pianist, conductor, and band director, born in 1957. She received her BA (1979) from the Cornish Institute in Seattle and did further study at the University of Washington. Her major composition teachers have been Bern Herbolsheimer, William Bergsma, and Diane Thome. Her works have been performed in the USA and abroad. A recipient of grants from the NEA and other major institutions, she teaches at Pacific Lutheran University and the Cornish Institute. (Cohen; Hixon)

Thome, Diane
USA composer, pianist, and music educator, born in 1942. She received her BMus (1963) from the Eastman School of Music, her MA in theory and composition (1965) from the University of

Pennsylvania, her MFA (1970) and her PhD (1973) from Princeton University, where she was the first woman to receive a doctorate degree. Her principal composition teachers were Robert Strassburg, Darius Milhaud, Roy Harris, A.U. Boscovich, and Milton Babbitt. Since 1977 she has taught theory and composition at the University of Washington School of Music. Her music is widely performed and she receives many commissions. (Boenke; Cohen; Hixon; Norton/Grove)

Thompson, Caroline Lorraine
Australian composer and pianist, born in 1948. She studied at New South Wales Conservatory where she received a diploma in education. She studied music theatre at Morley College in London and acting in Sydney. Jazz piano studies were with Chuck Yates and Serge Ermoll. Her principal composition teacher was Michael Hannon. She has performed in productions of her works and has written commercial songs. (Cohen; Hixon)

Thorkelsdóttir, Mist Barbara
Icelandic American composer, pianist, and music educator, born in 1960. She attended school in Iceland and received her BA from Hamline University, St. Paul, MN, studying composition with Russel Harris. In 1983 she studied with Morton Feldman and Lejaren Hiller at the State University of New York, Buffalo. She lives in Iceland, teaching piano and music

history at the Gardabaer Children's Music School. Several of her compositions have been performed on radio and television and at international festivals. (Cohen; Hixon)

Torres, Ana
Possibly Colombian composer, 20th century. Looking for more information. (*Guitar Review*, no. 97 [spring 1994])

Tower, Joan
USA composer, pianist, music educator, and administrator, born in 1938. Her BA (1961) is from Bennington College; her MA in theory and history of music (1967) and her DMA in composition (1978) are from Columbia University. Her principal teachers were Otto Luening, Jack Beeson, Vladimir Ussachevshy, Chou Wen-Chung, Charles Wourinen, Ralph Shapey, Allen Sapp, Ben Boretz, Henry Brant, Louis Calbro, Walllingford Riegger, and Darius Milhaud. She founded and was pianist for the Da Capo Chamber Players (1969-84). The ensemble commissioned and performed many new works and won major awards. Her compositions have been commissioned and premiered by some of the world's finest orchestras, including the New York Philharmonic in 1994. She has won many prestigious prizes, and since 1972 is on the faculty of Bard College. (Boenke; Cohen; Hixon; Le Page; Norton/Grove)

Ulehla, Ludmila
USA composer of Czech descent, born in 1923. She studied composition with Vittorio Giannini and received her BMus (1946) and MMus (1947) from the Manhattan School of Music, where she became Chair of the composition department (1970-89). She also has taught at the Hoff-Barthelson Music School in Scarsdale, NY (1968-91). She has received numerous awards and grants from ASCAP and Meet the Composer. (Norton/Grove)

Urreta, Alicia
Mexican composer, pianist, conductor, and music educator (1935-1986). (Norton/Grove says 1987.) She graduated from the National Conservatory in Mexico City, where she studied with R. Halffter and Sandor Roth. From 1957, when she made her debut as a pianist, she was the chosen performer in Mexico City for all avant-garde piano music. She studied electronic music in Paris at the Schola Cantorum and with Jean-Etienne at the RTF. She has taught chamber and electronic music at the National Autonomous University of Mexico. (Cohen; Hixon)

Uyttenhove, Yolande
Belgian composer and pianist, born in 1925. She studied at the Brussels Conservatory and at the Royal Academy of Music in London. She has won international awards for both piano and composition. (Norton/Grove)

van Appledorn, Mary Jeanne
USA composer, pianist, music educator, band director, and writer on music, born in 1927. She received her BM, MM, and PhD degrees from the Eastman School of Music. She made her Carnegie Hall debut as a pianist in 1956. Her principal teachers were Bernard Rogers and Alan Hovhaness. She is a professor of music and Chair of graduate studies in music at Texas Tech University in Lubbock, where she founded an annual symposium of contemporary music. The recipient of many recognitions, she has had premieres and recordings of her works by noted artists worldwide. Her publishers are Oxford University Press, Carl Fischer, and Molenaar's Muziekcentrale NV (The Netherlands). (Boenke; Cohen; Hixon; Norton/Grove)

Van der Mark, Maria (née de Jong)
Dutch South African composer and librettist, born in 1912. She studied at the Tonkunst Muzierkschool in Rotterdam before emigrating to South Africa in 1935. She studied composition with K. van Oostveen at the University of Witwatersrand in Johannesburg (1959-68). She is the composer of music and words used in the treatment of epileptic patients. (Boenke; Cohen; Hixon)

van Epen-de Groot, Else Antonia (pseud. Derek Laren)
Dutch composer, pianist, conductor, and music educator,

born in 1919. She studied first
with her father who was the
conductor and composer Hugo de
Groot. She pursued medicine for a
while, but in 1942, returned to
music, studying at the Hilversum
Music Lyceum. Her primary
teachers were her father, Hugo
Godron, and Jacques Beers.
(Boenke [uses Epen de Groot];
Cohen; Hixon)

van Schaijk-Lambermont, Herma
Looking for information about
this composer.

Vargas, Eva
German composer, 20th century.
(Cohen; Hixon)

Velásquez, Consuelo
Mexican composer born in 1920.
She studied piano at the Escuela
National de Música in Mexico
City. She worked at the Mexico
City radio station, XEQ, where
she formed her own ensemble and
broadcast her own music. Her
song, "Bésame mucho," was a
great hit in the USA during
World War II. She has had other
hits throughout her career and
her songs have been recorded by
dozens of artists, including Nat
King Cole, Ray Coniff, Jimmy
Dorsey, and The Beatles. A self-
taught composer, she has
achieved more popularity than
any Mexican woman composer to
date. (Cohen, 1981; Hixon;
Norton/Grove)

Verhaalem, Sister Marion
USA composer, music editor,
writer on music, music educator,
and music administrator, born in
1930. She received her BM in
piano (1954) from Alverno
College, Milwaukee, WI, and her
MM in piano (1962) from Catholic
University in Washington, D.C.
Her EdD in music education is
from Columbia Teachers ' College
(1971). She has been a teacher
since 1954. She has taught
workshops sponsored by the
National Piano Foundation of
Chicago both in the USA and in
Brazil, and she received a
research grant from the
Organization of American States
to study the music of Francisco
Minone and Camargo Guarnieri in
Brazil (1969-70). (Cohen; Hixon)

Viard, M. (Mme de)
French composer fl. ca. 1781.
(Jackson)

Vierk, Lois
USA composer, pianist, and
conductor, born in 1951. She
received her BA from University
of California, Los Angeles (1971),
and her MFA from Calfornia
Institute of the Arts (1978). She
has also studied at Tanglewood.
Some of her principal teachers
have been Jacob Druckman, Mel
Powell, Leonard Stein, and
Morton Subotnick. In 1971 she
became interested in Japanese
court music (gagaku) and studied
under Suenobu Togi at the
University of California. In 1982
she continued these studies in
Japan. (Boenke; Cohen; Hixon)

Vieu, Jane
French composer (1871-1955).

Little is known about her life, but she wrote over 100 works in a variety of genres, some under the pseudonym Pierre Valette. She wrote a solfège manual for the Paris Conservatory. It was dedicated to Gabriél Fauré. (Cohen; Hixon; Norton/Grove)

Vigneron-Ramackers, Josée (Christiane) (pseud. Jo Delande)
Belgian composer, singer, voice teacher, conductor, organist, and writer on music, born in 1914. She studied at the Limburg Organ School where she received her diploma in 1934. Her teacher for orchestration and fugue was Paul Gilson. She taught at the Koninklÿk Atheneum of Eisden and the Atheneum of Maaseik (1934-69). In 1945 she founded the Academy of Music in Eisden, which became the Gemeentelijke Muziekakademie Maasmechelen in 1972. She was the conductor of the Eisden orchestra and chamber orchestra (1945-70). (Cohen; Hixon; Norton/Grove)

Vito-Delvaux, Berthe di
Belgian composer, pianist, and music educator, born in 1915. She studied composition at the Royal Music Conservatory in Liège and later at the RMC in Brussels, under Leon Jongen. She taught in Liège from 1938. She won many awards and prizes including the Prix de Rome in 1943 and the Prix Modeste Grétry in 1962. (Boenke; Cohen; Hixon)

Volkstein, Pauline
German composer (1849-1925).

(Cohen says b. 1894.) She wrote over 1200 songs, 20 of them with guitar accompaniment. She lived in Dresden and Naples before moving to Weimer in 1905. (Cohen; Hixon)

von Zieritz, Grete
Austrian composer, pianist, piano teacher, and music educator, born in 1899. She studied at the Styrian Conservatory in Granz (1912-17). She then moved to Berlin to study with Martin Krause and R.M. Breithaupt (piano) and with Franz Schreker (composition). She taught at the Stern Conservatory in Berlin and won the Mendelssohn State Prize for composition in 1928. She was the first woman awarded the honorary title of Professor by the Austrian Federation President. She toured throughout Europe, often performing her own works. (Boenke; Cohen; Hixon; Norton/Grove) (Boenke, Hixon and Norton/Grove use Zieritz.)

Vorlová, Sláva (née Miroslava Johnová) (pseud. Mira Kord)
Czech composer, pianist, singer, choral conductor, and music educator (1894-1973). She studied singing at the Music Academy in Vienna, but pursued composition and piano after losing her voice. Her primary composition teachers were Vitezslav Novak and Jaroslav Ridky. In 1948 she wrote her *Symphony JM*, Op. 18 dedicated to Jan Masaryk, and was the first woman to graduate in composition from the Prague Conservatory. She wrote songs

and jazz compositions under the pseudonym, Mira Kord. (Boenke; Cohen; Hixon; Norton/Grove)

Waldo, Elisabeth
USA composer, violinist, folklorist, music educator, and writer on music, born in 1923. She won a scholarship to the Cornish Institute and later to the Curtis Institute, where she studied violin with Efrem Zimbalist. She was first violinist in the All American Youth Orchestra under Leopold Stokowski and later was first violinist with the Los Angeles Philharmonic Orchestra. She has also been violinist with Central and South American orchestras including the Mexico City Radio Network. She has been a researcher in Panama, in Mexico City, and at the Fine Arts Library at the University of New Mexico in Albuquerque. In the early 1970s she began blending indigenous instruments with her own orchestration. She has given workshops and lectures as a folklorist on the music and dance traditions of Latin America and the American Southwest. She founded and composed for the Pan-American Ensemble and the Pan-Asian Ensemble, both of which use traditional instruments of ancient cultures. Her compositions and TV and film musical scores have won many prizes and awards. She has also recorded some of her works, and distributes them through Southwind Studios, Inc. in Northridge, CA. (Cohen; Composer letter; Hixon)

Walker, Gwyneth
USA composer, music educator, and music administrator, born in 1947. Her BA is from Brown University and her MM (1970) and DMA (1976) are from the Hartt College of Music, University of Hartford. Her principal teacher was Arnold Franchetti. She taught at Oberlin (1976-80) and then at Hartt. In 1982 she moved to a Vermont dairy farm to concentrate on composing fulltime. She has over 90 commissioned works in her catalog and has won many awards. Her music is published by E.C. Schirmer of Boston and MMB Music of St. Louis. In 1988 she helped found the Consortium of Vermont Composers. (Boenke; Cohen; Composer letter; Hixon; Norton/Grove)

Walker, Louise (Luise)
Austrian guitarist, composer, and music educator, born in 1910. She studied at the Academy of Music and Performing Arts in Vienna under J. Ortner. She began guitar studies at age eight with Josef Zuth, a well-known Viennese guitarist. She also took lessons from Heinrich Albert and Miguel Llobet. She toured Europe, the USA, and Japan as a concert guitarist and taught at the Musikhochschule in Vienna and the Viennese Staatskademie for Music. Many of her compositions have been published, and there are recordings of her playing on the Turnabout and Epic labels. (Bone; Cohen; *Guitar Review*, no. 11 [1950]; Hixon; Summerfield)

Wallach, Joelle
USA composer, pianist, singer,
and music educator, born in 1946.
Her early training in music was
at the Juilliard Preparatory
School. Her BM is from Sarah
Lawrence College (1967) and her
MM is from Columbia University
(1969). In 1984 she received the
first doctorate in composition
from the Manhattan School of
Music. Her principal teachers of
composition were Chou Wen-
Chung, Jack Beeson, Stanley
Wolff, and John Corigliano. She
has won numerous competitions
and received awards for her
compositions. She has taught at
the City University of New York,
been a preconcert lecturer for the
New York Philharmonic, and
performs as both pianist and
singer. (Boenke; Cohen; Composer
letter; Hixon; Norton/Grove)

**Warren (Warren-Davis), Betsy
(pseud. Betsy Frost)**
USA composer born in the 1940s,
who sings professionally as Betsy
Frost. She received her BA and
MA from Radcliffe College. She
teaches voice. (Cohen; Hixon)

Weaver, Carol Ann
USA composer, pianist, and music
educator, born in 1948. She
attended Indiana University
where she received her bachelors
(1970), masters (1972), and Doctor
of Music in composition (1981).
She taught at Eastern Mennonite
University in Harrisonburg, VA,
(1972-76), at Concord College of
the University of Winnipeg,
(1977-81), and at the Wilfrid

Laurier University, Waterloo,
(1981-85). Currently she teaches
at Conrad Grebel College at the
University of Waterloo. She
immigrated to Canada in 1980.
While on sabbatical to Kenya,
Africa during 1992-93, Weaver
studied with a master drummer.
She has had numerous
commissions and grants and is
active as a pianist, performing
with her husband, the classical
mandolinist Lyle Friesen, in the
eclectic duo, Mooncoin. Her first
CD was released in January 1996.
(Cohen; Composer letter; Hixon)

Wegener-Frensel, Emmy Heil
Dutch composer, violinist, and
pianist (1901-1973?). She was the
daughter of composer Berta
Frensel Wegener-Koopman. She
studied with Sam Dresden.
(Boenke [uses Frensel-Wegener];
Cohen; Hixon [uses Wegener])

Weigl, Vally
Austrian American composer,
pianist, piano teacher, music
therapist, and music educator,
born in Vienna in 1894 and died in
New York in 1982. She studied at
Vienna University under Richard
Robert, Guido Adler, and Karl
Weigl. She received her MA from
Columbia University in 1955. She
lectured and taught at Vienna
University, at summer music
festivals near Salzburg, and at
the Institute for Avocational
Music. She was a music therapist
at NY Medical College and
Roosevelt Cerebral Palsy School
on Long Island and was Research
Director at Mt. Sinai Hospital in

New York. She was the recipient of numerous grants and awards. (Boenke; Cohen; Hixon; Norton/Grove)

Weir, Judith
Scottish composer and music educator, born in 1954. She briefly attended the Massachussetts Institute of Technology where Barry Vercoe sparked her interest in computer music. She studied composition at King's College in Cambridge (1973-76), and won the Koussevitsky Fellowship at Tanglewood in 1975. Her principal teachers were John Tavener and Robin Holloway. She taught at Glasgow University (1979-82) and has received major commissions. (Boenke; Cohen; Hixon; Norton/Grove)

Whitehead, Gillian
New Zealand composer and music educator, born in 1941. She studied at the University of Auckland and the University of Victoria, where she received her BMus (1963). Her MMus is from the University of Sydney (1965). Further studies were in London, Portugal, and Italy. She taught at Auckland University in 1975. Her principal teachers have been Peter Scutthorpe and Peter Maxwell Davies. She has won awards for her compositions. (Boenke; Cohen; Hixon; Norton/Grove)

Wiemann, Beth
USA composer born in 1959. She holds degrees in composition and

clarinet from Oberlin College (BM 1981) and Princeton University (MFA 1983, PhD 1994). She was a founding member of the Griffin Music Ensemble, a contemporary music group in Boston. Her works have won awards and been widely performed. Currently she teaches at Salisbury State University in Maryland, having previously taught at Reed College and College of the Holy Cross. (Composer letter)

Wilkins, Margaret Lucy
English composer born in 1939. She studied at Trinity College of Music and at the University of Nottingham (1957-60). She performed with the Scottish Early Music Consort (1969-76) and since 1989 has directed the contemporary music group, Polyphonia. She has taught at the University of Huddersfield. Her compositions have been regularly performed in England and abroad. (Norton/Grove)

Wilson, Mrs. Cornwall Baron
English composer and poet (1797-1846). She won prizes in bardic competitions in England and Wales. (Cohen; Hixon)

Winter, Sister Miriam Therese (Gloria Frances)
USA composer, singer, and music educator, born in 1938. She obtained her BA (1964) from Catholic University. Her MRE (1976) is from McMaster Divinity College and her PhD is from Princeton Seminary. In 1980 she

became an associate professor at the Hartford Seminary Foundation. She recorded a very popular album of her songs in the 1960s, including "Joy Is Like The Rain." (Cohen; Hixon)

Wolf, [L.], Anna (née Mrasek)
Austrian pianist and composer. She was born in 1774 and died in Vienna in 1808. (Hixon; Jackson)

Wolfe, Julia
USA composer born in 1958. She earned a BA (1980) from the University of Michigan and received her MM in composition (1986) from Yale University, where her principal teacher was Martin Breswick. She enrolled in the doctoral program at Princeton to study the music of Louis Andriessen. She has received a Fulbright Fellowship and many grants. She is co-founder of the Wild Swan Theater in Ann Arbor, MI, where she is playwright, actor, director and composer. She is also co-founder of the Bang on a Can Festival in New York, which presents many new works. She has received commissions and some of her works have been recorded. (Norton/Grove)

Wong, Hsiung-Zee
USA composer, artist, and designer, born in Hong Kong in 1947. She studied at the University of Hawaii with Ernst Krenek and Chou Wen-Chung. Studies in electronic music were at Mills College (1970) under Robert Sheff and Dane Rudhyar. Her FFA in industrial design is

from California College of Arts and Crafts. While at Mills she formed a women's creative arts group called Hysteresis. (Cohen; Hixon)

Wüsthoff-Oppelt, Sabine
Looking for information about this composer.

Wylie, Ruth Shaw
USA composer, flutist, pianist, music educator, and music administrator (1916-1989). Her BA (1937) and MA (1989) are from Wayne State University in Detroit, and her PhD (1943) is from the Eastman School of Music. Her principal teachers were Howard Hanson, Bernard Rogers, Arthur Honneger, Samuel Barber, and Aaron Copland. She taught at the University of Missouri (1943-49) and at Wayne State University (1958-69). She received many fellowships, awards, and grants. (Boenke; Cohen; Hixon; Norton/Grove)

Yamashita, Toyoko
Japanese composer born in 1942. She studied at the University of Art in Tokyo and at the Hochschule für Music in Stuttgart with professor Hubert Giesen (piano). She has lived in Berlin since 1967 and performs with a cellist. Winner of competitions and awards for her compositions, she produces a guitar festival every year in Berlin, which features her many works for guitar. (Brand, et al.)

Zaerr, Laura
Contemporary USA composer and harpist. She received her BM from the University of Oregon where she studied with Sally Maxwell. Later she studied harp in Paris (1981-82) with Bertille Fournier. Her master's degree is from the Eastman School of Music, where her principal teacher was Eileen Malone, and she recorded with Wynton Marsalis, Benita Valente, and James Galway. She also studied composition with Derek Healey at the University of Oregon. She plays Irish harp as well as classical concert harp and has built instruments with her father. She performs in the consort Psallite with her sister, a medievalist and storyteller. She teaches at Willamette University and at Linn-Benton Community College in her home town, Corvallis, Oregon. (Composer letter)

Zaffauk, Theresa
Austrian composer, 19th century. (Cohen; Hixon)

Zaidel-Rudolph, Jeanne
South African composer, pianist, conductor, and music educator, born in 1948. She studied at Pretoria University, at the Royal College of Music in London, and at Tanglewood. Her PhD (1979) is in composition from the University of Pretoria, where she was the first South African woman to receive a composition degree. Her major teachers were John Lambert, Tristram Carey, and Ligeti, with whom she studied at the Hamburg Hochschule. She has lectured at the University of Witwatersrand in Johannesburg. She has received numerous awards and commissions and had worldwide performances of her works. (Boenke; Cohen; Hixon)

Zaripova, Naila Gatinovna
Composer and music educator, born in 1932 in the Tartar Autonomous Republic of the former USSR. She studied at the Yazan Music School and at the Kazan Conservatory under A.S. Leman. After 1964 she taught in schools in Kazan. (Cohen; Hixon)

Zieritz, Grete von
See **von Zieritz, Grete**

Ziffrin, Marilyn Jane
USA composer, music educator, writer, and musicologist, born in 1926. She received a BM (1948) from the University of Wisconsin and an MA (1949) from Teachers College, Columbia University. Her primary composition teachers were Karl Ahrendt and Alexander Tcherepnin. She taught in public schools, was an assistant professor at Northeastern Illinois University (1961-66), then taught at New England College until 1982, when she decided to devote herself fulltime to composing. Her biography of Carl Ruggles, the distinguished American composer and painter, was published in 1994. She has received numerous prestigious awards and commissions. There are several

recordings of her works. (Boenke; Cohen; Composer letter; Hixon; Norton/Grove)

Zimmermann, Margrit
Swiss composer, conductor, and music educator, born in 1927. She studied in Berne with Jeanne Bovert and Walter Furrer and received a diploma in piano from the Ecole Normale de Musique in Paris. She studied composition in Paris with Arthur Honegger and at the Lausanne Conservatory with Denise Bidal and Alfred Cortot; then conducting, in Ossiach with Hans Swarowski and Aurelio Maggioni and in Monte Carlo with I. Markevitch. Opera conducting studies were in Milan with Umberto Cattini at the Verdi Conservatory, which granted her a diploma in composition in 1978. She has received many commissions, and several works have been recorded. (Cohen; Hixon)

Zivkovic, Mirjana
Croatian composer born in 1935. She studied at the Music Academy in Belgrade with Stanoljo Rajicic and in France with Olivier Messiaen and Nadia Boulanger. She teaches composition in Belgrade at the Music University. (Boenke; Letter from Professor Uros Dojcinovic)

Zubeldia, Emiliana de (pseud. Emily Bydewealth)
Mexican composer and pianist born in Spain (1888-1987). (Cohen and Hixon say b. 1948.) She studied piano at the Pamplona Academia Municipal de Música and later at the Madrid Real Conservatorio. She moved to Paris to study composition with Vincent d'Indy and piano with Blanche Selva, the Bach specialist at the Schola Cantorum. She then embarked on several successful concert tours, including appearances in the USA in 1931. In New York she met Augusto Novaro, the Mexican acoustician who had invented a changeable tone-color keyboard. She moved to Mexico City to study with him, becoming a Mexican citizen in 1942. He strongly influenced her compositional style. In 1947, after ten years teaching in Mexico City, she accepted a position at the University of Sonora in Hermosillo and remained there for forty years, Many of her compositions are in the University of Sonora library collection. (Cohen; Hixon; Norton/Grove)

Zucker, Laurel
USA composer and flutist, born in 1955. She is a graduate of the Juilliard School of Music where she studied flute with Samuel Baron (1975-78). She has also studied with Paula Robison at the New England Conservatory (1973-75) and with Marcel Moyse privately. She made a Carnegie Hall debut as winner of the American Music Center's Artist International Competition. Her MA in composition (1986) is from New York University. She currently teaches at California

State University in Sacramento. Zucker tours worldwide as a flutist and has made seventeen recordings for her own label, Cantilena Records, including one with guitarist, Richard Savino. She is the recipient of the Aaron Copland Award for 1996-97. (Composer letter)

Zumsteeg, Emilie
German composer, pianist, singer, choral conductor, and music educator (1796-1857). She was the daughter of court musician Johann Rudolf Zumsteeg of the Wurttemberg ducal court. She made early appearances at the Stuttgart Museum Concerts as a singer and pianist. Her compositions include lieder, piano pieces, and sacred music. She was a distinguished teacher and choir conductor in Stuttgart. (Cohen; Hixon; Norton/Grove)

Appendix 1

Composer Addresses

Elizabeth Alexander
206 N. Titus Avenue
Ithaca, NY 14850

Beth Anderson
(Barbara Elizabeth Anderson)
26 Second Avenue, #2B
New York, NY 10003

Ruth M. Anderson
2678 N. Beechwood Drive
Hollywood, CA 90068

Violet Balestreri Archer
10805 85th Avenue
Edmonton, Alberta
CANADA

Alice Artzt
180 Claremont Ave., No. 31
New York, NY 10027

Kristan Aspen
P. O. Box 15121
Portland, OR 97293-5121

Lydia Ayers
P. O. Box 340
Grand Central Station
New York, NY 10163

Carol Edith Barnett
3722 Pleasant Avenue S.
Minneapolis, MN 55409

Anna Bofill Levi
Edificio Walden 7, 10-11
08960 Sant Just Desvern
Barcelona   SPAIN

Teresa Borràs Fornell
Ptge. Comtes Mir i Borrell 8-b, 6-3
08302 Mataró (Barcelona)
SPAIN

Linda Bouchard
c/o Barbara Scales
Latitude 45
109 St. Joseph Street West
Montréal, Québec H2T 2P7
CANADA

Margaret Susan Brandman
P.O. Box 165
Glenbrook, NSW 2773
AUSTRALIA

Linnea Brooks
54647 S. W. Patton Valley Rd.
Gaston, OR 97119

Elisbetta Brusa
Via Pisacane 36
20129 Milano, ITALY

Ruth M. Byrchmore
Flat 1, 47 Lambs Conduit Street
Holborn, London WC1N 3NG
ENGLAND

Madelyn Byrne
481 Fourth St.
Brooklyn, NY 11215

Nancy Laird Chance
P.O. Box 96
Austerlitz, NY 12017

Maia Ciobanu
str. Suren Spandarian 7,
sc. G, et 9, ap. 301, sect 2
72248 Bucharest
HUNGARY

Theresa-Ann Clark
3322 35th Avenue S.
Seattle,WA 98144

Eleanor Thayer Cory
945 West End Avenue, #8B
New York, NY 10025

Mary Criswick
40 rue Piere Brossolette
94360 Bry sur Marne
FRANCE

D.C. Culbertson
6738 Glenkirk Rd.
Baltimore, MD 21239

Tina Davidson
508 Woodland Terrace
Philadelphia, PA 19104

Annette Degenhardt
Klosterstra. 1
D-55124 Mainz-Gonsenheim
GERMANY

Emma Lou Diemer
2249 Vista del Campo
Santa Barbara, CA 93101

Violeta Dinescu-Lucaci
Bütten Stra. 15 BP
76530 Baden-Baden
GERMANY

Grete Franke Dollitz
2305 Norman Ave.
Richmond, VA 23228

Eve Duncan
23 James Street
Templestowe
3106 Melbourne
AUSTRALIA

Therese Edell
1641 Rockford Place
Cincinnati, OH 45223

Marti Epstein
127 Thorndike Street
Brookline, MA 02146-2572

Tsippi Fleischer
7 Sderot Bat-Galim
Haifa 35012
ISRAEL

Tania Gabrielle French
1735 Pier Avenue
Santa Monica, CA 90405

Sherilyn Gail Fritz
172 Cornell Way
Port Moody B. C. V3H 3W2
CANADA

Kay Gardner
Box 33
Stonington, ME 04681

Ada Gentile
via Divisione Torino, 139
00143 Roma
ITALY

Janice Giteck
1833 Third Street
Kirkland, WA 98033

Lois Griffes-Kortering
1370 Ridge Ave.
Muskegon, MI 49441

Beverly Grigsby
17639 Osbourne St.
Northridge, CA 91325

Lynn Gumert
c/o Susan Grimm
2104 Spencer Lane
Finksburg, MD 21048

Ann Shrewsbury Hankinson
359 Tenth Avenue
Salt Lake City, UT 84103

Jane Smith Hart
120 Pelham Road
New Rochelle, NY 10805

Lynn Harting-Ware
84 Murellen Crescent
Toronto, Ontario M4A 2K5
CANADA

Sorrel Doris Hays
697 West End Avenue, PH-B
New York, NY 10025

Mara Helmuth
University of Cincinnati
College-Conservatory of Music
Cincinnati, OH 45221

Kathy Henkel
2367 Creston Drive
Los Angeles, CA 90068

Margaret Hontos
323 E. Palm Avenue
Monrovia, CA 91016

Katherine Hoover
160 West 95th St., Apt 5-B
New York, NY 10025

Adina Izarra
Av. Ocumare, QTA Kinanoke
Colinas de Bello Monte
Caracas 1041
VENEZUELA

Betsy Jolas
National Conservatory of Music
14 Rue de Madrid
75008 Paris
FRANCE

Yuriko Kojima
2-17-4-201 Jindaiji-Motomachi
Chofu City, Tokyo 182
JAPAN

Nagado Konishi
Sakai 738-1
Niigata City, 950-21
JAPAN

Annette Kruisbring
Vechstraab 1235491GC
Sint-Oedenrode
THE NETHERLANDS

Felicitas Kukuck
Am Hang 922587
Hamburg GERMANY

Yoko Kurimoto
1-1-2-101 Kanayama
Naka-ku, Nagoya
JAPAN

Elizabeth(Libby) Larsen
2205 Kenwood Pkwy.
Minneapolis, MN 55405

Anne Lauber
5170 Hutchison
Outremont, Québec H2V 4A9
CANADA

Hope Lee
27 Stradwick Rise
S. W. Calgary, Alberta
CANADA

Clarisse Leite
Academia Internacional de
Musica do Rio de Janeiro
Rio de Janeiro   BRAZIL

Rami Y. Levin
Dept. of Music
Lake Forest College
555 N. Sheridan
Lake Forest, IL 60045

Maria Linnemann
Edenstrasse 18
30161 Hannover
GERMANY

Ruth Lomon
2-A Forest Street
Cambridge, MA 02140

Janna MacAuslan
P.O. Box 15121
Portland, OR 97293-5121

Ursula Mamlok
315 East 86th St., #6-G E
New York, NY 10028

Myriam Marbe
Str. Grigore Alexandrescu,
3271128 Bucuresti, Sector 1.
Of 22 R.S. ROMANIA

Bunita Marcus
415 Ocean Parkway #3-D
Brooklyn, NY 11218

Chiara Maresca
Via del Boschetto, 60
00184 Roma, ITALY

Judith Markowitz
5801 N. Sheridan Rd, Suite 19A
Chicago, IL 60660

Janet Marlow
P. O. Box 945
Litchfield, CT 06759

Pamela J. Marshall
38 Dexter Road
Lexington, MA 02173

Margaret S. Meier
Music Department
Mt. San Antonio C. C.
1100 North Grand Ave.
Walnut, CA 91789-1399

Naomi Littlebear Morena
1815 N. Alberta
Portland, OR 97217

Junko Mori
2-15-17 Mitsuidai
Hachioji City,
Tokyo 192 JAPAN

Katherine Murdock
School of Music
Box 2098
Wichita State University
1845 Fairmount
Wichita, KS 67260-0053

Eva Noda
3000 N.E. 77th Place
Portland, OR 97213

Jane O'Leary
1 Avondale Road
Highland Park, Galway
IRELAND

Pauline Oliveros
156 Hunter Street
Kingston, NY 12401

Juanita Oribello
1037 Stanford
Oakland, CA 94608

Maria Luisa Ozaita
Marques Navarra 12-3 o izsher
Bilbao 48001 (Vizcaya)
SPAIN

Alice Parker
801 West End Ave., #9-D
New York, NY 10025

Alexandra Pierce
The Center of Balance
126 East Fern Avenue
Redlands, CA 92373

Debra Porter
17710 S.W. Independence Way
Beaverton, OR 97006

Deon Nielsen Price
10701 Ranch Rd.
Culver City, CA 90230

Teresa Procaccini
Vle Provincie 184
Roma ITALY

Eileen Betty Roe
St. Helen's Church
Kensington ENGLAND

Micheline Roi
R,R, #1 Lynden
Ontario L0R 1T0
CANADA

Danielle Roster
47, rue Eisknippchen
L-9517 Wiltz
LUXEMBURG

Anna Rubin
223 D Halsey St.
Princeton, NJ 08540

Alice Samter
Friedbergstrasse 14
14057 Berlin
GERMANY

Rhian Samuel
Music Dept., City University
Northampton Square
London EC1 OHB
ENGLAND

Felicia A. B. Sandler
6107 Plymouth
Stockton, CA 95207

Ruth Schonthal
12 Van Etten Blvd.
New Rochelle, NY 10804

Sharon Guertin Shafer
6818 Glencove Dr.
Clifton, VA 20124

Jeanne Ellison Shaffer
1062 Woodley Road
Montgomery, AL 36106

Ann Loomis Silsbee
915 Coddington Rd.
Ithaca, NY 14850

Jeanne Singer
64 Stuart Place
Manhasset, L.I., NY 11030

Letizia Spampinato
via Nuovalucello142
Catania (Sicily)
ITALY

Iris Szeghy
Tematínska 4,
851 01Bratislava
SLOVAKIA

Joan Szymko
Concord Community of Choirs
P.O. Box 2636
Portland, OR 97208-2636

Hilary Tann
627 Riverview Road
Rexford, NY 12148-1436

Gloria Tapia
Conservatorio Nacional
Avenida Pres. Masaryk 582
Mexico 5, D.F. MEXICO

Karen P. Thomas
1408 N. 36th Street
Seattle, WA 98103

Mary Jeanne van Appledorn
P.O. Box 1583
Lubbock, TX 79408

Herma van Schaijk-Lambermont
Laan ten Bogaerde 45491 GC
Sint-Oedenrode
THE NETHERLANDS

Elisabeth Waldo
P.O. Box 280-101
Northridge, CA 91328

Gwyneth Walker
R.D. 2, Box 263
Braintree, VT 05060-9209

Joelle Wallach
552 Riverside Drive, #5E
New York, NY 10027

Carol Ann Weaver
Music Department
Conrad Brebel College
University of Waterloo
Waterloo, Ontario N2L 3G6
CANADA

Beth Wiemann
510 Monticello Ave.
Salisbury, MD 21801

Laura Zaerr
5945 N. W. Rosewood Dr.
Corvallis, OR 97330

Jeanne Zaidel-Rudolph
17 Thelma Crescent, Bagleyston
2192 Johannesburg
SOUTH AFRICA

Marilyn Jane Ziffrin
P. O. Box 179
Bradford, NH 03221

Margrit Zimmermann
Ostermundigenstrasse 22
CH-3006 Bern
SWITZERLAND

Laurel Zucker
c/o Cantilena Records
972 Fourth Avenue
Sacramento, CA 95818

Appendix 2

Publisher Addresses

The source of these addresses is, in some cases, the original score. Current addresses for the same or related publishing houses and distributors have also been included. The best source of information on current availability of any music is a quality retail music store.

A. Broude
OUT OF BUSINESS

Acoma Company
P.O. Box 61, Station K
Toronto, Ontario M4P 2C1
CANADA

American Composers Alliance
170 West 74th Street
New York, NY 10023
Tel: (212) 362-8900

American Music Center Library
30 W. 26th Street, #1001
New York, NY 10010
Tel: (212) 366-5260

Ashley Dealers Service, Inc.
133 Industrial Avenue
P.O. Box 337
Hasbrouck Heights, NJ 07604

AstoriaVerlag
Brandenburgeschestr. 22 1000
Berlin 31 GERMANY

Barry Y Cia
Talcahuano 860, Bajo B
Buenos Aires 1013 Cap. Federal
ARGENTINA
US agent: Boosey and Hawkes

Belwin Mills
c/o Warner Bros.
15800 N.W. 48th Avenue
P.O. Box 4340
Miami, FL 33014

Bèrben Edizioni musicali
via Redipuglia 65
1-60100 Ancona ITALY
US agent: Presser

Billaudot
14 rue de l'Echiquier
75010 Paris FRANCE
US agent: Presser

Boosey and Hawkes
295 Regent Street
London W1R 8JH UK

Boosey and Hawkes
52 Cooper Square
New York, NY 10003
Tel: (212) 979-1090

Bote and Bock
Hardenbergstrasse 9A
D-1000 Berlin 12
GERMANY
US agent: Boosey and Hawkes

Breitkopf and Härtel
Auslieferung
Postfach 1103
6204 Taunusstein 4
GERMANY

Canadian Music Center
National Office
20 St. Joseph Street
Toronto, Ontario M4Y 1J9
CANADA
Tel: (416) 961-6601
FAX: (416) 961-7198

Cantilena Press
972 Fourth Avenue
Sacramento, CA 95818
Tel: (916) 441-6421

Carisch S.p.a.
Via General Fara, 39
Casella Postale 10170
1-20124 Milano ITALY

Carl Fischer, Inc.
62 Cooper Square
New York, NY 10003

Casa de la Guitarra
3-17-49 Shimo-ochiai,
Shinjuku
Tokyo 161 JAPAN
Tel: 03-3952 5595

Casa Nuñez
Buenos Aires ARGENTINA
Sold to Ricordi?

Casa Ricordi
Via Salomone 77
20138 Milano ITALY
US agent: Hal Leonard
(Boosey and Hawkes for
contemporary works.)

Chester, J. and W. Ltd.
7-9 Eagle Court
London EC1M 5QD UK
US agent: Shawnee Press

Chiappino
4-Via Gaudenzio Ferrari
4 Torino ITALY

Columbia Music Co.
P.O. Box 19126
Washington, D.C. 20036
Distributed by: Presser

Contemporary Music Adesso
Ch-6951 Corticiasca
Corticiasca
GERMANY
Tel/FAX: +41 91 944 1326

Contemporary Music Centre
95 Lower Baggot Street
Dublin 2
IRELAND
Tel: 01-661 2105
FAX: 01-676 2639

DearHorse Publications
P.O. Box 15121
Portland, OR 97215
Tel: (503) 233-1206
FAX: (503) 235-3292

Donemus
Paulus Potterstraat 14
NL-1071 CZ Amsterdam
THE NETHERLANDS
US agent: Presser

Durand and Cie
215 rue du Faubourg St. Honoré
F-75008 Paris FRANCE
US agent: Presser

E. C. Schirmer Music Co., Inc.
c/o E. C. S. Publishing
138 Ipswich Street
Boston, MA 02215-3534
Tel: (617) 236-1935

Editio Supraphon
Pulackeho 1
CS-112 99 Prague
CZECHOSLOVAKIA

Editions Henry Lemoine
17 rue Pigalle
75009 Paris FRANCE
US agent: Presser

Editions Max Eschig
215, rue du Faubourg St. Honoré
75008 Paris FRANCE
US agent: Presser

Editions Musicales
Transatlantiques
151 Avenue Jean Jaurés
75017 Paris FRANCE
US agent: Presser

Editions Orphée
407 N. Grant Ave., Suite 400
Columbus, OH 43221
Tel: (614) 224-4304
FAX: (614) 224-1009
Distributed by: Guitar Solo

Edizioni Curci
Galleria del Corso 4
I-20122 Milano   ITALY
US agent: Warner Bros.

Ed. Nota-Knjazevac
YUGOSLAVIA

European American Music Corp.
P.O. Box 850
Valley Forge, PA 19482

Faber Music Ltd.
3 Queen Square
London WC1N 3AU UK
Distributors: Hal Leonard,
educational; Boosey and
Hawkes, serious music

Fentone Music
Fleming Rd., Earlstrees Corby
Northants NN17 2SN   UK
US agent: Warner Bros.

Furore-verlag
Naumburger Strasse 40
D-34124 Kassel
GERMANY
Tel: 0561-897352
FAX: 0561-83472

General Music Publishing, Inc.
c/o Boston Music
172 Tremont St.
Boston, MA 02111

Guitar Foundation of America
c/o Peter Danner
Soundboard Editor-in-Chief
604 Tennyson Avenue
Palo Alto, CA 94301

Guitar Solo Publications
514 Bryant Street
San Francisco, CA 94107-1217
Tel: (415) 896-1144

Harold Branch
OUT OF BUSINESS

Hal Leonard Publishing Corp.
P.O. Box 13819
Milwaukee, WI 53213

Heinrichshofen's Verlag
Postfach 620
 26389 Wilhelmshaven
GERMANY
US agent: C.F. Peters

Irmãos Vitale editores
Rua Franca Pinto 42
São Paulo SP04016-000
BRAZIL

Korn
Buenos Aires
ARGENTINA
US agent: Ricordi Americana?

Marizzo Music
P.O. Box 945
Litchfield, CT 06759
Tel: (203) 567-5434
FAX: (203) 596-1447

Mel Bay
4 Industrial Drive
Pacific, MO 63069-0066
Tel: 1-800-325-5918

Mills Music
London UK
Used to be Belwin Mills, now
Warner Bros.

MMB Music, Inc.
10370 Page Industrial Blvd.
St. Louis, MO 63132

Möseler Verlag
Hoffman-von-Fallersleben-
Strasse 8-10/Postfach 1460.
D-3340 Wolfenbüttel
GERMANY

Music Fund/archives
Medená 29
811 02 Bratislava
SLOVAKIA
Tel/FAX: 42-7/533 26 45

Music Sales Corp.
P.O. Box 572
Chester, NY 10918

Musical New Services, Ltd.
20 Denmark Street
London WC2H 8NE UK

Norsk Musikkinformasion
Toftes gate 69
0552 Oslo NORWAY
Tel: +47 22 370909
FAX: +47 22 356938

Norsk Music Verlag, A.S.
Box 1499 Vika
NO116 Oslo 1 NORWAY

Novello and Co., Ltd.
Fairfield Road, Borough Green
Sevenoaks, Kent TN15 8DT
UK
US agent: Shawnee

Olivan Press
Universal Edition, Ltd.
2/3 Fareham St., Dean Street
London W1V 4DU UK

Oxford University Press
Music Department
37 Dover Street
London W1X 4AH UK

Oxford University Press
2001 Evans Road
Cary, NC 27513

Peer International Corps
c/o PeerMusic Classical
810 Seventh Ave.
New York, NY 10019
Distributed by: Presser

C. F. Peters
373 Park Ave. South
New York, NY 10016
Tel: (212) 686-4147
FAX: (212) 689-9412

Plymouth Music Co., Inc.
170 N.E. 33rd St.
P.O. Box 24330
Fort Lauderdale, FL 33334

Theodore Presser Company
1 Presser Place
Bryn Mawr, PA 19010-3490
Tel: (610) 525-3636

Primavera
(Editions Primavera)
US agent: General Music

Publication Contact
International
24 Avon Hill
Cambridge, MA 02140

Santa Barbara Music
Publishing
260 Loma Media
Santa Barbara, CA 93103

G. Schirmer/
Associated Music Publishing
257 Park Ave. S., 20th floor
New York, NY 10010
Tel: (212) 254-2100
Distributed by: Hal Leonard

Schott Frères
30 rue Saint-Jean
B-1000 Bruxelles
BRUSSELS
US agent: European Amercian
Music Corp.

L. Schott
Brunswick Road
Ashford, Kent TN23 1DX UK
US agent: European American
Music Corp.

B. Schotts Soehne
Postfach 3640
D-55026 Mainz
GERMANY

Scottish Music Information
Centre
1 Bowmont Gardens
Glascow G12 9LR
SCOTLAND, UK

Sea Gnomes Music
Box 33
Stonington, ME 04681
Tel: (207) 367-5076

Seesaw Music Corp.
2067 Broadway
New York, NY 10023
Tel: (212) 874-1200

Shawnee Press
Delaware Water Gap, PA
18327

Spanish Music Center
OUT OF BUSINESS

Thames Publishing
14 Barlby Road
London W10 6AR UK

Union Musical Espanõla
editores
Carrera de San Jeronimo 26
Madrid-14 SPAIN
US agent: Music Sales Corp.

Vanguard Music Corp
1595 Broadway, Room 313
New York, NY 10019

VDMK Manuskriptearchiv
München GERMANY

V. Hladky
Postfach 620
26389 Wilhelmshaven
GERMANY

Walker Music Publishing
R.D. 2, Box 263
Braintree, VT 05060
Tel: (802) 728-9841
FAX: (802)728-6231

Warner Brothers
15800 N.W. 48th Ave.
Miami, FL 33014

Bibliography

American Women Composers. *American Women Composers News/Forum.* (January and April 1985), Washington, DC: American Women Composers, 1980-93.

Archivio generale italiano delle fonti per chitarra. *Catalogo delle opere per chitarra.* Vigevano: Archivio generale italiano delle fonti per chitarra, 1984.

Armstrong, Tony, ed. *Hot Wire: A Journal of Women's Music and Culture.* Chicago: Empty Closet Enterprises, 1984-94.

Bellow, Alexander. *The Illustrated History of the Guitar.* New York: Franco Colombo Publications, Belwin Mills, 1970.

Boenke, Heidi. *Flute Music by Women Composers: An Annotated Catalog.* Westport, CT: Greenwood Press, 1988.

Bone, Philip J. *The Guitar and Mandolin.* 2d ed. London: Schott and Co., 1954.

Brand, Bettina, Martina Helmig, Barbara Kaiser, Birgit Salomon, and Adje Westerkamp, eds. *Komponistinnen in Berlin.* Berlin: Musikfrauen, 1987.

British Library. *The Catalog of Printed Music in the British Library to 1980.* London: K. G. Saur, 1981-87.

Button, Stewart. *The Guitar in England, 1800-1924*. New York: Garland Publications, 1989.

Clark, David Lindsey, comp. *Music for Guitar and Lute*. Exeter, England: Exeter City Library, 1972.

Cohen, Aaron I. *International Encyclopedia of Women Composers*. 2d ed., 2 vols. New York: Books & Music USA, 1987.

Danner, Peter. *The Guitar in America: A Historical Collection of Classical Guitar Music in Facsimile*. Melville, NY: Belwin Mills, 1978.

Gilmore, George, ed. *Guitar and Lute Magazine*, no. 11. Honolulu: Galliard Press, 1980.

Glasenapp, Lutz. *Die Gitarre als Ensemble- und Orchesterinstrument in der Neuen Musik*. Regensburg: Gustav Bosse Verlag, 1991.

Grunfeld, Frederic V. *The Art and Times of the Guitar*. New York: Collier-Macmillan, 1969.

Guitar Foundation of America. *Soundboard: Journal of the Guitar Foundation of America*. Claremont, CA: Guitar Foundation of America, 1974-96.

Guitar Solo Publications. *Mail Order Catalog*. San Francisco: Guitar Solo Publications, 1982-96.

Harrison, Frank Mott. *Reminiscences of Madame Sidney Pratten: Guitariste and Composer*. Bournemouth W., England: Barnes and Mullins, 1899.

Heck, Thomas F. "The Birth of the Classic Guitar and its Cultivation in Vienna Reflected in the Career and Compositions of Mauro Giuliani (d. 1829)." Ph.D. diss., Yale University, 1970. Ann Arbor: University Microfilms International, 1971.

Helleu, Laurence. *La guitare en concert: catalogue des oeuvres avec guitare du XX⁰ siècle*. Paris: Editions Musicales Transatlantiques, 1983.

Heresies Collective. Women and Music issue #10, *Heresies* 3, no. 2. New York: Heresies Collective, Inc., 1980.

Hixon, Donald L., and Don Hennessee. *Women in Music: An Encyclopedic Bibliography*. 2d ed., 2 vols. Metuchen, NJ: Scarecrow Press, 1993.

International Alliance of Women in Music.*The I.A.W.M. Journal* (formerly *International League of Women Composers Journal*). Wynnewood, PA: International Alliance of Women in Music, 1995-.

Jackson, Barbara Garvey. *"Say Can You Deny Me": A Guide to Surviving Music by Women from the 16th Through the 18th Centuries*. Fayetteville: University of Arkansas Press, 1994.

Jape, Mijndert. *Classical Guitar Music in Print*. Music-in-Print Series, vol. 7. Philadelphia: Musicdata, 1989.

Latin American Music Center. *Indiana University Latin American Music Center Catalog*. Bloomington: Indiana University Press, 1994.

LePage, Jane Weiner. *Women Composers, Conductors, and Musicians of the Twentieth Century: Selected Biographies*. 3 vol. Metuchen, NJ: Scarecrow Press, 1980-88.

Maslen, J. *Guitars and Guitar Playing: A List of Selected References and Music*. Melbourne: State Library of Victoria, 1966.

McCutchen, Meredith Alice. *Guitar and Vihuela: An Annotated Bibliography*. RILM Retrospectives, no. 3. New York: Pendragon Press, 1985.

Moser, Wolf. *Gitarre-Musik: ein internationaler Katalog*. 2 vol. Hamburg: Joachim-Trekel-Verlag, 1986.

New York Women Composers, Inc. *Catalog, Compositions of Concert Music*. North Tarrytown, NY: New York Women Composers, Inc.,1991.

Nolan, Deborah L. "The Contributions of Nineteenth-Century European Women to Guitar Performance, Composition, and Pedagogy." Master's thesis, California State University, Fullerton, 1983. Ann Arbor: University Microfilms International, 1983.

Olivier, Antje. *Komponistinnen: eine Bestandsaufnahme: die Sammlung des Europäischen Frauenmusikarchivs*. Düsseldorf: Tokkata-Verlag, 1990.

Olivier, Antje, and Karin Weingartz-Perschel, eds. *Komponistinnen von A bis Z: eine Korrektur der traditionellen Musikgeschichtsschreibung*. Düsseldorf: Tokkata-Verlag, 1988.

Ophee, Matanya, and Todd Harvey, eds. *The Orphée Catalogue*. Columbus, OH: Editions Orphée, Inc., 1993.

Pan American Union Music Section. *Compositores de America*. Vol. 9 and 17. Washington, DC: Organization of American States, 1955-77.

Pocci, Vincenzo. *Edizioni musicali per chitarra sola o con altri strumenti di autori dell XX secolo*. Roma: self-published, 1986.

Prat, Domingo. *Diccionario de guitarras*. Buenos Aires: Romero & Fernandez, 1934. Reprint, Columbus, OH: Editions Orphée, Inc., 1986.

Purcell, Ronald C., and Darien S. Mann, eds. *Guitar Music Collection of Vahdah Olcott-Bickford*. Vol. 1. Northridge, CA: International Guitar Research Archive, Music Department, California State University, 1991.

Radole, Giuseppe. *Liuto, chitarra e vihuela: storia e letterateine*. Milan: Edizoni Suvini Zerboni, 1979.

Rezits, Joseph. *The Guitarist's Resource Guide: Guitar Music in Print and Books on the Art of Guitar*. San Diego: Pallma Music Co., 1983; distributed by A. Kjos.

Rogatis, Teresa De. *Opere scelte per chitarra*. a cura di Angelo Gilardino, Stefano Aruta. Ancona: Edizioni Bèrben, 1993.

Sadie, Julie Anne, and Rhian Samuel, eds. *The Norton/Grove Dictionary of Women Composers*. New York: W.W. Norton, 1994.

Schneider, John. *The Contemporary Guitar*. Berkeley: University of California Press, 1985.

Schwarz, Werner. *Guitar Bibliography: An International Listing of Theoretical Literature on Classical Guitar from the Beginning to the Present*. Munich: K. G. Saur, 1984.

Smith, Dorman H., and Laurie Eagleson. *Guitar and Lute Music in Periodicals: An Index*. Fallen Leaf Reference Books in Music, vol. 13, Berkeley: Fallen Leaf Press, 1990.

Stewart-Green, Miriam. *Women Composers: A Checklist for the Solo Voice.* Boston: G.K. Hall, 1980.

Summerfield, Maurice J. *The Classical Guitar: Its Evolution and Its Players since 1800.* 2d ed. Newcastle-upon-Tyne, U.K.: Ashley Mark Publishing, 1991; distributed in U.S. by Hal Leonard Publishing.

Tapia Colman, Simón. *Música y músicos en México.* Mexico, D.F.: Panorama Editorial, 1991.

Theodore Front Musical Literature. *Music by Women Composers.* Van Nuys, CA: Theodore Front Musical Literature, Inc., spring 1994.

Torpp Larsson, Jytte. *Catalogue of the Rischel and Birket-Smith Collection of Guitar Music in the Royal Library of Copenhagen.* Edited by Peter Danner. Columbus: Editions Orphée, 1989.

Turnbull, Harvey. *The Guitar from the Renaissance to the Present Day.* New York: Charles Scribner's Sons, 1974.

Wade, Graham. *Traditions of the Classical Guitar.* London: John Calder, 1980.

Walker-Hill, Helen. *Piano Music by Black Women Composers: A Catalog of Solo and Ensemble Works.* Music Reference Collection, no. 35, New York: Greenwood Press, 1992.

Zaimont, Judith, and Karen Famera, eds. *Contemporary Concert Music by Women: A Directory of the Composers and Their Works.* Westport, CT: Greenwood Press, 1981.

Zaimont, Judith, and others, eds. *The Musical Woman: An International Perspective.* 3 vols. Westport, CT: Greenwood Press, 1984-91.

Zuth, Joseph. *Handbuch der Laute und Gitarre.* Wien: Verlag der Zeitschrift für die Gitarre, 1926.

Composer Index

Title Index

Titles are followed by the composer's name in bold type. In most languages articles are placed at the end of the title.

About the Compilers

JANNA MacAUSLAN and KRISTAN ASPEN are freelance academics, performers, and lecturers dedicated to increasing public awareness of women in the field of music. MacAuslan and Aspen formed the Musica Femina Flute Guitar Duo in 1983, and since then have toured the country performing works by women composers and lecturing about women in music. They have recorded two compact disks , *Returning the Muse to Music* (1989) and *Heartstreams* (1993).

ISBN 0-313-29385-6

90000>

EAN

9 780313 293856

HARDCOVER BAR CODE